MW00945842

When Things
Get *Real*

TANISHA STEWART

*When Things Get **Real***
Copyright © 2019 Tanisha Stewart

All rights reserved.

*When Things Get **Real*** is a work of fiction. Any resemblance to actual events, locations, or persons living or dead is coincidental. No part of this book may be reproduced in any written, electronic, recording, or photocopying form without written permission of the author, Tanisha Stewart.

Books may be purchased in quantity and/or special sales by contacting the publisher, Tanisha Stewart, by email at tanishastewart.author@gmail.com.

Cover Design: Tyora Moody
www.tywebbincreations.com

First Edition

Published in the United States of America
by Tanisha Stewart

When Things Get *Real*

Dedication and Acknowledgments

First and foremost, I dedicate this book to my Lord and Savior Jesus Christ. Without Him, I would not be here today.

Secondly, I would like to dedicate this novel to my family and friends. To my mother, Alice Jenkins, my beloved "Alice Jean," the driving force behind most of my life's accomplishments, you have been there through thick and thin, through good and bad, through struggle and triumph. Words cannot express how thankful and grateful I am for you. To my little sister, my "favorite girl" Goleana Grant, thank you for always supporting me. I am your biggest fan!

To my brothers James Auston, Thomas Stewart, Arthur Caldwell, and James Stewart, I love you all, and I thank you for supporting me in my endeavors. To my grandmother, Sue Stewart, thank you for your wisdom and your sense of humor, and for always encouraging me. To my father, James Stewart Jr., I love you, and I thank you for your constant encouragement and inspiration. To all of my extended family and friends, God bless you all. I dedicate this to you.

To my editor, Janet Angelo, thank you for providing constant encouragement, information, and support. Your thoughtful editing really helps to bring my stories to life. You go above and beyond in all that you do, and my books would not be the same without you. Also, thank you to my cover designer, Tyora Moody of Tywebbin Creations, for your excellent work.

Next, I would like to dedicate this book to all of my high school and college students past, present, and future. You guys wake me up every morning and keep me on my feet throughout the day. I love you all, and I thank you for inspiring me in your own unique ways.

I also cannot forget to mention my beta readers and reviewers. God bless each and every one of you. You've helped to develop me as an author, and you provide critical feedback regarding each story I write. I look forward to hearing from you with every published work.

Last but certainly not least, I dedicate this book to you, the reader. Without you, no one would hear the stories being told. I pray that this book will bless you, and that God will be glorified in and through your life. In Jesus's name, Amen.

When Things Get *Real*

**Where we left off in book one of this series,
When Things Go Left:**

Twon

I ain't want to do shit but go home and go to sleep. My life is entirely fucked up. It seems like everything is happening to me all at once, and I don't know how much more I can take. I swear, if one more thing happens … there's no telling what I will do. I got home and saw my mother's car in the parking lot. Damn. She must have stayed home today. I hoped she wouldn't say anything to me.

I quietly made my way into the house.

"Twon!" she said, as soon as I closed the front door.

"Yes," I said, my tone flat and uninterested, but she didn't get the hint.

"Come here."

I made my way to the living room where she was sitting on the couch. "What?" I said.

"Don't you 'what' me. I need you to go to the store and get me a pack of cigarettes."

"Ma, I'm tired, and I don't feel like going anywhere today. I just want to go upstairs to my room and go to sleep."

"I didn't ask you what the hell you wanted to do. I told you I needed you to go to the store to get me a pack of cigarettes. Now go."

I felt my body tremble as a wave of anger rose up inside of me. "Where's the money?" I said, trying to remain calm.

"I'm not trying to break a twenty, so you can just buy it."

"Well, I don't have it, so you're going to have to break a twenty today."

"Boy, I don't know who the fuck you think you been getting smart with lately! Get your fucking ass to the store and get me a pack of cigarettes."

"Ma, I told you, I don't have the money—"

"Well, you better got-damn find it!" she spat.

"FUCK THIS SHIT! I'M OUT!" I walked straight out of the house, slamming the door behind me. I didn't know where I was going, but I was getting the fuck up out of there. I swear, I can't take no more shit. I'm done.

***

I was driving so fast that I didn't even know where I was going. My head was clearly not in the game. I truly didn't give a fuck anymore. I had nothing left. It seemed like my life was never going to get better, so I decided that it was best to just let it go.

I'm sorry I couldn't be a better friend. I'm sorry I couldn't be a better boyfriend. I'm sorry I couldn't be a better son, but I did the best I could.

A tractor-trailer was coming swiftly toward me from the opposite direction on the bridge. I saw an opportunity, so I seized it.

I quickly swerved in front of him at the last possible moment and took a deep breath.

All I heard next was the sound of his horn then a loud crash and the smashing of metal, and I felt myself flying through the air.

Shaneece

I stared at the pregnancy test. There was no way I was seeing what I thought I was seeing — my eyes had to be playing tricks on me.

"Shaneece?" Shanelle knocked on the door.

"What?" I sniffled.

"What does it say?"

I was at her house for the rest of the week. My parents surprisingly let me go because they trusted my sister more than they trusted me. I told Shanelle that I had been feeling sick and throwing up lately, so she immediately took me to the store to get a pregnancy test. I stared at the result until my eyes turned blurry.

"Shaneece?"

I slowly got up and opened the door to face her. "My life is over," I said blankly, and handed her the test stick.

She looked shocked, but then her training as a nurse took over, and her expression turned calm. She looked at me.

"It's going to be okay, Shaneece."

"No, it's not! Dad is going to kill me!"

"No, he won't. He'll have to get through me first, and I won't let him!" She smiled to ease the tension, and I gave a nervous little laugh. "We will get through this together, Shaneece. We just have to get you set up with doctor's appointments, a proper eating plan, and some prenatal vitamins, and then we have to start planning the future. Are you still with the father?"

I hung my head in shame. "I don't know who the father is," I mumbled.

"What?"

"I don't know who the father is, Shanelle!" I snapped.

She looked disappointed, but her expression turned calm again. "Well, do you at least have an idea?"

I swallowed slowly. "It's between two guys. They're best friends."

Shanelle sighed. "Oh, Shaneece … well, do you want to try to call them? Or do you want to wait until later?"

"No, I might as well get it over with now." I wasn't thinking clearly. I grabbed my new cell phone that she bought me and dialed Twon's number first, praying that he would pick up. Of course, he didn't. But then I remembered that he had blocked my number, so he had no idea I was calling.

Next I called Hype. He answered on the third ring. "What?" he said.

"Hype, I need to talk to you."

"We got nothing to talk about, Shaneece."

"Actually, yes, we do. Look, this is important. I know you're mad at me now, but I have something to tell you."

"What the fuck you got to tell me, Shaneece?"

"I'm pregnant."

He was silent for a few moments.

"Hype?" I said, wondering if the connection was lost.

"I don't know why you telling *me* that shit. It ain't mine."

"Hype, stop playing games. We need to figure out how to handle this."

"No, *we* don't need to figure out shit! You fucked me and you fucked that nigga too. Sounds like a personal problem." *CLICK.*

I stared at the phone, wondering where I could possibly go from here.

TANISHA STEWART

When Things Get *Real*

When Things
Get *Real*

When Things Get *Real*

Trigger Warning

This book contains a wide range of very serious situations experienced by its characters, including, but not limited to suicidal behavior, physical and emotional abuse, neglect, violence, and other serious forms of trauma.

Some of these situations, and their associated imagery/visual descriptions, may be triggering or traumatic for readers who have experienced similar situations. This message is written to inform readers of potential triggers for these traumatic events, so he or she will know ahead of time whether he or she should continue reading this story.

When Things Get *Real*

Hype

I stared at the phone in my hand after hanging up on Shaneece. "Man, this bitch is wilin'." I sucked my teeth and flipped the phone onto the coffee table.

"Who?" Charles turned to look at me, if you could call it that. His eyes were so glazed over from being high that I doubted he could see much of anything.

"Nigga, you high as fuck!" I said, chuckling at him. "You want me to get you some eye drops or something? You know G-Ma be popping up almost every day, and she won't approve."

"Man, ffffuck…" He stopped his cuss word before he said it when he saw the smile disappear from my face.

"I'm grown," he said, changing his tone.

"I understand that, but I'm not trying to hear all that yelling and shit."

"Me either." Charles attempted to sit up straighter on the couch. "That's why I don't come around her like that."

"G-Ma's cool though," I said. "She just be trying to look out."

"Nigga, my own *mother* don't be trying to look out for me. I stay drunk and high as fuck at her house, and she don't say shit. Excuse my French, but what the fuck G-Ma gonna tell me?"

"I mean, my mother doesn't really say shit to me either, but still. At least G-Ma tries."

"You can deal with that shit if you want to," he said, leaning forward with his elbows resting on his knees. "But I ain't trying to have nobody all in my business."

"You still be with Chief and them?" I said, referring to the guys Charles sold drugs with.

"Yeah, why? You trying to get put on?"

"Nah, that shit ain't for me."

Charles chuckled. "Yeah, that's right. You a school boy." He nudged me.

"I wouldn't say all that, but—"

"Who was that on the phone though?" he said suddenly.

"Oh, that was Shaneece. Bitch talking bout she pregnant."

"Pregnant? You wasn't strapping up?"

I turned my head slightly. "Not really."

"Fuck you mean, not really, nigga?" Charles looked serious all of a sudden. "Wasn't you just all shook and shit cuz you thought you had AIDS a couple of months ago?"

"I mean, I figured since I was only with one chick now, I ain't have to worry about that shit."

"Yeah, but the bitch turned out to be a THOT, so now you back to square one. What you gonna do if it's yours?"

"I mean, ain't shit I *can* do. What's done is done."

"Shit, you might *need* me to put you on if it is yours. Babies cost mad money, bruh." Charles looked worried for me.

Just then, we heard someone frantically twisting the doorknob. Both of us jumped up, ready for action as Quaid burst into the living room.

"Guys!" He was panting for breath, sweat dripping down his face. "You gotta come quick!"

"Come quick?" I said, looking back and forth between Quaid and Charles. "Where? Fuck wrong with you?"

"It's Twon!" He said, shock and fear all over his face. "He's in the hospital. I think…I think he killed himself, man…" Quaid rubbed his hands from the top of his head down his face, and he blinked back some tears.

Charles and I froze at those words, but Charles spoke first.

"Fuck you mean, Twon killed himself, Quaid?" For the first time in my life, I saw fear in Charles' eyes. That sent chills all through my body.

"What happened, Quaid?" I persisted.

"I was driving behind Twon on a bridge. He was speeding and driving crazy. Then, all of a sudden, he swerved out in front of a tractor-trailer. I swerved out of the way when they made contact. All I saw…" He choked back tears. "I saw his car flip over the bridge and go into the water. I called the ambulance, but they wouldn't let anybody go near. I saw them put him on a stretcher, and I didn't know what to do, so I came here." A tear finally escaped. I watched it roll down his cheek as if I were mesmerized. I couldn't think straight; I was in that much shock.

"Yo . . . you sure that shit was Twon, nigga?" said Charles, pacing back and forth.

"Yes," said Quaid, taking a quick swipe at his tears and hoping they didn't notice. "I was right behind him."

"Why the fuck would he kill himself?"

"I don't know."

Charles shook his head in disbelief. "Yo, my nigga can't be dead. You're not telling me this, Quaid. You're not telling me this." He shook his head again.

"What do you think we should do?" I said.

"Let's go to the hospital," Charles said with complete clarity, his high apparently wiped out by the seriousness of the situation. He grabbed up his keys from the coffee table and started for the door.

"Wait…what if they don't—" Quaid began.

"LET'S GO!" said Charles, causing both of us to jump. Quaid took the hint and headed for the front door. They both stopped and turned around when they realized that I wasn't behind them.

"What the fuck you doing, Hype?" said Charles. "Let's go!" I could see the anxiety all over his face. So many thoughts were swirling in my mind in that moment.

"I can't see that shit," I said. "I can't..." My voice trailed off.

"Pull yourself together, man, we gotta go," said Quaid. "We don't know what we're gonna find when we get there, but we gotta go. This is our boy Twon we're talking about. You gonna let him lay there alone thinking we don't care?"

"I can't see that shit," I repeated, like I was in a daze.

"Yo, I'm not finna sit here arguing with this nigga. Let's go, Quaid." Charles pushed Quaid toward the door, and Quaid followed him reluctantly, looking back at me as he walked out the door.

"You fucked up, Hype," Charles shot in my direction. "Fucked up." He slammed the door, and a few seconds later, I heard him crank his engine and take off down the street squealing tires as he rounded the corner. I sank down onto the couch, reeling in shock.

Everything had gone wrong lately – every damn thing. It was all a mess – Twon and Shaneece, Tierra, the fight, and now Twon – everything.

I didn't know what else to do, so I picked up my phone and called Tierra.

Tierra

I sighed as I typed the last sentence of my paper for my English class. "Finally," I breathed, as I quickly saved the document before closing it. I rubbed my tired eyes. I had been writing this stupid paper for over four hours. Usually, it didn't take me that long to write papers, but my mind was so consumed with all that had been happening lately that I could barely think straight.

I still could not believe that Twon actually slept with Shaneece! I couldn't figure out who I was more angry with – Twon for throwing our two-year relationship down the drain, or Shaneece for pretending to be my best friend, all while scheming on my man.

Angry tears surfaced in my eyes, but I blinked them back. I was not doing this today.

I picked up my phone to check my notifications. I had it face down and silent on my desk because I didn't want to be even more distracted than I already was. I looked at my notifications and rolled my eyes when I saw three missed calls from Twon. My heart panged when I saw two missed calls from Quaid. That was another person I had been avoiding, for a different reason.

My relationship with Quaid had become more and more tense over the last few months, mainly because we both carried pent-up feelings for each other the entire time that Twon and I were together. I shook my head as I finally came to grips with the fact that Quaid and I had been playing this game for too long.

I mean, of course I never cheated on Twon with Quaid, but we came really close a few times . . . I blushed as I thought about the water fight we had after the first time he cooked for me, and then my mind traveled to the time we were sitting in his car, and he asked me if I liked him. I think we both caught each other off guard that day, because neither of us was willing to admit it…

I jumped as my phone buzzed in my hand with a call from Hype. "Hello?"

"Tierra…" said Hype, but his voice was all the way off.

Something wasn't right. I pressed the phone closer to my ear to hear him better. "Hype, what's wrong? Why do you sound like that?"

"Some shit just went down with Twon."

"What do you mean? What happened? Where are you?" Hype was scaring me with how serious he sounded.

"Quaid said Twon might have killed himself."

Nothing could have prepared me for those words. My stomach felt like it literally flipped. My mind immediately became frantic as I jumped up out of my seat pulling a sweater over my head. "What?!?" I exclaimed. "What are you talking about, Hype?" I practically screamed into the phone. "Where is Twon?" My voice shook and my breathing grew heavier as I desperately tried to process what Hype had just said to me.

"Quaid said Twon pulled in front of a tractor-trailer, then his car flipped over the bridge. He saw it happen, Tierra. He saw the car plunge into the water—"

"Where is he? Where is Quaid?"

"Quaid and Charles went to the hospital to see what was going on. I stayed at home. I just couldn't be there. So I called you."

"Why did you stay at home, Hype?" I implored, and then it hit me full force. "Why did he do this?" My voice shot up to a higher pitch than I'd ever heard in my life, and tears sprang from my eyes as it hit me what was happening.

"I don't know, Tierra."

"We have to go down there to see what's going on."

"I can't see that shit."

"So you're not going to go?!" I stared at the phone in disbelief before putting it back to my ear.

"I can't."

"Well, I'm going. I'll talk to you later." I ended the call and walked to my mother's bedroom door.

"Ma..." I said, knocking. "Ma!"

"What?" I heard her get up from her bed and walk over to open the door.

"What's wrong with you?" she said, rubbing her eyes.

"I need to go to the hospital," I said, as calmly as possible.

She looked confused. "Why? Who's at the hospital?"

"Hype said Twon tried to kill himself." I swallowed a lump in my throat.

"What?" Her eyes grew wide, and her mouth literally fell open in shock.

"Yes. I need to go," I said.

"Hold on, let me throw something on right quick." She flipped on her light and grabbed some clothes from her drawer.

I ran downstairs, grabbed the keys, went outside, and started the car, waiting in the passenger seat until she came outside. She emerged from the house about five minutes later. She looked at me as she put her seatbelt on.

"Ma, what if it's true?" I said, trembling.

"All we can do is pray, Tierra." She began praying as she pulled out of our driveway and headed down the street in the direction of the hospital.

Shaneece

I felt like such a filthy fucking whore. I had truly hit rock bottom with this stunt. I cheated on Hype with Twon, and I secretly slept with this guy named Markus a few times too. Now I'm pregnant, and I don't know who the father is. But there's no way Markus could be the father, because I stopped sleeping with him a couple of weeks after I got with Hype.

I was disgusted with myself. How could I let myself go this far, to get pregnant and not know who the father was? I didn't know which was worse – being pregnant and not knowing who the father was, or sleeping with two best friends and actually thinking I could get away with it.

"What are you thinking?" said Shanelle, staring at me.

"I feel disgusting."

"We all make mistakes, Shaneece."

"Not like this." I sighed and shook my head. "Who betrays their best friend by sleeping with the best friend of the man that she is in love with?"

"In love with?"

"I'm in love with him, Shanelle!" I wailed. "I have been since the first time I saw him!"

"Which one? Twon, or the Hype guy you just called?"

"Twon," I said, sniffling. "And now he will never talk to me again."

"Well, if you guys are in love, I'm sure he'll—"

"No, he's not in love. I'm the only fool who can say that." I buried my face in my hands, my shoulders shaking as I broke down.

"Shaneece…" Shanelle rubbed my back. "You have got to pull yourself together. This is tough, I know it is, but you will get through this. It will work out."

"How, when he hates me!"

"I'm sure he doesn't hate you."

"He blocked my number in his phone, quit the job where we worked together, and cussed me out in front of the whole school. Yeah, I think he hates me, Shanelle."

"It's probably just due to the situation, Shaneece."

"Can't you fucking hear me?!" I yelled so loud I made her flinch. "Sorry. But for real, though, he doesn't want anything to do with me."

"I'm just trying to help," said Shanelle. "I don't mean to upset you. We can talk about something else if you want."

"Thank you."

We sat there in silence until I couldn't stand it any longer. "Can we just turn on the TV or something?"

Shanelle grabbed the remote and flipped on the TV. It was on the news channel. Just as she was about to flip to the guide to find something good to watch, something caught my eye. I grabbed Shanelle's arm.

"Wait!" My eyes were glued to the screen. "Turn that up!" My heart raced as I stared at the news report, my mouth open. They were showing Twon's car being lifted out of the water at a bridge a few blocks from where he lived. The headline of the story running across the screen was *18-Year-Old Man Attempts Suicide*.

"Oh, my God!" I said, not believing what I was seeing.

"What? What is it?" Shanelle looked confused.

"That's Twon! He tried to kill himself!"

"How do you know it's him? It doesn't say his name—"

"That's his car, Shanelle. I would recognize it anywhere. And that bridge is over by his house." I stood up. "I need to go back home and get to the hospital. I need to see him."

"Shaneece—"

"I have to go, Shanelle! I need to see him!"

"Okay, but I'm coming with you." She grabbed her purse from the table, and we made our way outside to her car.

"I understand you're upset," said Shanelle as she started the car and checked her mirrors. "But are you sure you want to go there tonight? I mean, we have no idea what condition he's in. It could be really bad, Shaneece. Are you sure you're ready for that?"

"Yes, Shanelle," I said, feeling calmer now. "I have to be there, no matter what."

Tierra

My mother and I got to the hospital in about fifteen minutes. As soon as we parked, I jumped out of the car and strode toward the building.

"Hold on, Tierra!" said my mother, hurrying up behind me.

"Sorry," I said, slowing down.

"It's okay," she said. "How are you feeling?"

I had barely said two words the entire ride to the hospital because my mind was totally focused on Twon. I had prayed silently as my mother prayed out loud that he would be okay, and that God would not let him die.

"I'm alright, Ma. I just need to see him."

I waited while my mother asked about Twon's location. The receptionist told us he was in the ICU, and said we could go wait with the rest of the family in the waiting area there. *Rest of the family?* I replied inwardly, and my facial expression probably gave away my surprise. As far as I knew, Twon's only family was his mother. He had never met his father, and he had no brothers or sisters, so I had no idea what family the receptionist was referring to. *I guess I'll find out soon enough.*

As soon as my mom and I rounded the corner to the ICU, I saw Quaid and Charles sitting in the waiting area. Both were visibly nervous. As soon as Quaid saw me, he jumped up out of his seat.

"Tierra," he said, pulling me into his arms and holding me for a moment. "Are you okay? How did you find out?"

"Hype called me." I stepped out of Quaid's embrace and briefly hugged Charles then remembered that he'd never met my mom. "Charles, this is my mother." They all briefly hugged, and I turned my attention back to Quaid. I was almost too afraid to ask, but I had to know.

"Is he okay?" I said, my voice barely above a whisper.

"He's . . . alive, at least." Quaid's eyes told me it was too painful to say more.

I let out a sigh of relief.

"Thank you, God!" I bent over with one arm holding onto Quaid's shoulder, not realizing the huge weight that I was feeling until it was lifted off of me.

"Where's Twon's mother?" said my mom. "Is she here?"

"She left," said Charles, his expression blank. "She was here for a minute, then as soon as the doctor said he was alive, she bounced."

"She *left?*" My mother and I said in unison, neither of us believing our ears.

"Yup," said Charles, his voice devoid of emotion. "She said she had to get back to work, so she left."

"Wow," said my mother, shaking her head. I could tell by her facial expression that she wanted to go off, but she was keeping her cool for our sake.

"Will they let anybody go in to see him?" I said.

"Not 'til he's stable," said Quaid. "His mother didn't leave any specific details with the doctors about who can or can't visit, but they still aren't letting anyone see him yet."

"So she doesn't even…" My mother started again. Her fists were balled up, and I could tell she was angry, but she took a deep breath and kept her cool. "Well, I guess that's a good thing. We can be here for him."

"Did they say whether or not he is awake or conscious?" I said.

"They said he had some swelling in his brain, so he might need surgery, and he broke both of his legs. As long as his brain is not damaged, he should turn out okay. It's a miracle, because the way that car flipped…" Quaid's voice cracked then trailed off. He ran his hand over his head. I reached out and held his hand. He looked down at me, gratefulness in his eyes.

"So, you saw what happened?" said my mother.

"Yes, ma'am," said Quaid, putting his head down. "I was right behind him when he pulled in front of the tractor-trailer."

"Why would he do this?" I said.

"Nobody knows," said Charles, his expression stony, his arms crossed.

"Well, how about we stay here a few hours together," said my mother. "Then we can come back in shifts to make sure that somebody is here when he wakes up." All of us nodded because no one wanted Twon to be alone when he woke up.

We all sat back down and waited for the doctors to come with news on Twon's condition.

Shaneece

We got to the hospital in a few hours, with me holding my breath practically the entire way. I felt kind of bad for basically forcing Shanelle to make a three-hour trip all the way back here when she had just driven me here the day before after the fight with our parents. I knew she probably didn't feel like driving all that way again so soon, but she didn't complain. I loved my sister, and I thanked God that she was there for me when I needed her.

We made our way to the front desk and asked about Twon. When we found out he was in the ICU, we followed the signs in the corridor, and I felt more nervous with every step we took to make our way there. I knew that the ICU meant Twon's condition was serious. My heart rate increased as soon as we turned the corner and I saw Tierra, Charles, and Quaid, and a woman who I assumed was Tierra's mother because she looked just like an older version of her.

Tierra turned when she heard us approach, and as soon as she saw me, she jumped up out of her seat. "What the hell do you think you're doing here?" she said, coming at me, her eyes narrowed. Her mother jumped up as well.

"Tierra, watch your mouth."

"No, Ma. She has no right to be here."

"I have just as much a right as you," I said boldly. "I am the mother of his child!"

"Shaneece," Shanelle said, trying to calm me down, but it was no use.

"Mother of his child?" Tierra said, anger and hurt flashing through her eyes.

"Yeah, you heard it right," I fired back at her.

She lunged toward me, but her mother held her back. "Tierra, you better calm down now," she said. "This is not the time or the place."

"Yeah, you better listen to your mother," I said, full of attitude, but that's exactly how I intended it.

"Who the—" Tierra lunged toward me again, but her mother held her back.

"I said stop it, girl! Now, you are not about to act a fool in here!"

"Shaneece, let's go," said Shanelle, tugging at my arm.

"No!" I said. "We just got here."

"This isn't a good time. We can get a hotel room and come back in the morning. We don't want to get kicked out of the hospital."

I stood there glaring at Tierra as she glared at me. I couldn't let her feel like she'd won this round. "Fine," I said after our staring contest, and turned around with enough attitude to make my point. "I don't want to be in the same vicinity as that girl anyway."

Shanelle sighed and looked at Tierra's mother apologetically as we made our way back down the hall.

Twon

I blinked as my eyes focused on the brightness of the room. I was trying to figure out whether I was in heaven or hell, but then I heard what sounded like a heart monitor, so I guessed it was neither.

"Shit," I said, sucking my teeth.

"You're awake?" I heard a voice off to my side. I quickly turned my head and immediately regretted it as pain shot through my entire body. Quaid was sitting next to my bed looking nervous.

"What are you doing here, Quaid?" I said, starting to feel irritated. This was one of the last muthafuckas I wanted to see at a time like this.

"I was there when you . . . I saw the accident."

"Well, if you saw what happened, you should know it wasn't an accident."

He sighed. "Look, Twon, I'm sorry about everything, okay?"

"You mean when you and Hype fucking jumped me at the basketball court, or when you was plotting and scheming on stealing my girl? Which one is it, Quaid, just so I can be clear?"

"I'm sorry about everything, Twon. I never meant for any of this to happen."

"Yeah, whatever, sneaky ass nigga."

"How you *wake up* talking shit?" said Charles, standing in the doorway.

"Hey," I said, not really sure how to address Charles. My beef was more with Hype and Quaid, but I wasn't sure where Charles stood in the situation, because he was their cousin.

"Wassup, my dude?" he said, nodding his head at me, letting me know that we were cool. "Glad to see you awake."

"Thanks."

"The doctor said your legs are all fucked up, so I guess you won't be playing ball no time soon. But you better heal up quick, cuz you got an ass whooping coming." Charles smirked.

I could tell that he was trying to lighten the mood and ease the tension between me and Quaid, so I smirked back at him, but at the moment, basketball was the last thing on my mind.

"So I guess a nigga ain't dead then," I said, and my heart filled with pain.

"Nope," said Charles. "And we're all glad to see that."

I was almost afraid to ask the next question. "My mother been by here?"

I could tell by the expression on Charles' face that he was trying to choose his words carefully. "I mean…" He scratched his head, glancing back and forth between Quaid and me. "She been having to work a lot and shit. She came through a few times though. Tierra been here a lot, and her moms, and even Shaneece's THOT ass had to be forced away from your bedside every time she came."

"How long have I been here? And what about Hype?"

"You been in a coma for about three days. The doctor said you had swelling in your brain and shit. They wasn't sure if you was gonna make it for a minute. They also said some shit about permanent brain damage, but since you woke up talking shit, they must have been wrong."

I chuckled. "And what about Hype?" I repeated. He was the person I most wanted to see outside of Tierra. Hype was my best friend, like a brother to me since elementary school. I was close with Quaid and Charles, but not like with Hype.

"He came through," said Charles. "He's supposed to be stopping by again later tonight, but his ass been trying to avoid Shaneece."

"Why?"

"I mean, I'm not sure if I should tell you, seeing that you just woke up and shit. Not trying to make your ass fade to black again."

"What is it?" I said, looking back and forth between Quaid and Charles. Quaid had been totally silent since Charles entered the room, and now he looked nervous.

"I think we should wait 'til later," said Charles, easing away from the subject. "Your ass just came back from the dead. Give yourself time to breathe and shit."

"Come on, Charles, stop playing," I said. "Whatever it is, I'm going to find out sooner or later anyway, so you might as well tell me now."

Charles looked at Quaid then Quaid looked at me and nodded his head at Charles.

"A'ight." Charles sighed. "Shaneece says she's pregnant, and either you are the baby's father, or Hype is."

Hype

If I thought my life was fucked up before, the shit is definitely fucked up now. Shaneece's ass is pregnant, and either me or Twon is the baby daddy. If this ain't some shit, I don't know what is…

I really don't even know how to process this shit. I mean, me and Twon was literally in the middle of beef when all this went down. Me and Quaid just jumped him at the basketball court a couple of weeks ago, and now the nigga tried to commit suicide. I knew Twon was dealing with a lot with his moms and Tierra and now with our situation, but I never thought it was affecting him this deeply. Despite my beef with him, that man has been like a brother to me since day one, ever since the first time we met in kindergarten.

I feel like an asshole for even having beef with him now, especially since all this was happening. I remember right before he did this shit, he was calling me on the phone trying to tell me something, but my ass was so caught up in the Shaneece situation that I wasn't trying to hear what he had to say. I feel mad guilty and mad selfish over that shit yo, word up.

I don't know why I seriously believed that Twon went behind my back with Shaneece. I guess I was so mad that I was blinded, cuz that girl really broke my heart and shit. Never thought I'd see the day that I would get my heart broken by a female, but I guess that's why they say never say never.

I been low-key avoiding Shaneece ever since she said that she was pregnant, because I don't know how to deal with it. First of all, how the hell am I supposed to raise a kid when I barely even know my damn self? I mean, it's not like I can ask my daddy for advice. That nigga was never in my life to begin with, so it's not like I can go to him now.

And what about college? Do I just give that shit up, or what? I don't know what the workload is gonna be like, or even if I will get any acceptance letters, but if I do, what do I do? Just turn them down and get a job? Or what? Should I put my life on hold 'til I get some DNA results, or should I just go if I get accepted, and see what happens? I really don't know what to do. G-Ma gonna be heated at me…

I do know one thing though: If I am the father, I'm gonna be in my kid's life, yo, straight up. We gotta break this cycle of niggas just dropping babies left and right, and leaving the mother alone to take care of them. I mean, granted, I've heard crazy stories of ratchet baby mommas, and bitches who use their kids as pawns, but I know for sure that it can't all be the female's fault. Look at my situation: None of my friends have had their father in their life. Well, except Shaneece's lying ass, but she don't count. Outside of her, none of the people in my close family have their father in their life, and that shit has to stop.

Facts.

Shaneece

Well, I guess the cat is out of the bag now. I didn't plan for it to come out this way that I was pregnant, but it did. I don't know . . . just seeing Tierra at the hospital angered me. I know I was the one in the wrong in this situation, but I still feel resentment toward her for some reason. I really have no right to – it was *me* who slept with *her* man, not the other way around, but I still do…

"Hey. You ready?" Shanelle said. She was bringing me back to my parents' house. Winter break was over, which meant that it was time to go back to school and face reality. I could only imagine how people were going to treat me, especially if it came out that I was possibly pregnant with my ex-best friend's boyfriend or his best friend.

And don't even get me started about my parents. My father would kill me if he found out I'm pregnant, so I had to beg Shanelle not to say anything to either of my parents. I don't even know how to have that conversation. I mean, I know I won't be able to hide it for too long, but I plan to hold out for as long as I can. Shanelle got me a prepaid phone that I'm hiding to use for all of my contacts with the hospital. I have no idea how I am going to hide my doctor visits and ultrasounds, but I'm going to try, because I'm scared shitless of the alternative.

"I'm as ready as I'll ever be, Shanelle." I took a deep breath and let it out as we took off. The ride was pretty uneventful. We mainly just listened to music and didn't talk much. I think we both had a lot on our mind. When we finally pulled up to our parents' house, I gulped.

"Shaneece…" Shanelle began. "I know this is difficult for you, but I honestly believe that you should just tell Mom and Dad that you are pregnant. They will undoubtedly be mad about it at first, but I think it will be more stressful for you if you try to hold it in and hide everything from them than if you just come out and say it."

"I understand what you're trying to do, Shanelle, but I'm just not ready to face this with them yet. I mean, what if they try to make me get an abortion? I'm not killing my baby." I swallowed a lump in my throat as I trembled internally at the mere thought of going through such a horrible procedure.

"I understand that, and legally, I don't believe they can do that."

"But what if they *can* though?! I know that Dad will probably jump on that opportunity if it's within his rights to do so."

"Well, we could do some research on it, but outside of Dad and what he might do, have you thought about what *you* are going to do? I mean, you just said that you are going to keep the baby, but how are you going to care for him or her? Are you still going to college? Are you going to find a job? How are you going to handle the situation when you find out who the father is?"

"I don't know, Shanelle. I don't even know how to deal with this situation. That's why I don't want Mom and Dad to know right off the bat. They'll try to pressure me, and I don't even fully understand the situation myself yet. I need time to sort all of this out."

Shanelle sighed. "Okay. Even though I disagree with you, I respect your decision."

"Thank you."

"Are you ready to go in the house?"

"Barely," I chuckled. "But there's no place else for me to go." We got out of the car. I looked down at my shirt and adjusted it to make sure there was no bulge showing from my prepaid cell phone that I had hidden in my bra. *Good thing I have ample cleavage*, I thought with a smirk.

"What are you smiling about?" Shanelle said, wondering how I'd gone from nervous to flippant in mere minutes.

"It's nothing," I said. "Just trying to wrap my head around this crazy situation."

As soon as we walked into the house, my father started in on me. "I hope you had fun over Shanelle's house, Shaneece, because there are going to be some serious changes in this house. You no longer have a laptop except for use in front of your mother or me, and for homework purposes only. Same thing with your phone. We already saw that Shanelle bought you a new one."

I looked at Shanelle. *You see what I mean?* I shouted through my eyes. She offered an encouraging smile.

"Okay, Dad," I said. "I'm sorry."

"Also, I went ahead and deactivated all of your social media accounts since you will no longer be needing them. You left all of them open on your desktop, so I didn't have to hack them to get in. I deleted all of your pictures and everything before I deactivated the accounts, so there will be no excuse for you to try to go back in. Do you understand?" The expression on his face made it clear that he was daring me to challenge him.

I felt the hurt and pain from his words rising up in my throat, but I decided that I couldn't break down now. I had to be strong for my baby, and I had to find a way to get the hell away from my father so I could be done with this situation once and for all.

"Okay," I said, nodding my head as if I understood, though on the inside, I was boiling with rage. I struggled not to let my negative emotions show, reminding myself that I had to keep my stress levels low for the baby. So I decided to just let it go.

"Okay," I repeated, my tone more final this time.

Tierra

I think Twon and I are really over for good. I mean, it was one thing to sleep with someone else while we were temporarily broken up, but it's another thing to have a baby behind my back. I don't think he purposefully got her pregnant, and besides, Hype could be the father, but still – he didn't even bother to use protection!

And no matter how hard I try, even after the situation with Twon trying to kill himself, I still cannot get those images out of my head of Twon and Shaneece in the bed together. That filthy bitch had her mouth all over my man…

And don't even get me started on *that* bitch. Who the hell does she think she is, waltzing into the hospital like she owns the place, acting like she has any right to be there for Twon? I wanted to fight her *so bad*, but my mother held me back. I don't give a damn if she is pregnant. I know I'm probably wrong to think that way, but having all of these angry feelings toward her and not being able to put my hands on her just because she is pregnant is driving me crazy.

"There you go with that look on your face again," said my mother, interrupting my thoughts.

"Hey," I said.

"You still thinking about that girl?"

"Yes."

"Well, what are you going to do if Twon *is* the father?"

"I have no idea, Ma."

"And how are you feeling about Quaid?"

"I don't know. I feel like I'm caught between both of them. Me and Twon were together for two years, but I've always had feelings for Quaid, ever since we first met. I just couldn't bring myself to admit it until recently."

"Well, which one do you think is better for you?"

"I don't know. I still love Twon, despite everything that happened, but I can't deny my feelings for Quaid either."

"Have you prayed about it?"

My head snapped back in surprise. "*Prayed* about it?"

"Yes."

"Do you think God will even answer this kind of prayer? I mean, I'm pretty sure He has much more important things to deal with than trying to help me figure out which man I should be with."

"Why don't you just try it and let Him decide whether what you're going through is important to Him?"

"I'm not sure I want to do that. I mean, what if He like, strikes me with a lightning bolt or something?"

My mother burst out laughing. "What if He *strikes* you?!" She gasped for air, holding her stomach, she was laughing so hard. "Girrrl, you are really a trip. God is not going to strike you down just because you ask Him a question."

"Oh." I looked at her sheepishly.

"Ain't you been going to church lately? I thought they would've taught you that by now."

"Ma, can I ask you a question?" Her last statement reminded me of something I had been dying to know since my early childhood. My mother never went to church with me, ever. She always said that she used to go to church when she was younger, and then she stopped, but she never told me why, and I was eager to find out.

"What's going on?" she said, looking like she was slightly uncomfortable all of a sudden.

"I know I've asked you this multiple times before, and you always tell me the same thing, but I really want to know: Why did you stop going to church? And did you ever get saved?"

"Why do you ask? Are you thinking about getting saved?" I was very close to my mother, and I could read her body language better than she knew. It was obvious that she was trying to inch away from my real question. So I decided to go for it and ask her again.

"Yes, getting saved has been heavy on my mind for a while, but I really want to know why you stopped going to church all those years ago, and why you've never gone with me."

She sighed. "Tierra, I don't think you would understand. But as far as your situation, I believe you should definitely go for it. If you've been wanting to be saved for a while, that probably means that God has been calling you. You should answer Him and get saved."

"But why don't you think I would understand?"

"I don't really want to get into all of that right now. Maybe later."

My shoulders slumped in defeat when I realized that she wasn't going to answer. "Well, can you at least tell me if you ever got saved?"

"Yes. Yes, I'm saved." Her response was a bit too brisk. She wasn't telling me something.

This was so confusing to me. My mother had always been on top of my spiritual life – I mean, she didn't always force me to go to church, but when I was younger, she made sure I always did my Bible study lessons, and even after I stopped going to church, she always tried to answer my questions when I asked for spiritual advice. Even now, she was trying to encourage me to pray about the whole Twon/Quaid situation, but she wouldn't go to church for herself, and she wouldn't tell me why she wouldn't go.

I persisted. "Well, if you're saved, why don't you go to church then?"

"Like I said, I don't really want to get into it. You just go ahead and get saved. It will be the best decision you ever made in your life, trust me."

"Okay, Ma." I had to accept her answer for now, but I wanted to know the truth eventually.

T*won*

I definitely wasn't expecting those words to come out of Charles' mouth. Shaneece was *pregnant*? And I could be a *father*? This is crazy. I literally only had sex with her one time, and now I might have a baby on the way.

Shit, I guess it's a good thing that my plan to kill myself didn't work, because if it did, I would have put my child through what I went through, growing up without my father in my life. That's the one possible good thing to come out of this whole situation aside from the fact that Hype doesn't seem to have beef with me anymore.

I honestly don't know how I'm going to handle this situation – I mean, the doctor said that my legs should heal within six to eight weeks because of the type of fractures I have, so I guess after my legs are healed, I can try to go back to work. But the thing is, even if they let me back to the factory, which I pray that they will, I will definitely need to up my hours to full time because there's no way I can save up for a baby working twelve-hour shifts on weekends, much less afford the rent my mother is charging me. And then there's school on top of that. How am I going to keep up with my classes *and* my grades *and* work fulltime hours? Shit, my ass just might have been better off dead…

"I see you're finally awake now." My head popped up at the sound of my mother's voice, and I was instantly filled with pain. I had to keep reminding myself not to make quick movements like that because my body hurt all over.

"Ma!" I was surprised to see her. I hadn't seen her since I first woke up from the coma, and that was almost two weeks ago. That shit hurt my feelings like you wouldn't believe, but I tried to push the pain away and focus on being grateful that she was here now, at least.

"Hmph," she said, taking a few more steps into the room.

"How have you been doing?" I said. "I haven't seen you in a while."

"Damn right, you haven't."

My mouth dropped open slightly at those words. I was trying to figure out why she was coming at me like this, but she wasted no time making sure I understood.

"You think you slick driving your fucking car over a bridge to get out of paying me my money? You got another muthafucking thing coming if you think you about to play me. I ain't taking care of no grown ass man, so you're gonna need to find a place to stay when you get out of here."

Her words hit me like a ton of bricks. "Ma! The doctor said they're going to discharge me in a couple of days. I don't have any money saved, and I have nowhere else to go."

"You should have thought about that shit before you drove over a fucking bridge!"

"Ma," I said, fighting back tears. "You would really kick me out on the street with two broken legs and nowhere to go?"

"Don't try to blame me. You did this to yourself. You say you're so responsible, and you think you're so damn smart. Figure it out, because I'm done. I've raised you all this time. You can figure it out for yourself now."

"You *raised*—?" I started, but she was already heading for the door.

"That's all I came here to say," she said, waving her hand at me dismissively. "You're still seventeen. Maybe you can get in foster care or something. All I know is I'm done with your bullshit."

"Ma! You just said it yourself — I'm only seventeen! I'm not a grown ass man. So you're just going to leave?"

She didn't even look back at me. She just sashayed out the door and kept walking. I could hear her four-inch heels clicking all the way down the hospital corridor, and then I heard her stop and speak to someone.

"Oh, hey, how are you?" she said in her fake professional voice that she uses when she's talking to someone important.

"I'm fine."

Who's that? I thought, my mind racing to put a name to the familiar voice. Then it hit me. *She's talking to Hype's grandmother G-Ma.*

"I came here to see Twon," said G-Ma in her warm, caring voice.

"Oh, he's right inside. He'll be so glad to see you," said my mother, all fake sweetness and concern.

"Mm hm."

G-Ma sees right through her. I smirked at the thought. G-Ma doesn't miss anything.

"Well, I've got to get to work, but I'll be back later!" said my mother, brisk and professional.

"Mm hm," G-Ma repeated. I was dying to see the expression on her face.

"Hey," said G-Ma in a soft voice as she came into my room. She stood next to my bed and smiled down at me.

"Hey, G-Ma. Thanks for coming." I was still trying to process everything my mother said to me, and it took all my effort to smile and be polite when I felt like punching my pillow and yelling at the top of my lungs.

"How are you doing?" Without waiting for an answer, she added, "I heard what your mother said before she left your room. You can come and stay with me."

I stared at her in shock. "Huh?"

"You can come and stay with me, boy. I'm not about to have you out here in these streets. We will get you healed up, inside and out."

I blinked back tears. "Thank you," I managed to croak. There was no point in trying to protest, because she sounded like her mind was made up, and because I really had nowhere else to go. I had no other family besides my mother. Her side of the family lived on the other side of the country, and I had never met any of them. I knew nothing about my father's side of the family.

"No problem," she said. "You're a good man, Twon. You always have been."

"Thank you." I swallowed a lump in my throat at those words. That was the nicest thing an older person had ever said to me.

Hype

Yo, I have always been raised to have respect for my elders and to never put my hands on no female, but on my life, I want to hook off on Twon's mother. Straight up.

Who in the FUCK kicks their seventeen-year-old son out on the streets with two broken legs, no money saved, and nowhere to go? This woman has done plenty of fucked up shit to Twon over the years, but I have never seen her go this low. What the fuck is wrong with this lady, for real?

I mean, plenty of people have bad ass kids, but Twon couldn't have been *that* damn bad. If Twon didn't have us, where would he have gone? And that ain't even the worst part about it. As if that wasn't enough, she already had all of his shit laid out in front of her house when me, Charles, and Quaid went to pick it up for him. She had my nigga's draws outside, bruh. We were able to get most of his stuff, but of course, all his games and shit were stolen because she just left the shit out there in plain sight. Wow.

I have never seen no shit like this before in my life. I thought Shaneece's father was bad, but shit, he ain't got nothing on Twon's mother, in my opinion.

I made my way over to G-Ma's house after school. I was bringing Twon's assignments to him since he was working from home 'til his legs healed up. I guess the administrators felt bad for him, so they gave him that option.

I knocked on the door and waited for somebody to come open it.

The door was opened by none other than Shaneece! I was instantly heated at just the sight of her.

"What the hell are you doing at my grandmother's house?" I said.

"I gave her my address," said G-Ma, coming up behind Shaneece with her hand on her hip. "And boy, you better watch your mouth, cussing in *my* house."

"How does your daddy feel about this?" I glared at Shaneece with daggers in my eyes. She broke eye contact then finally looked at me.

"I haven't told my parents yet."

"And when are you planning on telling them?" I demanded. My patience was wearing thin by the second. I really could not stand the sight of this bitch.

"I don't know, Hype!" she exclaimed, clearly upset.

"Boy, get in this house and get out of that girl's business. And stop talking to her all mean. She could possibly be the mother of your child. Is this how you want your relationship to go?"

"G-Ma…" I started, but I couldn't think of anything to say.

"Listen, I understand that you all are in a very difficult situation, but being mad at each other and mean to each other is not going to help. Y'all need to learn how to forgive and get along for the sake of that child. You don't want this girl stressing every time she comes over here while she's pregnant. That could have a negative effect on the baby."

I reflected on her words. I had never thought of it that way, that taking my anger out on Shaneece could be hurting the baby. I definitely didn't want my kid coming out with issues, and I would hate myself if I knew that I was the cause of it, so I decided to swallow my pride and my hurt and just let it go.

"Alright." I finally said. "I'm sorry."

Shaneece had tears in her eyes. "You really forgive me?" She looked shocked.

"I'm going to try to for the sake of the baby."

"Thank you," said Shaneece, and she went into the kitchen to make herself a snack.

Deep down inside, I cared about Shaneece, even though I knew I could never be with her again. For one, she played me, and for two, she already seemed to have her heart set on Twon. *Damn!* I thought. *What this nigga be* doing *to these bitches?*

I chuckled at that thought, but I kept it to myself. I guess I just needed to learn to be a man about this situation.

Shaneece

Finally, there is some light at the end of the tunnel. I thank God for Hype's grandmother. She has really taken me under her wing. She tried to convince me to tell my parents about the pregnancy, just like Shanelle did, but when I told her my situation and emphasized that I was not ready to deal with that just yet, she said that she understood, and that she would support me no matter what.

Seeing Hype's grandmother kind of gave me a glimpse of how a parent is supposed to be. I mean, granted, she's not his mother — she's his grandmother, but I can tell that they are close to each other, and I can also tell that she has a really good heart, because she immediately welcomed me with open arms without any judgment, and she's even letting Twon stay with her, when he's not even part of the family!

I feel kind of like a lame to share this, but I bawled my eyes out when I first met her, and she said that she accepted me, and that she was willing to give me advice and be like a mother to me if I needed it. I literally broke down right there in front of her, because I could tell that she wasn't just saying it to be nice — she really meant it. I know, that's really lame, and it may even just be the hormones, but either way, it touched my heart, because I've never had that before.

I'm sure my parents love me on some level, but I have never felt that they actually accepted me. It was always about how I just wasn't good enough because I didn't bring home perfect grades like Shanelle. It's refreshing to see that someone sees something good in me. I am truly grateful for G-Ma.

"Look at this THOT ass bitch." I heard a voice behind me. I closed my locker and slowly turned around, taking in a deep breath and trying to remain calm.

Standing in front of me was Jarmica, the same girl I saw sneering at me in the waiting room at the doctor's office when I was there for my prenatal vitamins.

"Do Hype and Twon know that you're pregnant?" she said with a smirk. "Do you even know which one is the father?" She chuckled in derision.

"I would be more worried about who's the father of *your* child," I retorted. "Rumors have it that you've been around the block a few times yourself. What were *you* doing at the doctor's office that day?"

"Bitch, who the fuck do you think you're talking to like that?" she said, stepping into my personal space.

"Obviously you, bitch!" I said, refusing to back down. "You're the one all up in my business like you have none of your own."

"Bitch, don't think you can't get it just because you're pregnant. I'll have my girl Shatina fuck your ass up. She fights pregnant bitches."

My anxiety increased when I saw Shatina stepping toward me like she was ready for action.

"I don't have time for this," I said, stepping around Jarmica.

"Yeah, that's right, bitch. You better back down." She pushed my head roughly, but I just kept walking. I wasn't about to let anybody hurt my baby.

I honestly don't know how much longer I can stay in school. Ever since I set foot on campus after winter break, so many girls have come up to me calling me a THOT, a slut, a whore, everything. And now that the word was pretty much out that I was pregnant, I could only imagine it would get worse.

I never would have thought that my last year of high school would be like this.

Hype

I went over Charles' house after school. Me and him been hanging kind of heavy lately, especially since the beef I'd had with Twon. I downed the last of my Cheetos, threw the bag in the trash, and grabbed my Pepsi from the coffee table.

"You 'bout to rot out all your muthafuckin teeth, nigga," said Charles, sipping on a Bud Light. He burped.

"I know you ain't talking about me when you 'bout to fuck up your whole damn liver." I took a long drink, savoring the taste as it went down my throat. This was life.

"Yo, let me holla at you about something," Charles said, looking serious all of a sudden.

"What's up?" I shot my empty Pepsi bottle into the trashcan. "YES!" I couldn't resist congratulating myself when it went in.

"I'm saying…." He hesitated. "You might be 'bout to have a baby and shit. How you gonna provide for it?"

"I don't know, man. I guess I'm gonna have to get a job or something."

"Well, how about instead of all that, you come make some easy money with me?"

"I don't know, Charles. I'm not really with that drug dealer shit."

"It's better than having to deal with all them niggas trying to clown you at some corny ass fast food restaurant!" He smirked. "Am I right?"

I'd had two jobs at fast food joints when I was in tenth grade. At both of them, I got fired the same way — some guys my age came into the place and tried to play me because I was behind the counter. Both times, I hopped over that shit and hooked off on them.

"I don't know, Charles. Why you want me to do this so bad all of a sudden?"

"Look…" He sighed. "Shit ain't the same. Chief just got locked up because he got caught violating his probation. I been trying to hold shit down, but one of my other niggas just got robbed, and I got beef with these other niggas from a couple blocks over. I need somebody I can trust on my team, and you the only nigga I know besides Chief that I would actually trust with something like this."

"Damn. I feel you," I said, buying some time to process what he said. I mean, I never was the drug dealing type, but I definitely wasn't trying to have Charles out there with nobody really holding him down. I reflected on his words for a few moments, then we both looked when the front door opened. Charles' mother, my Auntie Shameka, walked in carrying a shopping bag.

"Hey," she said to us.

"Hey, Auntie," I said.

"Hey Ma," said Charles.

"Charles, when exactly do you plan to go back to school? You haven't been there in three days. It's a miracle that your ass made it to senior year!"

"Ma, stop all that naggin'! Shit."

"I'm just saying, though, when are you going back?"

He sucked his teeth. "I'll go back tomorrow, okay? Happy now?"

Her expression softened. She eyed the beer in his hand. "Any more of those left in the fridge?"

"I think like two."

"Good. Cuz I'm about to relax."

She walked into the kitchen carrying her shopping bag.

"So you made a decision yet?" Charles said in a low voice, turning back to me.

"Nah, not yet. Give me some time to think about it."

"A'ight, nigga, but don't take forever."

"I won't."

Twon

Shaneece and I been trying to act cordial since the conversation between her, Hype, and G-Ma about getting along for the sake of the child. I wasn't trying to be no cause of issues for the baby either, so I was trying my best to swallow my anger toward Shaneece about the mess we were all caught up in.

I mean, even though the situation is fucked up, Shaneece is really not all the way bad. I can tell that she genuinely cares for me by the way she acts, and I care for her too since we've been through similar things with our parents. On the one hand, I wish this situation would just go away, but on the other hand, I'm kind of looking forward to having a kid.

I tried to call my mother a few times since I been here, just to let her know I was here and to see if she would let me come back to the house, but she never answered the phone. Then, the last time I called, the automated message said the number was no longer in service, so I guess she had the house phone disconnected. When I called her cell phone, it went to voicemail every time. I guess once my legs get fully healed, I'll make a trip over there to see if we can talk.

"Hey!" said Shaneece after G-Ma let her in the door. She hugged G-Ma then came over to give me a hug. I patted her back a couple times, but I was still conflicted about my feelings for her, so I wasn't really trying to hug her like that.

"How's your physical therapy going?" she said.

Thankfully, that was the one thing my mother didn't cut me off from — her health insurance.

"It's alright. Thanks for asking."

"How are your legs feeling?" Without waiting for an answer or an invitation, she leaned down and gently massaged my legs, starting with my calves.

"What are you—?"

"Does that help the pain?" She smiled up at me, her fingers working some kind of magic on my legs.

I knew what she was trying to do. I blinked back some tears. "Yeah. Thanks."

"No problem!"

"Hmph!" That was G-Ma, smiling at us from the doorway before she made her way back to the kitchen.

We stared at each other awkwardly, both of us kind of embarrassed, then Shaneece continued to massage my legs. That shit was feeling good, so I wasn't even 'bout to tell her to stop. We heard a knock at the door, but we thought nothing of it, figuring it was probably Hype or somebody, but we got a rude awakening when Tierra strode into the room. She stopped in her tracks when she saw Shaneece massaging up near my thigh.

"What are you doing?" she said, looking shocked and hurt.

"She was just giving me a massage, Tierra. It's no big thing."

"Oh, is *that* what you're doing?" Her eyes dared Shaneece to challenge her.

"Look, I'm not trying to get into this with you today, girl." Shaneece retorted. Her amazing fingers stopped. "Twon, I have to go." She grabbed her purse and walked out of the house without another word, digging for her keys as she strode to the door.

"So I see that you and Shaneece are getting really acquainted," Tierra said, her voice laced with sarcasm. "I can just hear your thoughts now. *Oooh, that feels so good, Shaneece. Keep massaging right on up my thigh, girl.*"

"Yeah, just like you and Quaid getting all cozy," I shot back.

"Whatever, Twon. That wasn't the same situation, so don't even try to compare the two."

"How is it not the same? You and Quaid was messing around for who knows how long."

"Me and Quaid were not messing around, so you don't even know what you're talking about!" she spat. "We kept trying to tell you—"

"Look, I'm not trying to do this today. I was having a peaceful time 'til you came in here."

I could tell that those words hurt her. "Yeah, I bet you were. You were having a peaceful time getting a personal massage from Shaneece." She whirled around and made her way to the door.

I felt bad now. "Tierra, wait…."I didn't mean to hurt her feelings, especially since I felt like I was mostly to blame for our situation. "Tierra, please don't leave. I didn't mean it like that. For real."

"It sure sounded like that to me," she said, her hand on the doorknob.

"I don't want to fight."

"Me either."

"I'm sorry for everything that went down."

"So am I, but I don't really want to get into it right now."

"So when do you want to get into it?"

"Just not now."

"Have you been around Quaid since then?"

"Why, Twon?" She flung out her arms in frustration. "Why are you asking me this?" She shifted her handbag to her shoulder. "You know what? I have to go." She opened the door and walked out, and even if I'd had a comeback, it would've been useless because she was gone that fast.

Tierra

This nigga got a lot of fucking nerve, asking me about Quaid when I just caught Shaneece with her hands practically up his pants! And don't even get me started on that BITCH! It literally takes everything inside me not to try to hurt her. She just can't keep her fucking hands off my man. If that bitch wasn't pregnant….

She really just has no clue.

And Twon didn't make it any better, taking her side over mine. I refuse to let him continue to hurt me with this girl. Sooner or later, me and him are going to have to figure out what we're going to do, because if we do end up together, she is not going to be allowed near him, child or not.

My cell phone buzzed in my pocket as I stood at the bus stop. I pulled it out and stared at the caller ID. I figured it would have been Twon calling me trying to get me to come back to G-Ma's house, but it was Quaid. "So this nigga doesn't even care," I said, referring to Twon. "Probably still feeling all mellow from that bitch's fingers up his leg." A lady standing near me glanced at me talking to myself. I turned away and wiped a tear as I answered Quaid's call.

"Hey," I said.

"Hey, how are you? Everything okay? Your voice sounds different."

"No, it's okay. I'm good."

"You don't sound good. Where are you?"

"Leaving G-Ma's house. I'm outside at the bus stop."

"Did something happen?"

"Nothing. Just got into an argument with Twon over Shaneece."

"Oh, was she there?"

"I caught her giving him a massage." I snorted. "If that's what they want to call it."

"Do you need me to come and get you? We could talk about it."

My heart panged at those words. Quaid was giving me the type of treatment that I should have been getting from Twon. Quaid was always there to pick up the pieces, but Twon seemed hell-bent on breaking my heart...

"Tierra?"

"Oh, no, that's okay. I'm fine. But thank you for asking though."

"Do you need a ride home?"

"No, the bus is pulling up now." I stepped forward as it stopped in front of me. The doors opened, and I stepped inside, paid my fare, and walked toward an empty seat.

"Okay then, if you're sure." Quaid sounded disappointed.

"I'm sure. I'm already on the bus now. What's wrong?"

"Nothing. Do you want me to talk to you until you get home?"

I smiled. Quaid was so sweet. "Sure. That's fine with me."

We chatted during my entire bus ride home, and by the time we got to my street, I was feeling so much better. But that's how all of my conversations are with Quaid. He always finds a way to uplift me and make me feel better.

I talked to him until I got in the house. After we said our goodbyes, I reflected on the day's events. I definitely had some thinking to do.

Shaneece

I sniffled as I scrubbed my locker door, trying to clean up all the mess. Somebody had written "THOT ASS BITCH" in huge capital letters all over my locker in red lipstick. I really don't know how much more of this shit I can take. I am so ready to leave this school…

Splat! I felt something smack the back of my head, and then I heard laughter and feet running down the hall. I quickly whipped around and saw this boy from my English class smirking at me. I felt something slimy dripping down the back of my neck. I ran my hand through my hair, and sure enough, it was an egg.

"ARGGH!" I screamed. I took off after the boy, full of anger. He looked kind of surprised, and when he saw I was headed toward him like a freight train, he started to run, but he tripped over his feet and fell to the floor. I jumped on top of him raining blows on his head. I busted his nose in the process, and I would've kept pounding him if I hadn't felt strong arms lift me up and pull me off of him.

"What is going on here?" It was one of the school cops.

"HE THREW A FUCKING EGG AT MY HEAD!" I screamed, lunging toward the boy again, but the cop held me back.

"This stupid bitch busted my nose!" said the boy, holding his hand over his nose to stop the blood.

They took us to mediation, where neither of us wanted to say anything to anybody. Since we refused to speak, they sent us both to in-house detention for the rest of the day.

I could only imagine what I would face when I got home to my father.

***

"SHANEECE!" He screamed louder than usual, before I was even all the way in the house. "ARE YOU FUCKING CRAZY?"

Suddenly, vomit rushed up my throat. I bolted to the bathroom and threw up. My father stood at the door, watching. "What the hell is wrong with you?" He had brought his voice way down and actually sounded concerned.

"I'm feeling sick," I said. "I think it was something I ate at school." I prayed to God that he wouldn't pry further, because I was nowhere near ready to tell him I was pregnant.

"What the hell are you doing fighting boys?"

"He threw an egg at my head, Dad. It was some stupid senior prank thing," I added, hoping it sounded convincing.

"Oh." He chuckled. "I used to do that kind of stuff when I was in high school. Well, don't get into any more fights, okay? I hope you feel better."

I was thoroughly surprised that he actually believed me, and that he let me off the hook that easily. I let out a deep breath.

Then my eyes welled with tears when I realized that my father would've been even angrier if he'd known I had been in a fight with a baby growing inside of me. Sure, he would be furious that I was pregnant, but knowing that I might have endangered my baby would send him over the edge because after all, he was a good father, and I knew that he would be a proud grandfather — eventually, when the shock wore off.

And then I ugly cried like I hadn't cried in a long time. Where the hell was my life going to turn up from here?

Tierra

I sat in my living room watching TV while waiting for my mother to come home from work. I really wanted to talk to her about Twon and Shaneece, the possibility of the baby being Twon's, and my feelings about Quaid. I felt so conflicted and confused, and she always gave me great advice.

I heard a knock on the front door, and it startled me because I wasn't expecting anyone to come over. I pressed mute on the remote and went to the door. "Who is it?" I called out.

"It's me, Quaid." I froze. Quaid and I hadn't really been alone together since that night Twon saw him giving me a ride home from the store. We had talked on the phone a few times, but that wasn't the same. I wasn't sure I was ready to face him just yet, but I wasn't about to leave him standing outside either. I opened the door.

"Hey," I said, trying to mask my surprise. "What are you doing here?"

"I think we need to talk."

I let him in the house and closed the door behind him.

"How about we go in the living room? My mom should be home soon."

We made our way over to the couch and sat down at either end, partially facing each other.

"So, how have you been doing lately?" I said, trying to break the awkward silence.

"I've been okay." He stared at the living room rug. "I kind of go back and forth. I mean, I know that Twon is alive and he's okay, but I can't get those images of his car flipping over the bridge out of my head. It keeps replaying in my mind over and over again. Even when I go to sleep, I dream about it, and when I wake up, it's still heavy on my mind."

"Wow," I said, my heart filling with compassion for him. I hadn't even thought about how Quaid might have felt since he was actually there when the accident happened. Everyone was so focused on themselves and their own feelings, and of course on Twon and his feelings, but I don't think anyone had stopped to check on Quaid. "That must have been really traumatic for you."

"It was, Tierra." He turned toward me slightly, and I could see sadness and tiredness in his eyes. He didn't look like his usual self at all.

"Is something else bothering you?" I don't know why, but in my heart, I just felt that seeing the accident wasn't the only thing on Quaid's mind. There had to be something else that was bothering him too.

"I don't know . . . I guess the other thing is that I kind of feel like I may have played a part in what happened to him." He swallowed a lump in his throat.

"Why do you think that?"

"Because right before this happened, we had the whole situation with you guys breaking up over me, and also with me and Hype jumping him at the basketball court. I just feel like if I hadn't been in the middle of you guys' relationship, none of this would have happened." A tear slid down his face, and he wiped it away, but he kept his eyes averted.

"Oh, Quaid…" I scooted closer to him and gently rubbed his back. "Quaid, Twon and I had way more problems than the situation with you. If you remember, he was cheating on me with Shaneece, and we were having our own problems on top of that. Also, he goes through a lot with his mom — look at how she just kicked him out a few weeks ago! That's a lot. I would definitely not say that you were the one at fault."

He sat there silent for a few moments then finally turned to face me. "Can we pray?"

I was taken aback by his words. I was totally not expecting him to say that — I mean, I know Quaid is a Christian, but I had no idea why he wanted to pray all of a sudden. "Um . . . okay," I said.

"We don't have to if you don't want to," he said quickly, as if he almost regretted bringing it up.

"Oh, no. I want to. It's just that I'm not really experienced with prayer like that."

"That's fine. I just have a lot on my mind, and I've found that God always hears me when I cry out to Him."

I couldn't argue with that, so I followed his lead and stood up. We faced each other, and he held out his hands. I placed mine in his, and the reaction was so sudden and immediate that it took me by surprise. I felt all tingly inside. His hands were so strong and warm, and I wanted to hold them forever. I tried not to stare at him as he bowed his head. He closed his eyes, so I decided to close mine too so that I wouldn't get distracted.

Quaid began to pray, and I swear, his voice was so strong and powerful, it was like I could feel every word. He prayed for Twon and his mother, and he also prayed for his family. He even prayed for me! I was so engrossed in his words that I barely remembered to say "Amen" when he was done.

We opened our eyes and looked at each other, and then we smiled.

"Wow," I said. "That was great."

"Yes, it was." This time he didn't break eye contact, and the moment felt amazing and real, like it was eternal somehow.

Twon

G-Ma brought me some lunch on a tray as I was doing some assignments for school. "Here you go, boy," she said, setting the tray down in front of me. "Can't have you starving in here."

"Thank you," I said, smiling at her. "You know I could have gone to the kitchen on these crutches." I had recently transitioned to crutches, and sometimes I could get by with just one crutch because one of my legs was healing a little faster than the other.

"I know." She said, sitting down across from me with her own tray of food. "But I brought it to you because I want to talk to you."

My heart dropped slightly. *Is she 'bout to kick me out?* My mind raced as I tried to think of where I could possibly go from here. My mother was still not answering my phone calls. I had lost my car when I flipped it over the bridge, and the insurance company refused to pay out a claim because it was attempted suicide, so I didn't have a car to sleep in. I didn't know what I was going to do if this was why she wanted to talk to me.

I braced myself for the worst. "What's going on?" I said, trying to sound nonchalant.

G-Ma came right out with it. "I want to talk to you about how you got to the point where you wanted to end your life."

I stared at her in shock. "I don't really know where to start," I said finally.

"That's fine, but I want you to begin to let it out. It's not good to hold all of those feelings inside of you."

"I appreciate it," I said, feeling kind of numb. It was totally new to me to have someone like G-Ma, someone like a mother figure, actually care about me.

"So, do you want to try to talk about it?" Her eyes were full of patience and compassion, to the point where I felt like I could tell her anything, and not have it come back on me later on down the road.

I didn't really know how to start, so I just plunged in and told her how I found out about my father, and how my mother held it from me all these years. After that, I described how I started having flashbacks of all the things my mother did to me when I was younger, and how she treated me. By the time I was done talking, it was dark outside, and I felt exhausted, but also like a burden had been lifted from my shoulders. I had no idea I even remembered all the stuff I told G-Ma — it was like it all just came back to me, and there was more. I hadn't even told her half of the story, but I figured the rest could wait for another day.

The whole time I was talking, she just sat there and listened, with no interruptions. After I was finished, she offered me a few encouraging words, then we ate dinner together before I drifted off to sleep. That night was one of the most peaceful nights of my life.

Tierra

Quaid came over my house again a couple of days after the time we prayed. "Is this going to become a routine?" I joked as I opened the door for him.

"Possibly." He had a happy smile on his face as we made our way to the living room. Again, my mother was at work, so we were alone together.

"So, I see that you look like you're feeling better!" I said, giving him a once-over. He was actually looking sexy as hell in a fitted cap, a white T-shirt, some black jeans, and some fresh white Air Forces. For some reason, the contrast of that white shirt against his dark chocolate skin was driving me crazy on the inside. Also, for some inexplicable reason, the fitted cap brought out the length of his lashes and the juiciness of his lips. *Pull yourself together, girl,* I scolded myself inwardly. *Focus!*

"Tierra?"

I was so drawn in by his looks that I didn't even realize that he had been talking to me the whole time.

"Huh?" I said.

"Are you okay?" He looked concerned.

I suddenly felt embarrassed. Here I was lusting over him while he was probably trying to talk about something important.

"I'm sorry. I was just . . . I got a bit distracted there for a moment. What were you saying?" I leaned forward and was all serious attention to prove that I hadn't completely lost my mind.

"Oh, that's cool," he said. "I was just asking if you've had a conversation with Twon."

"About what?"

"About whether you guys are getting back together."

"Actually, no . . . we haven't had that conversation yet. Why? Has he said something to you?"

"No . . . he doesn't really talk to me like that. I think Twon and I need to have a one-on-one ourselves."

"So why are you asking about *me* and Twon?"

"Because, I just…" He looked nervous. He sighed and turned to face me. "Look, Tierra, I want to be completely honest with you. I've had feelings for you since the first moment I met you. I was too afraid to say anything to you about it, and before I could, you and Twon got together. But my feelings never went away. I apologize for telling you this now, because I know this is probably not the best time, but I feel like I can't hold it in any longer, and I really want to know how you feel about me."

Damn. I didn't even know what to say. He really just laid it all out there, just like that. I suddenly felt trapped. I mean, I knew that we had been dancing around this issue the whole time we'd been friends, but now that it was finally out in the open, I wasn't sure if I was ready to have this conversation with him.

"Quaid . . . this is really a lot to take in right now."

"I know, and I'm sorry. And believe me, I'm really not trying to pressure you. But I also want to be true to myself too. I feel like I've kind of been on hold this whole time that you guys were together, because I never got to see if you had any feelings for me. If you don't, that's fine, and I'll back off. But if you do, I just want to let you know that I want to be with you."

Damn, Quaid was really dropping truth bombs today! I had never seen him be this blunt before. I was totally taken aback. He had hinted plenty of times that he had feelings for me, but now he was coming full force, and I didn't know what to do.

"I'm not sure what to say, Quaid. This feels like it's kind of out of nowhere."

"Well, if I remember correctly, it was you who actually brought up this subject the first time, that day in the car. I just want to follow up on it, put it out on the table, and see where we can go from here."

"I understand, but I don't think I meant . . . I mean, um, I don't think this is the best time to discuss this."

"Well, can you at least tell me if you have feelings for me too, or if you ever did?"

The look in his eyes was so intense that I had to glance away. I really wasn't used to him being this bold.

"Why don't we do this another time? I'm really not sure if I'm ready to have this conversation."

He looked kind of disappointed at my words. I felt bad because he had just poured his heart out to me, and I felt like I was brushing him off. I wanted to just give in and tell him that I had been feeling him too, but at the same time, I couldn't deny that I still had deep feelings for Twon, and I wasn't sure if I was willing to let him go — especially if he was going to end up with that stupid bitch Shaneece.

After a long pause, he finally spoke. "Okay. I won't pressure you. I know I just showed up here unexpectedly and dropped this on you. I didn't mean to catch you off guard like that. I'm sorry. We're cool. I'm glad you're my friend."

"Thank you . . . me too," I said in an awkward attempt to make him feel better, but my heart was filled with guilt.

Hype

I know that this is probably the dumbest shit I've ever done in my life, but I took Charles up on his offer. It's not like I wanted to really sell drugs like that, but at the same time, I didn't want to leave my cousin hanging. I can't lie though — I've only been doing it for like a week, but I'm already paranoid as fuck. I feel like I gotta constantly watch my back for the cops and shit. I mean, I know niggas sell drugs every day, but shit, niggas get caught every day too.

BZZZZZZ. BZZZZZZ.

I looked at the caller ID on my phone. It was a number I ain't recognize. I picked it up anyway, in case it was important.

"Hello?"

"Hello, may I speak to Hype?" The voice was an older black dude. It sounded familiar, but I couldn't place it.

"Yeah, this is him."

"Hype, how you doing. I'm not sure if you remember me, but my name is Dr. Chris Young, and I came to your school a little while ago to talk to your class about being a college student."

"Oh, yeah, I remember!" *How the hell this nigga get my number?*

"You're probably wondering how I got your number," he said with a slight chuckle, and I chuckled too. "I saw that you applied to be a Sociology major at the school, so I wanted to reach out to you."

"Oh, yeah, true, I did do that. Thanks."

"No problem. I just wanted to let you know that the admissions office is still processing applications, so the decisions are not final yet, but you have a definite chance of getting into the school, and we would love to have you as part of the Sociology program."

"Wow. Thanks, sir." *I was supposed to call him sir, right?*

He chuckled again. "Feel free to call me Chris, or Dr. Young, man."

That made me feel more comfortable. "Okay, thanks, Chris. Dr. Young." I felt kind of stupid saying both names, but I wanted to put some type of respect on it too.

"No problem. I also wanted to let you know that if you do get accepted, which you should find out in about a month or so, you'll need to fill out the form in the packet that says you accept your acceptance."

"Wait . . . say that again? You said I gotta accept my acceptance?"

"Yeah. I know it sounds confusing, but it's basically a way for us to know exactly who is coming to the school, because many students get accepted to multiple institutions, and we may not be their first choice."

"Oh, that makes sense. Well, thanks for looking out."

"No problem. On the form, it has an option to either mail it back, email your response, or call in your response. I just wanted to let you know what to expect if and when you get the letter."

"Okay, cool. Thanks, man."

"No problem. And if you have any other questions about the process, you can give me a call or shoot me an email."

"I will. Thanks."

After we hung up, I felt stupid as hell. Here I am out here selling drugs when there is a chance that my black ass could actually get into college.

Charles is my cousin, so I definitely want to hold it down, but at the same time, I gotta start thinking about my own future too, especially if I actually get accepted.

Damn, this shit was confusing as hell, and that's without even throwing a possible baby in the mix.

Shaneece

I sat in my usual place in the front of my English class, and as usual, I could feel Tierra's eyes boring into my back. I wish I could just switch out of this stupid class so I wouldn't have to see her anymore, but I already talked to my guidance counselor, and he told me it was too late in the semester. Part of me just wants to drop out of school altogether and just get my GED or something, but I'm not sure if I would need my parent's permission for something like that...

"Okay, so today we are going to start a new paper assignment, but this time, there will be a little bit of a twist." My English teacher stood up in the front of the class, obviously pleased with himself for coming up with whatever idea he had in mind. I almost rolled my eyes at him. The last time he had a 'brilliant' idea, it almost ended up in a fight between me and Tierra because he tried to put us in a group together. I so hoped that whatever he cooked up this time was an individual assignment.

"This assignment is going to be a research paper, but it will be a little different," he continued. "I want each of you to pick a social issue pertaining to adolescents in this country, conduct some research on it, and produce a five-page paper by the end of the week. But the catch is this: Everyone has to pick their topic today, and each student has to have a unique topic, so no two people can write about the same thing."

Groans could be heard throughout the classroom. It was pretty much a consensus that nobody thought his idea was all that great except him.

"Oh, come on guys, this will be fun!" He tried to joke, but it was a total fail. "Does anyone want to call first dibs on a topic now?"

The kid next to me raised his hand. "I do."

"Thank you, Michael. What's your idea, so I can write it on the board?"

Michael shot me a sly look before he spoke. "Can I do mine on teen pregnancy?"

I felt my ears growing hot. This was about to be some bullshit. I could feel it. The teacher, however, was totally excited about Michael's topic.

After Michael, other people started to pick up on it. One girl said that she wanted to do hers on STDs. Another guy chose promiscuity among teens based on gender. Yet another student tried to suggest a topic on teen girls becoming pregnant without knowing the father, and how that would affect the future children, but the teacher put a halt to that topic, and told him that he needed to broaden his scope.

"Shaneece?" He pinned me with his eyes and waited.

I felt my face growing hot as I looked up at him.

"You've been quiet this class period. Do you have a topic in mind?"

"Probably THOTism," said a girl to the side of me, and I heard snickers across the room.

He wrinkled his nose. "THOTism? What is that? I'm not familiar with that term."

This of course led to ripples of laughter across the class.

"Actually, I'll do my paper on bullying among high school students," I spat, glaring at the girl who basically just called me a THOT. "That seems to be running rampant nowadays."

The rest of the class period was uneventful, but I still couldn't shake my growing anger at having to deal with shit like this every day. When was it ever going to end?

***

I decided to call Shanelle on my bus ride home. I seriously wanted to look into dropping out and getting a GED, but I couldn't search it on my laptop at home because with the new household rules, my parents were breathing down my back with every move I made.

"Hello?" she said, sounding kind of sad.

"What's wrong with you?" I said, immediately feeling concerned.

"Nothing . . . just going through a lot right now."

"What is it? Something at work?"

"No, work is great. It's when I get home that the issues begin."

"What's going on?"

"I don't want to burden you with my problems when you've got enough of your own."

"Shanelle, you can talk to me. As many times as I have cried on your shoulder, I am definitely here for you."

She sighed. "It's Steve. I caught him cheating again." Steve was Shanelle's on-again, off-again boyfriend of three years. Things had started off great between them, but then Shanelle found out he was cheating on her, and then he cheated again after that. This was the third time he betrayed her trust.

"You need to just leave him, girl."

"I know, but it's easier said than done, Shaneece. I'm in love with him."

"I definitely understand that."

"I know . . . anyway, what's up with you? How's everything with school?"

"Same old stuff. These people have nothing better to do with their lives."

"Did something new happen?"

I told her about the incident in English class. She joked about coming to my school to beat a few people down for me. That made me chuckle, but I knew it wouldn't solve the problem. "Do you know anything about whether you need a parent's permission to drop out and get a GED?"

"I have no idea. Are you sure you want to go that route?"

"Yeah. I think I do because I know the stress can't be good, especially with the baby and all."

"True." She paused. "Well, I will do some research on it and get back with you. In the meantime, think about whether there is any way that you can at least finish your senior year. You've come this far, and you've barely got half a year left."

"I will," I said, but in my heart, I had already made my decision. I had to get out of this school.

Tierra

I decided that it was time to finally have a conversation with Twon. His legs were almost healed, and he seemed to be feeling better, so we needed to decide what we were going to do about this relationship.

"Hey," I said, after G-Ma let me in the house. I was relieved to see that Shaneece wasn't there.

"Hey," he said, looking up at me from where he sat on the couch.

I went over and sat down beside him. "We need to talk." I sighed.

"I know. A lot has happened."

We stared at each other for a few moments, then Twon spoke first. "Tierra, I know you probably won't believe me when I tell you this, but I really do love you, and I never meant for all that to go down with Shaneece. I mean, I know there's no excuse, but I really wish I could take back that day when you saw us in my room."

I blinked as I had a flashback of that day. "Me too." I grimaced at the thought of them naked in the bed together. "Do you still have feelings for her?"

"Do you still have feelings for Quaid?"

I could feel myself getting hot when he asked that question. "Twon, I asked you about Shaneece. We're not talking about Quaid right now."

"I understand that, but the reason we broke up the first time was because of Quaid."

"No, the reason we broke up was because of YOUR paranoia. You refused to accept the fact that I wasn't messing with him."

He sucked his teeth and rolled his eyes. "Oh my gosh, Tierra. Why can't you just admit it?"

"There's nothing to admit, Twon!" I stood up. This conversation was not going at all the way that I planned. "I'm sick and tired of trying to convince you over and over that I was NOT messing with Quaid. We never kissed, we never had sex, we never did anything. All that was YOU and Shaneece, NOT me and Quaid."

"Whatever, yo." He stretched out his legs and folded his arms, gazing across the room like he was deciding on something. When he collected his thoughts, he sat up straight and looked at me so fast that it startled me. "Okay, so y'all never did nothing physical, but did you have feelings for him? Because it's obvious that he has feelings for you."

"That's none of your business." I scooted a few inches away from him to put some space between us.

He leaned toward me, clearly getting more and more angry by the second. "And how exactly is that none of my fucking business when you was supposed to be MY girl?"

"See, that's why I can't ever talk to you, Twon."

"No, it's not that you can't talk to me. It's that you can't admit when you're clearly fucking wrong."

"How am I wrong when you fucked Shaneece on our anniversary?"

"I admitted that, and I fully apologize, but I need you to admit your part in the situation before we can move forward."

"I have no part in the situation if I didn't cheat on you."

"Look, do you even want to be together anymore, or not? Because from this conversation, it don't look like it to me."

"Don't you sit there and act like I'm the one who's causing all the issues here."

"Whatever, Tierra." He looked like he was exhausted. "I'm not going to talk in circles with you."

"There you go, always beating me down. Every time I talk to you, you have something negative to say about me."

"Well, what the hell am I supposed to do when you won't ever admit you're wrong? Huh?" He was clearly heated now. "I admitted my fault, and all I asked you to do was admit yours too. But instead of doing that, you want to act like you're so fucking innocent and I'm just this stupid ass jealous ass boyfriend, like I don't have a clue. You may not have been fucking him, but you definitely wanted the nigga. Can you just admit that, or would you rather sit there and continue to pretend that I'm the bad guy?"

I stared at him for a few moments, taking in his words. As hard as it was for me to admit it, I knew I had to. Twon was right. I did have feelings for Quaid.

"Okay," I said finally. "Yes, I have feelings for him."

"So who do you want to be with, Tierra, me or him?"

"Who would you rather be with, me or Shaneece?"

He stared at me for several long moments then shook his head and spoke with an air of finality in his voice. "Well, I guess this is how it's always going to be between us, so we might as well just let it go."

I felt a pang in my heart at his words, but at the same time, I had to agree. I knew it would break my heart to say the next words I was about to say, but they had to be said. Me and Twon were just not meant to be, and as much as it hurts, I have to let him go.

"You're right. We should just let it go," I said finally.

I could see the indecision in his eyes. I could tell that he was trying to decide whether this was the best move for us. After a few moments, I saw his expression change slightly, like he had made his choice. "Alright," he said. "I guess I'll see you."

Despite all the things I had just said, it still hurt that he actually agreed that he didn't want to be with me anymore. This was almost too heavy to bear, but in my heart, I believed that it had to be done.

I swallowed. "I'll see you."

I left G-Ma's house.

Twon

I been kind of depressed since that conversation with Tierra. I mean, I knew the chance of us getting back together was slim to none, but I was still kind of holding out hope. Two years down the damn drain. It seems like I can't ever catch a break in life.

"Boy, you done barely touched your lunch. I know you hungry." G-Ma walked into the room, checking up on me. I definitely needed to get her a card or a gift or something when I got back on my feet, because she didn't have to do anything she was doing for me, but she did it anyway.

"Sorry. I was just sitting here thinking."

"What you thinking about?" She sat down across from me. "Do you need to talk?"

I've gotten closer to G-Ma since I been here in her house. G-Ma has always been cool over the years, but I never really had full-fledged conversations with her until she let me live here.

"It just seems like I can't hold on to nothing in my life. I lost my father the day I was born. I just lost my girlfriend. I lost my car. I basically lost my mother, and I almost lost two of my best friends, all at the same time. It really seems like I can't catch a break."

"Have you ever tried to contact your father's side of the family?"

"No. I mean, the first time I even looked him up was a couple of months ago, right before I went over the bridge. I don't even know if he still has any family around here."

"He does."

I looked at her in surprise, my heart pounding. "He does? How do you know?"

"I've always known."

"What? What do you mean? You knew my father?"

"I knew your mother and father when they were younger. They were both at my church. They were set to get married before he . . . before he passed."

"My mother was in the *church*?"

G-Ma nodded her head. I was in total shock. "She used to sing in the choir, then after she had you, she just disappeared. I know it was because of what happened with your father."

My mind was swimming. "Wait, do Hype and them know about this?"

"No, no. I never told any of them. Not even my daughters know except Gina." Gina was Quaid's mother.

"Well, how come y'all never told me you knew my father, after all these years? I been coming around since I was five years old!" I felt betrayed. As many times as I had dreamed about my father, about finally meeting him one day, and I could have known a long time ago that it wouldn't be possible.

"I felt like it wasn't my place. I wanted to tell you, but I wanted to respect your mother's wishes too, even though I totally disagreed with how she treated you."

"Wow." I said, sitting back in my seat. "Well, what was he like?"

"Your father was a good man — saved, full of the Holy Ghost. He loved your mother, and he couldn't wait to meet you. He was a hard-working man too, always willing to help out anybody who needed it."

Her words touched my heart. Even though it wasn't a whole lot, it felt good to actually hear about my father from somebody who knew him.

"Thank you for telling me that, G-Ma. You have no idea how much that means."

She paused. "Twon . . . there's more to the story."

The hairs on the back of my neck prickled at those words. I could tell that whatever she was about to tell me was huge.

"What is it?" I said, bracing myself.

"You have an older brother. His name is Trav. He still goes to my church."

My jaw dropped in shock at those words. "You serious?"

She nodded.

So many thoughts swirled through my mind that I didn't know what to say next. "An older brother — are you sure? How old is he? Does he know about me? Wait, did my mom have him too?"

"I know, it's a lot. And believe me, I wanted nothing more than for you to know this a long time ago, but I didn't want to go against your mother. Even though I didn't appreciate the way she treated you, I felt that it wasn't my place. Trav is twenty years old. He doesn't know about you either, or at least I don't think he does. He's a junior in college. Sweet boy, saved too. He has a different mother, a girl that your father was with before he met your mother." She chuckled. "You two actually look alike — I'm not sure how Quaid never picked up on it."

"Quaid knows my brother?"

"He doesn't know that he's your brother, but he knows him."

"Wow." This was almost too much to bear. "Well, can we set up a meeting? Do you think he'll want to meet me?"

"I'm sure he will. He's an only child, so I'm sure he'll be happy to find out he has a younger brother. I don't know his mother's story, or whether she wants you two to meet, but I figure that too many years have already passed without you boys knowing each other, and I have been feeling guilty about it myself, knowing it all this time and not telling you. I hope you can forgive me and understand where I was coming from."

"Definitely," I said without even having to think about it. "You've already done a lot for me that you didn't even have to do. I really just want to meet him. I never knew I had a brother."

"Well, I will talk to him the next time I go to church and see what he says. I'm sure he'll want to meet you too."

"Thank you," I said, tears in my eyes as it really started to hit me.

Hype

So Twon's ass has a brother. Wow. There's really no words to describe his mother for holding that kind of information back from him. I know personally that Twon has always wanted a brother because we used to have conversations about it when we were younger. He saw that I had Quaid and Charles, which were basically like brothers to me even though they were my cousins, but on his side, he had nobody, so I kind of became his brother, and he became mine.

I know this is going to sound like some real hater shit, but please bear with me. I'm happy for Twon that he has a brother. For real. But on the other side, I kind of feel some type of way about it, because where does that leave me? Me and Twon been like brothers since we first met, so now that this new nigga is in the mix, I don't know how that's going to affect our relationship.

I know it's fucked up, but I don't know how else to feel about it. We already kind of on edge with the whole Shaneece situation, since one of us is the father of her baby (as long as she wasn't fucking nobody else), and now this shit happens. And on another side, I wonder why G-Ma never told *me*. I feel some type of way about that shit too.

Anyways, I'm still out here hustling with Charles. I know I can't do this shit for too long though. I hope his boy hurries up and gets out, cuz this shit is not really what I'm about.

Tierra

I cried myself to sleep the night that me and Twon broke up for good. I mean, I guess it was inevitable that it was going to happen, but it still hurts like hell. I really thought we would be together forever, or at least for longer than this, but I guess some things just aren't meant to be.

I wonder if he's going to go running to Shaneece now that we are officially over. I pray that he doesn't. I know that I have no hold over him anymore, but I would hate for us to break up just for him to end up with that bitch. She singlehandedly ruined our relationship. If she wasn't all up in Twon's face every chance she got, maybe me and him could have had a better outcome. I feel like such a fool for trusting her, but never again.

"Tierra, Quaid's here!" My mother called from downstairs. I sat up quickly in my bed. What was he doing here?

I quickly threw on some jeans and a cute shirt, went to the bathroom to brush my teeth and fix my hair, then I made my way downstairs, trying to play it off like I didn't just fix myself up to see him.

He had on that fitted cap again, and it was driving me crazy again.

"Hey," I said, hands in the pockets of my jeans, trying to act casual.

"Hey. I hope I'm not bothering you."

"No, you're good." I said. "What's up?"

"I was wondering if you wanted to take a walk with me."

"Take a walk?" I repeated, wondering what this was all about.

"Yes, if that's okay."

"Okay," I said. "Ma!" I called into the kitchen. "I'm 'bout to leave with Quaid. I'll be back in a little bit."

"Okay, don't stay out too late!" she said, not leaving the kitchen.

When we went outside, I noticed that Quaid's car wasn't parked in front of the house.

"Did you walk here?" I said, giving him a strange look.

"Yeah," he said, and he blushed slightly.

"Well, what if I would have said no? You would have walked all the way back home?"

"I guess so." He chuckled, and that's when I realized that he had a dimple on his left cheek. *Mmm. Chocolate and dimples.* It was almost too much for me.

We strolled down the sidewalk together, then he spoke up. "Tierra, I want to talk to you about our conversation the other day."

"Oh, really?"

"Yeah. I realize that that was a bad time for you, and I apologize. I don't want you to feel like I'm pressuring you. I know you and Twon are still in the process of figuring things out, and I don't want to intrude—"

"Me and Twon broke up for good."

He looked surprised. "You did?"

"Yeah. A couple of days ago."

He stopped and really looked at me. "Are you okay? Do you want to talk about it?"

"Not really. We just decided that it was best to let it go. Every time we make up, we end up right back in the same arguments, so the relationship really wasn't going anywhere. It was time to let it go."

"Well, I'm sorry to hear that."

"Are you really?" I countered.

"Yes! I mean . . . yeah, I have feelings for you, but at the same time, I would never want to see you hurt either. Even if you decided to get back with Twon, I would rather see you happy with him than miserable with me just because I want you."

My heart panged at those words. I was falling for Quaid the more time I spent with him, but what he just said also made me feel guilty, because I knew that I was partially harboring resentment toward Twon because I did not want him to be with Shaneece.

I stepped a little closer to him and looked into those gorgeous eyes of his. "I like you too," I said softly, finally ready to admit it.

"Huh? Did I hear you right?"

"I have feelings for you too, Quaid. I had feelings for you when we first met, and I still have those same feelings now. I've just been too stubborn to admit it, or something crazy like that."

"That's good to know," he said, looking as awkward as he sounded.

We continued to walk together in silence, and I noticed we were touching shoulders; then I felt him touch my hand with his. I looked over at him, and he was looking down at me to see if it was okay. I nodded, and he intertwined his fingers with mine. I felt that tingly feeling again, holding hands with him like this. I felt safe and protected, and like I didn't want to let him go.

We got to a park, and it was empty. "You want to go on the swings?" he said, grinning at me.

"Sure." I grinned back. We raced to the swings.

"Let's see who can swing the highest first," he said, a challenge in his eyes.

"Now you know you are going to win with those long legs of yours." I gave him a side eye.

He chuckled. "I'll give you a head start."

I rolled my eyes. "Okay, whatever." I started to swing, and I went higher and higher, then Quaid jumped in and started swinging too. Of course, he quickly caught up to me and surpassed me in height. As hard as I pumped my legs, I was no match for him, but it felt fun and free and happy, like being a carefree child again. It took my mind off the whole Twon situation, and then it occurred to me that Quaid always knew how to do that for me — to make me feel like everything was going to be alright.

After we finished swinging, we walked around the park talking and laughing together. Then he got serious with me again.

"So . . . I know it's probably too soon, but what do you think about us being together? Like . . . in a relationship."

He stared at me intently.

"Um . . . I don't know. Don't you think that would be kind of awkward?"

"How so?" He stepped a little closer to me.

"I mean, like . . . with you and Twon. How would he feel about that?"

"I understand what you're saying, but it's not really about how Twon feels. The only people that would be in the relationship are you and me."

Something about the way he said "you and me" turned me on. Quaid just had this sexiness about him without even trying. He was shy, and he was sweet, and he was awkward, but he was sexy.

"Quaid…" I looked down, not sure how to continue.

He gently cupped my chin with his hand and lifted my face up. He stared into my eyes, and I wanted to look away, but I couldn't. He slowly leaned his head down, and before I knew it, his lips were covering mine with a kiss.

His lips were so soft and smooth, and it felt like I could kiss him forever. I savored the moment, but then I started to feel guilty, so I pulled out of the kiss.

"What's wrong?" he said.

"We have to stop. We're moving too fast."

He looked hurt, but I could tell he understood.

"Okay."

"Sorry," I said.

"No need to apologize. You're right. We were moving too fast."

"Thank you," I said, glad that he wasn't mad at me.

"How about we get you home? I don't want your mother thinking I kidnapped you." He chuckled.

I smiled at him, and we made our way back to my house. When we got there, after we said our goodbyes, Quaid gave me a hug and a kiss on the cheek.

I watched his tall, muscular frame for a few moments as he walked down the street toward his house, and I was about to step inside when he turned and waved goodbye.

He must've felt me gazing at him! I was embarrassed that he caught me staring at him, but I smiled and waved back, then went into the house.

Shaneece

Shanelle got me the info about whether you needed a parent's permission to drop out of high school and get a GED, and also whether parents could force you to have an abortion. It turns out that they can't force me to get an abortion, but they do have to give me permission to drop out and get my GED.

My life is so fucking screwed. How the hell did I go from being an A-B student on her way to college to getting pregnant and not knowing who the father is, and on the verge of being a high school dropout? I have no idea how to handle this situation. Eventually, my parents are going to find out that I'm pregnant, and I can't drop out and get my GED without their permission. So yeah, basically I'm screwed.

I trudged into the house after school, and already felt annoyed just being there. *I am so fed up with that place, it's not even funny.*

"Shaneece. Come here." My father didn't waste any time barking commands when he heard me open the front door. My heart dropped slightly. I was trying to gauge what this could possibly be about based on his tone, but I couldn't read it. I walked into the kitchen where he and my mother were sitting at the table. They looked at me with quiet, seething anger in their eyes.

"Yes, Dad?" I said, trying to keep my tone light. I hoped he wasn't about to blow up at me over something stupid. I had been walking on eggshells ever since I got back home from winter break, trying to follow all of his stupid rules to a T.

"What's been going on at school?"

"What do you mean?" My heart raced as I racked my brain to figure out where he could be coming from.

"Your English teacher called us and said that you've been having issues in his class. He said you almost got into a fight with another girl before winter break, and you recently wrote a paper on high school bullying, and it seemed like you were speaking from personal experience. What's going on?"

"Nothing." I prayed to God internally that the English teacher didn't tell him why I almost got into a fight with Tierra.

My mother took her turn. "Shaneece, we know it's not nothing. You haven't been acting like yourself lately at all. We took away your laptop, and you barely have use of your phone, but you don't seem to have a problem with it. You don't put up any kind of a fight, and that's not like you. Is everything okay?"

This was almost too much for me. These motherfuckers had the nerve to ask me about bullying in school when they had been bullying me my whole fucking life!

"No!" I said, irritated. "Nothing's wrong. It was just a stupid paper. I was just trying to get an A."

"But what about the fight with the girl? And the other fight you got into with the boy who threw the egg at you?"

"Look, I'm not being bullied!" I exclaimed, feeling trapped all of a sudden. There was no way in hell I was telling them what was going on in my life. Not like they gave a damn anyway, as long as I got the grades they wanted. *All I am to them is a stupid fucking piece of paper with a grade at the top. Nothing more, and I've never been anything more.*

"Shaneece, we—" My father stopped mid-sentence. "Why is your shirt lighting up?"

"What?" I said, trying to turn around so he wouldn't see the prepaid phone through my shirt, but it was too late.

"Do you have another fucking phone?!" My father jumped up from the table, all sympathy gone from his voice as he made his way toward me.

"No, Dad, I—"

"Take that fucking phone out of your shirt, now. NOW!"

I reluctantly pulled the phone out of my bra. I had just missed a call from the doctor's office. *Shit. That was a close call.*

"Who the fuck just called you?" he said. "And it better not be that fucking Twon boy either, or I'm finding his ass."

"No, Dad, it's not."

"Who the fuck was it then?" He quickly snatched the phone from my hand before I could think of a lie. "They left you a voicemail. Check it. Now. And put it on speaker phone." He extended the phone toward me, fire in his eyes.

My breathing became more labored as I started to panic. My eyes darted back and forth between my mother, my father, and the phone.

"I said call the fucking voicemail, Shaneece!" He barked at me so loud that I jumped. My vision became blurry as my eyes filled with tears. I couldn't move. I just stood there staring at him.

He impatiently swiped the screen to unlock the phone, then he held down the 1 button to call the voicemail. Once it dialed, he pressed the speaker button.

"What's your fucking password, Shaneece?"

I just stood there.

"What's your fucking password?!"

I looked at my mother, but she just stared at me with a disappointed expression on her face.

"If you don't tell me your motherfucking password—"

"Nine three four two," I stammered, and put my head down in shame as he quickly dialed the numbers. My face reddened as I heard the receptionist confirming my appointment for my first ultrasound scheduled for next week. I had scheduled an early one because I wanted to know the due date so that I could trace it back and see if there was a chance that Twon was the father.

When my father hung up the phone after hearing the message, he looked at me with utter disgust.

"You're fucking pregnant?" He took a step toward me, and I took a step back.

"How long has this been going on? What the fuck is Twon's address?"

"Dad, I—"

"And you've been hiding this shit right under our fucking noses this whole time? You sneaky little bitch!" He lunged toward me, but my mother came out of nowhere and tackled him to the floor. She caught him off guard, and he fell on his side.

"She's pregnant!" she exclaimed. "You're not going to hit her!"

"It doesn't matter if I fucking hit her! She's getting rid of it anyway!"

"No, I'm not!" There was no way I was getting rid of my baby.

"Oh yes, the FUCK you are!" My father clambered up from the floor and my mother had to help him a little. If I weren't so shaken, it would've made me laugh because they looked so ridiculous.

"You are getting a fucking abortion, and that little fucker Twon is helping to pay for it," he bellowed. "Do his parents know?"

"He may not even be the father!" I spat, before I realized what I said.

My mother looked shocked, and my father's eyes almost popped out of his head. "What the hell do you mean he might not be the father?"

"It's either him or another guy." I couldn't meet their eyes.

"You filthy fucking whore." He swiped my phone screen again and called the doctor's office.

"What are you doing?!" I screeched.

"You're getting a fucking abortion. You're not about to be in my house under my roof pregnant."

He switched to an upbeat, professional voice when he got through to the receptionist. He identified himself as my father, and told her that I changed my mind about wanting the ultrasound and that I wanted to schedule an abortion instead. He answered a few more questions, wrote down the time, date, and address of where the abortion would be scheduled, then he hung up the phone.

"In two fucking weeks, this shit is over. You are going down there with me, and you are getting a fucking abortion. I can't fucking believe you. Get the fuck out of my face."

I looked at him, then at my mother, then I turned around and walked upstairs to my room.

Twon

I nervously stood on one of my crutches at the door of the restaurant where I was supposed to be meeting my brother, Trav, for the first time. G-Ma hooked me up with some cash to pay for my meal since I ain't have nothing. I felt embarrassed as fuck taking the money from her, but she said she wouldn't have it any other way. Bless God for that woman, yo, word up. She's the closest thing I have ever had to a mother. All this shit she been doing for me be having me crying like a bitch. I gotta get up out of her house ASAP, because I'm turning soft as a mutha.

I saw a black Acura, the same model as the one I had, pull into the parking lot. My heart jumped because I knew it had to be my brother. I don't know how I knew, but I knew. He parked, then the door opened, and he got out, looked toward the restaurant, and saw me. I held my breath but released it when he smiled mad hard and started walking toward me blinking like he couldn't believe his eyes. I couldn't believe mine either — this dude looked JUST like me, except he was a little lighter and didn't have braids. We were the same height and everything.

"Yoooooo, this is bananas, son!" he said when he got closer to me. He quickly picked me up in a bear hug, causing me to almost drop my crutch. "Oh, my bad." He quickly helped me to find my balance. "I don't be thinking sometimes. What happened to your leg?"

I stared at him for a few moments, frozen. My throat got tight and my nose stung as tears came to my eyes. I tried to blink them back and swallow, but I was overcome with emotion. All my life I wanted a family. I had dreamed about having a brother since I was a child, and now I had one, and he was standing right in front of me.

"You really my brother?" That did it, and I broke down. Trav grabbed me up in a hug once again, and I hugged him back. This shit was surreal, yo. My brother was right there in front of me, hugging me. I'd never felt anything like this before.

After we stopped hugging, we wiped our tears with the back of our hand in one swift motion, as if we'd timed it perfectly. My heart panged as I realized that we must have got that from our father. "Man, these people going to think we a bunch of pussies," I said.

Trav busted out laughing, and his laugh was so funny that I started laughing. From his demeanor, it seemed like he was a real goofy dude, and I could tell that he was the type that was always laughing about something.

After we got through laughing, he reached out to shake my hand. "Oh yeah. My name is Trav."

This caused me to bust out laughing again because of how serious his face turned so quickly. "Twon, bro." I shook his hand.

We made our way into the restaurant, and the girl who seated us made a comment about how much we looked alike, which made us both smile, especially because her smile said, *And you both look good, too.*

"So, you never knew about me either?" said Trav, sliding into his seat as I sat in mine across from him.

"No, and the crazy thing is that I always wished for a brother."

"Me too." Trav nodded. "I used to beg my mother for one, but she never paid me no mind."

"Did you . . . do you remember anything about our father?"

"Yeah. I was almost four when he died, so I have some memories of him. I brought a picture so you could see." Trav pulled out his wallet, took a picture out, and handed it to me.

I stared at it for a long time. It was a picture of my father holding Trav as a baby. Both of them were smiling.

"Wow," I said. "Do you have any more of these?"

"Oh yeah," said Trav. "You can actually keep that one. I have another copy of it."

"Thanks, man."

"So, what's up with you, Baby Bro?" He nudged my shoulder lightly. "You got a girlfriend? You in school, right? What happened to your leg? Wassup?"

I took a deep breath and told him a little about myself and what had been going on with me lately. He cracked a few jokes to make me laugh, and I cracked a few with him too. We were in the restaurant for hours, just kicking it. I was in shock because of how easily we vibed. Even though we literally just met that day, it felt like I had known Trav all my life. He told me about his girlfriend, Stephanie, and our two cousins, Slink and Wolf, from our father's side of the family. My mind was blown by all the information. The family I had always wished for was right in front of me.

I can't wait to tell Hype about this shit, because he knew how much I been wanting a brother.

Hype

I went over G-Ma's house after Twon got home from meeting his brother Trav. He told me all about it, how his brother was so cool, and how he wanted me to meet him and his cousins Slink and Wolf. We was all supposed to be meeting up today.

I know I'm hating like a mutha when I say this, but I hope Twon don't replace me with these niggas. We got history — fuck them niggas.

Sorry, I know that was harsh, but I guess I really did see Twon as my brother all these years, and now I find out he got a real brother. I guess I just don't want to be kicked to the curb.

I'm trying to be optimistic about this shit, and that's why I agreed to meet with these niggas. This is gonna be Twon's first time meeting Slink and Wolf, and my first time meeting all of them.

Me and Twon waited by the basketball court as three dudes pulled up in a car and hopped out.

"That's them!" said Twon, looking excited. One of them looked just like Twon, so I guessed it was Trav, and the other two looked related, but not the same as them.

"Wassup, lil niggas?" said one of them, a blunt hanging from his mouth. He held out his hand to give me and Twon dap.

"Lil niggas?" I repeated, instantly not liking this cocky muthafucka.

"My bad," he said, not looking sorry at all. "I didn't mean to offend you. I'm Slink. This is my brother, Wolf, and my cousin, Trav."

"Hype," I said. That was all he was getting out of me until I was cool with this dude.

"You burn?" He extended the blunt toward me.

"No, I don't smoke with niggas I don't know." I said that to let the nigga know not to fuck with me cuz I still wasn't fucking with him.

"Twon, bruh, why your boy so uptight?" said Wolf, chuckling. It was obvious he was high too. His eyes were red and low. Trav's eyes were clean and clear, so I didn't take him for a smoker.

"Ain't shit uptight about me, nigga. And if you got a question, you can ask me directly."

"Excuse me," said Wolf, holding his hands up like he was mocking me. "Sorry for trying to start a conversation."

"So it's nice to meet you, Hype," said Trav, looking excited. "Twon told me all about you when we met the other day."

"Nice to meet you too," I said, sizing him up with my eyes and deciding that I actually liked him. He reminded me of Twon, except he was lighter skinned, didn't have braids, and seemed kind of goofy.

"Ned Flanders ass nigga," said Slink, and he and Wolf started laughing.

Even though me, Twon, and Charles often made fun of Quaid for being a Christian, we were also cool with Quaid, and he knew it. I didn't like these niggas, so I didn't laugh at their little joke about Trav.

"So what type of shit are y'all niggas into?" said Twon, still looking excited to meet his cousins.

I decided not to say any more sarcastic shit for the rest of the meeting, but I already knew I didn't like Twon's cousins. Something about them rubbed me the wrong way. They seemed like some grimy niggas.

Tierra

I can't stop thinking about my breakup with Twon, and the feeling of Quaid's lips pressed against mine. I don't think we should have kissed that soon. I'm not even fully over Twon, and I've already basically started a relationship with Quaid. I just hope Twon didn't go running to that bitch Shaneece. For all I know, they planned our breakup so they could be together…

"Tierra, this seems to be a pattern with you," said my mother as she walked into the kitchen after getting home from work.

"What do you mean?"

"Every time I come into this house you're sitting in that same seat with that same expression on your face. I don't like how all of this is affecting you. I think you might need to take a break from boys altogether."

My head snapped at her last words. "Take a break from boys *altogether*? Why would I need to do that?"

"Because it's making you bitter, that's why."

My heart hurt at those words. "You think I'm bitter?" My eyes welled with tears.

"This situation is having a negative effect on you. If you allow yourself to stay in these negative emotions, it will lead to bitterness. Trust me, I know all about it."

"Well, I don't know what I'm supposed to do, Ma. I've never been in this situation before."

"Well, I have, and I'm telling you that I think it's best for you to leave Twon and Quaid alone and focus on God."

For some reason, her words irritated me. "How are you going to tell me to focus on God when you don't even go to church?"

She made her way over to me with the quickness. "Girl, I know you been going through a lot lately, but you better watch your mouth when you talk to me. I am still your mother, and you know I don't play about disrespect."

"Ma, I'm not trying to disrespect you. But I don't think you understand where I'm coming from."

"I understand exactly where you're coming from, Tierra! I've been there myself. In fact, I've been through even worse. You need to leave both of those boys alone and focus on God and graduating from school. You're about to go to college. You don't need to be worried about all of this right now."

"Well, I can't just break things off with Quaid when we just started our relationship."

"Why can't you?"

"Because, Ma! We just started."

"I'm sure that Quaid will understand if you need to take a break."

"I'm not sure if that's what I want, though."

She stood there staring at me then sighed. "Okay, Tierra. The decision is up to you. I said my piece, but some things I guess you just have to learn on your own."

She turned and walked upstairs to her room, closing the door behind her.

I sat there at the kitchen table for a few minutes longer out of stubborn determination. *I can sit in this chair all night if I want to,* I argued with my mom in my head. Then I felt guilty because I knew she spoke the truth. I needed to just focus on God and school. I had been wrestling with the idea of being saved for a while, and I often still felt like there was an urge inside of me to go through with it, but I was too scared. I kind of felt like I just needed somebody to hold my hand through the situation. My mother always urged me to go to church and get saved, but she wouldn't even go herself, so she was no help.

I picked up my phone and called Quaid.

"Hello?" Quaid said after the first ring.

I smiled, but my heart felt sad because I was basically about to break up with him. "Quaid, are you busy?"

"Um . . . no, not really. Just finishing up some homework. Why? How are you? How's your day going?"

"It's alright." I sighed. "I just needed to talk to you. Can you come over, and maybe we could take a walk or something?"

"Sure! I'll be there in like ten minutes."

"Okay. See ya." I felt guilty because he sounded so eager and excited to see me.

***

Almost exactly ten minutes later, Quaid knocked on the door. I went outside with him to take our walk. He hugged me and kissed me on the cheek. That caused me to blush, but I felt bad because I was about to break up with him.

We walked in silence for a few minutes, then Quaid spoke first. "So, what's up? What did you need to talk to me about?"

I stopped and turned to face him. "Quaid..." And then my mind went blank. I didn't really know what to say. I didn't really want to break up with him, but at the same time, I felt like I had to. I put my head down to collect my thoughts because it was very hard to do that while looking at him.

"Tierra, what's wrong?" he said softly. He gently cupped my chin with his hand and raised my face up so that we could look in each other's eyes.

"I just feel like . . . I think we might be moving too fast with all of this."

"What do you mean? With our relationship?"

"Yeah. I mean, I just broke up with Twon, and me and you already kissed."

"So . . . do you regret it?" He looked like he was bracing himself for the worst.

"No, no, it's not that I regret it. I actually enjoyed it, and I want to do it again. But, don't you think we should at least clear things with Twon first?"

Quaid's head snapped back in surprise as he let go of my face, his hands resting at his sides. "Clear things with *Twon* first?" He looked at me like I was crazy.

"Yes," I said, and now I felt kind of upset with him for his reaction. "I mean, don't you even care that this messed up you guys' friendship?"

"Tierra, if you don't really want to be with me, all you have to do is just say it."

"That's not what I said, Quaid." I crossed my arms over my chest. "I said, don't you think we should at least see if Twon is okay with us being together, seeing that you are part of the reason that we broke up, and y'all are supposed to be best friends."

"Look, I don't need Twon's permission to live my life. He sure didn't ask for *my* permission when he..."

"When he *what*, Quaid?"

"Nothing." He put his hands in his pockets, looking kind of uneasy.

"No, you were going to say something, then you stopped. What did Twon need *your* permission for?" My eyes narrowed at him.

He stared at me, then he snapped. "Look, Twon knew I wanted you from the start, okay? He knew I liked you. I told him and Charles, then he just up and went after you like it was nothing. That's why I say that I don't need Twon's permission for anything I do. He did me wrong, so he doesn't deserve my respect in this situation."

My ears grew hot at this revelation. "So you mean to tell me that you and Twon just saw me as some kind of piece of meat or something? Like y'all could just pass me back and forth? Once Twon was done with me, it was your turn? Huh, Quaid? Is that how you really see me?"

"No! The only thing I've *ever* seen you as is the most beautiful woman I have ever met in my life!" His eyes were full of passion, and I could tell he meant every word.

I was taken aback by Quaid's boldness. I wasn't used to him being this blunt. I was mad at him a few seconds ago, but with those words he just said, I was turned on. I grabbed him by the back of his neck and pulled his head down for a kiss. It was hungry, it was passionate, and it drove me crazy on the inside.

When we finished, we pulled back and stared at each other, then we went in for another kiss, this time more gentle than the last one, but still full of passion.

"I can't get enough of you, girl," said Quaid, his voice husky.

"I can't get enough of you either."

Oh well. I guess that break-up was a fail.

Shaneece

I don't know how I'm going to handle this situation with my father, but one thing that I do know is there is no way in hell he is about to make me get an abortion. He may have been able to control me in many things in life, but this is where I draw the line. This is *my* baby. He's just going to have to face the music.

I snuck over G-Ma's house after school the next day to tell Twon what my dad was trying to do. I prayed that he would be there alone so that we could figure this out together, but of course Hype was there too.

I mean, yeah, there is a chance that he is the father too, but I know in my heart that it's Twon's.

"Your father did *what?*" said Twon, looking heated.

"I don't know what I'm going to do, Twon." I sat next to him on his futon and crossed my arms over my chest. Hype stood against the wall, his arms crossed over his chest, and one of his feet crossed over the other.

"I mean . . . don't you think this might be a blessing in disguise?"

Twon and I looked at him like he was crazy. "What do you mean, a blessing in disguise?" I said.

"Listen, we in our senior year of high school. None of us is ready for no damn baby anyway. Your pops is probably looking out by making you get rid of it."

I can't fucking stand Hype. He was acting totally nonchalant about the whole situation, like killing a baby was as easy as walking down the street. "It's not a fucking *it*, Hype! It's a he or a she, a son or a daughter. How can you just want an abortion so easily?"

"Like I said, none of us is ready for no damn kid, or at least I ain't. I don't know what y'all muthafuckas got planned."

"It's not about having a plan. This is a *life*, Hype! Can't you see that?"

"Yes, I see that very clearly. But I also see clearly that none of us is in a position to deal with this shit."

Twon finally spoke up. "Well, I'm not getting rid of my kid."

"Nigga, what if the shit ain't yours?" said Hype. "Huh? Then this bitch got *me* stuck with a damn baby. I ain't ask for this shit."

"I didn't stick you with anything!" I was feeling heated now. "It takes two to make a baby, and I damn sure didn't rape you."

"Nobody said all that! What I'm saying is that neither one of y'all seem to realize that this is not a game! This is real life. Y'all niggas talking about keeping the baby like we got money like that. When it gets here, who's going to take care of it, huh? Do you got money saved, Twon? Huh? How about you, Shaneece?"

"We can make a way," I said, not backing down for anything.

"Real talk," said Twon. "We can all get jobs and start saving now."

Hype just stood there stewing for a few moments, then he'd had enough. "Man, whatever. Y'all do what y'all wanna do then."

He stormed out of the house and slammed the door behind him.

I snorted sarcastically. "Yeah, real mature, Hype."

"Hey, we're all under a lot of stress," said Twon. "I can see where he's coming from."

"So you're taking Hype's side now that he's gone?" I stared at him in disbelief. "You want me to get rid of our baby too?"

"No, no, that's not what I'm saying." He paused. "What I'm saying is that even though I totally disagree with Hype about the abortion, I can see that he's just scared. I think we all are. None of us was planning this, and truth be told, none of us is really ready for this. Me and you are willing to get ready, but we can't really fault Hype if he hasn't processed the situation yet. Shit, I haven't even processed it fully yet."

"So . . . what do you think our plan should be?"

"Well, I was planning to go to the factory to see if I can get my job back now that I'm off the crutches. Do you think you can find a job anywhere real quick that you could work after school or something?"

"Well, I'm planning on dropping out anyway, so…"

He looked at me in shock. "You dropping out? Why?"

"You haven't been there, Twon. You don't see how these people treat me. I have girls and guys on my back practically every day calling me all kinds of THOTS and whores and sluts, and I can't even count how many fights I've almost gotten into." I told him about the guy who threw the egg at my head. When I finished the story, he was fuming.

"What was his name?"

"Don't worry about it, Twon. It's over."

"I don't give a fuck. That nigga had no right to disrespect you like that."

"Look, we've got bigger fish to fry. Let's just focus on the baby."

He fumed in silence then sucked his teeth like he'd given up. "Well, I'll let it go for now, but if he does anything else to you, you better let me know, and I'm-a fuck that nigga up."

I blushed and eyed him seductively. "Oh really?" I sauntered over and stood in front of where he sat on the sofa. I struck a pose that showed off my curves to their best advantage. "How are you going to do that with your limp and all?"

"I may be limping, but I can still get shit handled." He stood up and faced me licking his lips. He put his hands on my waist and went in for a kiss, and I immediately felt nauseous and clapped my hand over my mouth.

"What's wrong?" he said. "I got bad breath or something?"

I held my finger up and rushed to the bathroom to throw up. Twon followed and held my hair back as I vomited in G-Ma's toilet. He watched me as I washed my mouth out in the sink, and when I had washed and dried my face, he grabbed me from behind and pulled me into his arms, kissing me with so much fire and passion that I almost lost my footing.

After we kissed, I felt dizzy. "You are totally disgusting for doing that," I said, chuckling at him.

"How so?"

"Kissing me after I just threw up?"

He chuckled. "Girl, you lucky this is G-Ma's house, or I would have had to show you just how disgusting I can be."

Twon was lucky it was G-Ma's house too, because I was definitely up for a challenge. For some reason, I was feeling a whole lot better about this situation, and about life in general. I always believed that Twon and I were meant to be together, and that we could get through anything.

We stared into each other's eyes for a few moments then walked hand in hand back to Twon's room.

"Well, unfortunately, I have to go home before my father gets suspicious and starts tracking me," I said. "But I'll see you later."

"A'ight. See you." He kissed me one more time, causing me knees to get weak, before I let go of his embrace and made my way home.

Hype

I really can't stand that fucking bitch, Shaneece, yo. She really think she got this whole shit figured out, like once she has the baby, we gonna be this big fucking happy family. Well, newsflash, bitch: You still fucked my best friend, so this shit ain't never gonna be totally alright.

I mean, I know I said that I was going to forgive and forget for the sake of the baby, but every time I encounter that bitch, I can't get it out of my head that she played me for Twon. Not knocking my dude or anything, even though I was pissed off at him for a while, but that bitch really did a number on me.

I made my way to Quaid's house. Charles' car was outside, which added to my irritation. Not that we beefing or anything, but I'm really not cut out for this drug dealing shit. I'm trying to find a way to tell him that I want out. I ain't got caught or nothing, but I'm tired of being all paranoid all the damn time. I got enough on my brain with Twon and his newfound fucking family, Shaneece and her bullshit ass fantasies, and waiting to hear back from these colleges to see if my black ass got a future. And now this nigga got me selling drugs. I'm stressed to the max yo, straight up.

I walked into Quaid's living room where he and Charles were playing video games.

"What you doing here?" I said to Charles, a little too aggressively.

"Fuck wrong with you?" said Charles.

"Nothing," I said, trying to calm down. I turned to face Quaid. "Just got a lot on my mind."

Charles snickered. "Well, speak your piece, nigga!"

I tried to find the words to tell Charles that I really only wanted to talk to Quaid, but I couldn't bring myself to do it, cuz no matter how I said it, it was going to sound fucked up.

All my life, Charles and Quaid have been major influences in my decisions. As much as I love Charles and see him as my brother rather than my cousin, that nigga be giving some corrupt ass advice sometimes. I mean, look at what I'm going through now: this nigga's form of preparation for a baby was to sell drugs and get money.

I mean, granted, he really does mean well, but Charles' mindset was never really about doing the right thing. It was always about getting money and bitches, and getting over. I definitely fed into that mentality myself many times, but I also relied on Quaid real heavy when it came to doing the right thing. As much shit as all of us talked about Quaid being a Christian, the nigga is wise beyond his years. Whatever he told me, I knew it was going to be on some righteous shit, and that's what I really needed to hear right now.

"Well, nigga?" said Charles. "You gonna talk, or what?"

Against my better judgment, I decided to spill the beans. "Man, I got all types of shit going on." I let loose and told them all about Twon and his family, Shaneece and the abortion, and the whole college thing. I left out the drug thing, because I knew Quaid would snitch on me to G-Ma, and I didn't want to deal with that headache.

I been low-key avoiding her house, fronting like I just didn't want to be around Shaneece, but it was really because G-Ma's ass got a sixth sense for knowing shit. I don't know how she does it, but she picks up on everybody's bullshit from a mile away, and she can always tell when I'm doing wrong. She always says it's the God in her, but either way, I ain't trying to hear all that right now.

I also didn't want to bring it up because I wanted to talk to Charles alone about that, and I still wasn't sure how to say it. After I finished my rant, Charles was already going in before Quaid could even open his mouth.

"Man, fuck that bitch!" he said, referring to Shaneece. "Her daddy was willing to give her a way out, and she didn't take it? And what the fuck is this nigga Twon on? Her pussy can't be that damn good for him to let her trap him into a baby. And fuck college right now. Apparently the bitch ain't going through with the abortion, so you gonna need to save up money for that shit too."

See what I mean? Like I said, Charles definitely means well, but his advice is always corrupt as fuck.

Quaid sat there taking everything in before he spoke. "Well, how about we tackle these situations one by one?"

Charles cut in. "Nigga, did you hear anything I just said? I just gave him the best advice he's gonna get."

"I heard you," said Quaid, and I could tell that he was trying to choose his words carefully. "But I have a different perspective about the situations."

"Okay, Jesus Junior." Charles snorted and smirked. "Tell this nigga how much of a sinner he is, and how he needs to repent from his wicked ways."

"Come on, Charles," I said. "This is not the time for that." I could tell that Quaid was heated at Charles for insulting his Christianity. Normally, I would have laughed at some shit like that, but these situations were way too serious for jokes.

"Whatever, nigga." Charles leaned back in his seat. "This nigga ain't gonna tell you nothing that I ain't already said."

"Actually, I disagree with everything you said," Quaid replied, still trying to hold back his anger.

"Okay, Church Boy, you're on." Charles stared him down.

Quaid looked at me. "Well, like I was saying, I think we should tackle these situations one by one. First let's start with the most pressing matter. What do *you* want to do about the baby? Do you feel like you are ready to be a father, or at least willing to try? I know you are mad that she didn't want the abortion, but have you considered other options? What about adoption?"

This nigga Quaid really needs to be some kind of counselor or something. I never even thought of adoption as an option. I felt myself relax a little bit. Now I feel like this is something I can actually get through. If we have the baby and shit don't work out, we can give it up for adoption.

"I never even thought of that," I said. "I don't think I'm ready to be nobody's daddy, and if it is mine, I would definitely be interested in adoption. I mean, I ain't no heartless nigga. I only agreed to the abortion because I didn't see no other way out."

Charles sucked his teeth, obviously mad that I was going with Quaid's advice. "And if it is yours and you give it up for adoption, what if the kid gets fucked up in the system? We knew niggas that grew up like that. Half of them is all fucked up in the head cuz they been passed around and abused. What about that, Quaid?"

That was something else I hadn't thought about. I definitely didn't want my kid getting abused, even if I did fuck up his life by giving him up for adoption.

"But it's not guaranteed that the child will be abused," Quaid countered. "There are plenty of children who go to loving homes when they are adopted."

"But it's still a fifty-fifty chance though," Charles shot back.

"Don't you think life is better than death, regardless? Would you have rather been aborted?"

"This ain't about me."

"You're right. It's not about either of us. This is Hype's decision. We're just here to help."

"I'll have to think more about it," I said.

"So, on to the Twon situation," said Quaid. "I understand that you don't like his cousins, but do you think it's just jealousy, or do you actually see something off about them?"

"What this nigga got to be jealous about?" Charles interjected. "Them niggas ain't shit, and if they try something, they can catch these fucking hands. Simple as that."

Quaid sighed. It took a lot of effort to control his temper. "Look, Charles, I didn't say anything while you gave your speech. Can you at least give me the courtesy and stop interrupting mine?"

"Whatever, nigga. Fuck it. I was just stating the obvious."

"I don't think it's jealousy," I said. "I really just don't like them niggas. I mean, his brother Trav is cool. I didn't get no bad vibe from him. But both of them cousins ain't shit, and I can tell."

I meant what I said. There really was something that rubbed me the wrong way about Twon's cousins.

"Okay." Quaid nodded as he took this in. "So how do you plan to handle your interactions with them moving forward?"

Charles answered. "Like I said before, if the niggas try to pop off, we hook off, simple as that."

"I don't know," I said, trying to tone down Charles because he was really starting to piss me off. "I guess I'll just try not to be around them that much."

Quaid nodded in agreement. "That makes sense. That way, it reduces the tension."

Charles rolled his eyes. "This nigga…" he muttered under his breath.

"About college," said Quaid, trying to maintain his composure, but I could tell that Charles was really getting under his skin with all his sarcasm.

"We'll talk about that later," I said, deciding to cut the conversation short. I could tell that regardless of what Quaid said, Charles was going to talk shit, and I didn't feel like hearing them argue today. Them niggas ain't never really saw eye to eye, and I don't think they ever will.

"You sure?" said Quaid.

"Yep, he's sure," said Charles, hopping up out of his seat. "Come on, nigga," he said, turning to me. "Let's go get this money."

"What do you mean, 'get this money'?" Quaid sensed something. "Hype doesn't have a job yet."

"It's nothing," I said, trying to rush to leave. "We just gotta go."

"Nigga, he's a grown ass man," Charles shot at Quaid. "You ain't his momma or his daddy, and neither one of those muthafuckas seem to care what he does anyway."

Quaid looked mad heated now, as realization dawned. He stood up, furious. "Hype, don't tell me you're selling drugs." His voice was short, and he looked at Charles like he wanted to hook off on him.

"So what if he is?" said Charles. "What you gonna do? Snitch to G-Ma? She ain't his mother."

"Leave G-Ma out of this," I said, thoroughly heated that Charles had just outed me.

"Hype, are you crazy?" Quaid looked at me like I had lost my mind.

"Look, Quaid, I gotta do what I gotta do, okay?" I moved toward the door, trying to get out of there, but Quaid wasn't having it. I was feeling more and more guilty by the second.

"No, you don't HAVE to sell drugs, Hype. You are on your way to COLLEGE. I'm not going to let you throw your life away because of this garbage."

"And what the fuck you gonna do to stop him, huh?" said Charles, looking heated as he stepped around me to get in Quaid's face. I immediately stepped between them. Charles and Quaid fought one time when we were younger, because Charles kept provoking Quaid. I never really spoke on it, but Quaid got him that day, and I know for sure that Charles been wanting a rematch ever since.

"Chill, let's go," I said, trying to diffuse the situation.

Quaid looked worried and disappointed. "No, Hype. You've got to stop this."

"We'll talk about it later," I said, pushing Charles toward the door before he could say anymore sarcastic shit.

"I don't want you to get locked up, Hype."

"Nigga, stop being so fucking scary!" Charles snapped. "Ain't nothing gonna happen to him cuz I'm not going to let it."

Quaid snorted. "And what are you going to do, as many times as you've been arrested and we've had to bail you out!"

"Man, fuck this nigga—" Charles tried to get around me to hook off on Quaid, but Quaid looked like he was ready, and I wasn't letting this happen today. Too much is already going on to be having my family fighting and shit.

"Charles, let's GO!" I roughly pushed him toward the door, opened it, and forced him outside.

"I'll get back to you later, Quaid," I called over my shoulder as I pushed Charles toward his car.

"Yeah," was all Quaid said, angry and disappointed. He slammed the door.

Charles and I got into the car.

"Nigga, you really need to stop provoking Quaid like that," I said to Charles. "He does nothing to you."

"Man, fuck that nigga." Charles was still pissed off that he didn't get to hook off on Quaid.

"Fuck your cousin that's basically like a brother to you? That's how you feel, Charles?"

"That nigga never liked me, so I don't have to play nice with his ass."

"Well, maybe if you stopped fucking provoking him every chance you got, you wouldn't have to play nice with him." I paused. "Still fucking holding a grudge from childhood," I muttered.

"Ain't nobody holding no fucking grudge. The nigga came at me, so I came at him."

"But he's fucking family though."

"So is Twon, and y'all niggas still jumped on him."

"Look, I'm not trying to sit here and argue with you about this shit. You and Quaid need to find a way to get along, cuz I'm tired of y'all niggas always beefing."

"Well, we wouldn't always be beefing if—"

"Look I'm done talking about this shit. Let's just go."

"Whatever, nigga," said Charles, and he turned his music up.

Twon

As confusing as this situation is, I really feel like life is starting to turn around for me. I got my friendship back with Hype, I found out I have a brother and two cousins, me and Shaneece are basically together, and we might be 'bout to have a baby on the way. I always wanted a family of my own, and it seems like it's all coming at me at once.

I've been thinking about a lot of things lately: college, getting my job back, trying to get another whip, and my mother. It almost seems like too much, but I'm trying to find a way to prioritize it all.

I really need to see my mother, ASAP. I know most people would tell me just to let it go because she's pretty much shown me all my life that she wants nothing to do with me, but she's still my mother. I'm glad my legs are healed. Since she cut off the house phone and doesn't answer her cell phone, I'm going to have to pop up on her at the crib. Not even on no negative shit. I really just want to see if we can have a relationship. Maybe now that I'm out of her house, she can find a way to tolerate me...

"That bitch ain't in the bathroom or nothing, is she?" said Hype, poking his head into my room.

"Nah, she ain't here. What you doing back so soon?"

"That nigga Charles is tripping. Him and Quaid got into it a little while ago."

"Over what?"

"I was telling them about all these situations that are going on, college and the baby and shit. And you know how they always at each other's throats."

I chuckled. "Yeah, they always did fight over you."

"Not over me. They got their own issues. Remember that time Charles and Quaid fought?"

"When we was like *twelve*, nigga?" I scrunched my nose in disbelief. "They still beefing over that shit?"

"Yeah . . . I mean, they never really got along, but I know for a fact that Charles been holding a grudge ever since."

I chuckled again as I thought back to that day. Quaid had surprised us all when he finally hooked off on Charles for talking hella shit. What was even more surprising was that he actually won the fight. We had always wrestled each other and play fought, but Quaid was so soft that none of us thought he could fight.

"Charles learned that day," I said, and chuckled at the memory.

"I know, but we got to find a way to help these niggas resolve their issues. They can't be beefing for the rest of their lives over some bullshit."

"I mean . . . well me and Quaid still got low-key beef over Tierra, so I don't know how much help I can be."

"Y'all niggas still on that?" Hype looked shocked and confused. "I thought y'all got over that."

"No, that nigga stole my girl, Hype. He went against the code."

"I mean, well, from what he told me a little while ago, you stole her from him first."

"I stole her? What is this nigga talking about?" It was my turn to be shocked and confused.

"Quaid said that he told you and Charles that he was feeling Tierra heavy, but you snatched her up before he could get with her."

"What?" I said, sucking my teeth. "That's not how it happened."

"Well, that's what he said, and Quaid ain't never been no lying nigga."

"Well, he may not be a liar, but he's definitely a sneaky nigga."

"In that case, you qualify as a sneaky nigga too, when your ass was slithering around with Shaneece."

"Hype, as long as you known me, you know I ain't never been no fucking snake. I never knew Shaneece was the girl you was talking about."

"How come you never said you was feeling her then?"

"I don't know. It all just happened. How come you never told us she was your girl? If I would have known that, I never would have got with her like that."

"Y'all still fuckin?!" Hype looked totally pissed off at that prospect.

"Look nigga. I know you was feeling her, but I really didn't know y'all was together. If I would have known, I would have treated the situation accordingly."

"Like you did with Quaid?"

"I told you I don't know what the fuck Quaid is talking about! Yeah, he told us he liked her, but he didn't say it was that serious. I took it as he just saw her as a pretty girl."

"Well, obviously you were wrong."

"Right." I paused, taking it in and seeing my wrong. "I see what you're saying, but I can't take back the past."

"Well, how about you at least talk to him so y'all can get over this?"

"I'm willing to do that. He still messing with Tierra?"

"You still fucking Shaneece?"

"Point taken." I really had no right to say anything in this situation. "But on some real shit, are you still feeling Shaneece?" I knew damn well that Hype still had some type of feelings for her, but now I was really starting to feel her too, so I wanted to hear what he had to say about it.

"I mean, the bitch has obviously made her fucking choice. She never really wanted me from jump, and I never been the type of nigga to chase a bitch. I see you feeling her from how y'all talk to each other, so I guess I'm just going to have to get over it."

"But is me and you still cool though, if I were to get with Shaneece?"

"Nigga, I ain't stupid. I know you probably already been fucking her. You just better hope G-Ma never catches y'all nasty asses, or you might be homeless again."

I busted out laughing at that last comment. "Fuck you, Hype. No, I haven't had sex with her again, but I'm really starting to feel her though. But I don't want to try to get with her if it's going to cause more beef with me and you."

"I appreciate that. Well, if you squash shit with Quaid, then you have my full permission to fuck Shaneece."

I busted out laughing again. "Fuck you, Hype!" I repeated, nudging his shoulder. He started laughing too.

"But for real though. I need you and Quaid to be good. We brothers."

I could tell that Hype was trying to be a man about the situation, but I could also tell that he was still hurting over Shaneece. I really wish that she hadn't been so damn sneaky; then none of this would have been going down like this. I decided to change the subject.

"Oh, I almost forgot to tell you: Trav, Slink, and Wolf said they want to link up and play some video games. You down?"

He paused. "Listen, man, I'm good with Trav, but I don't like them niggas Slink and Wolf."

"Why not?"

"They came at me the wrong way."

"Man, they was just playing!"

"Look, I know you excited about meeting your family and all that, but I'm really not feeling your cousins."

"Can't you just give them the benefit of the doubt? It might be that y'all just started off on a bad foot."

Hype looked like he wasn't convinced at all, but his expression finally softened. "Fine, I'll give these niggas another chance. How 'bout y'all come through to my crib and we can play some shit?"

"Thanks!" I said. "I'll call them up."

***

Me, Slink, Wolf, and Trav made our way to Hype's house to play video games. I excitedly turned the knob to open the door.

"This nigga don't keep his door locked?" said Slink.

"No, we never do. We always just roll though each other's houses."

"Wow. That's brave." He said, looking like he really wanted to say, "That's stupid." We walked in, and Hype hopped up from the couch.

"What's up?" he said to me, shooting a glance at Slink and Wolf.

"What's up?" I said, dapping him up. "Where's Charles and Quaid?"

"Quaid had to work, and Charles is on the block."

"You ready to get that ass busted, nigga?" said Wolf, eyeing Hype.

Hype looked like he wanted to say something sarcastic, but he tried to play it cool. "Yeah, nigga. We'll see."

The atmosphere for the rest of the day remained the same. Hype tried to be cordial, but I could tell that he just didn't like Slink and Wolf. They didn't help the situation either, because they kept throwing low-key shots at him. I know for a fact that Hype would have hooked off on them and kicked them out of his house if they weren't my cousins, but he held himself back because of me. He seemed to get along with Trav though. They cracked a few jokes back and forth at each other, and even partnered up against Slink and Wolf in one of the games. When they left, I already knew what Hype was going to say.

"Listen, man," he started. "I tried, but that's the last time I'm letting your bitch ass cousins in my house. Trav is cool all day any day, but I really don't want to ever see those corny ass niggas again."

I knew there was no point in arguing, so I decided to just let it go.

Shaneece

Today is supposed to be the day of my abortion, but I still have no idea what I'm going to say to my father. All I know is that there is no way in hell I am killing my baby. All my life, my parents have run me. They have forced and controlled me in every way possible. Well, that's stopping today. This is *my* body and this is *my* baby, and there's nothing they can do to stop me…

"Shaneece, I know you heard me calling you. Come on, let's go." I jumped at the sound of my father's voice. He had suddenly appeared at my doorway. My heart rate increased. I searched for words to say, but I couldn't think of anything good enough.

"Shaneece. Let's go." My father's expression was solemn. I could see that there was no way he would even think of compromising with me, so I would just have to come out and say it.

"I'm not going." I was trembling on the inside and hoping that my voice and demeanor looked strong enough on the outside.

"What did you just say?"

"I said I'm not going. I'm not getting an abortion."

"Look, Shaneece, you don't have an option here—"

"I do have options because you can't legally force me to kill my baby."

"Legally force? I am your father! First of all, it's not even a baby yet! It's nothing more than a fucking parasite at this point. You're barely even three months pregnant, talking about killing a baby. Get your fucking shoes on, and let's go. I'm not rescheduling this appointment."

"There was no need to schedule it in the first place because I'm *not* getting an abortion." My father really pissed me off when he called my baby a fucking parasite.

"Michelle!" My father called out to my mother.

My mother came to my room a few seconds later. "What? What's going on?"

"Get your fucking daughter before I have to drag her out of that bed and into the car so we can get to this abortion appointment. Now, I said I wouldn't lay hands on her, but if she keeps coming at me with this attitude, she's going to leave me with no choice."

My mother turned to me with a pained expression. "Shaneece, let's just—"

"*No*, Mom! I said I'm not going, and I meant it. You guys can't make me do this, and I'm not doing it!"

"Shaneece, honey, I understand that you don't want to do this, but you have to think about what's best in this situation."

My mother's eyes pleaded with me, but I wasn't having it this time.

"I said no."

"How are you going to support a fucking baby? Huh?" My father stepped closer toward me. I moved back in my bed. "You can barely even take care of your fucking self," he continued. "You're irresponsible and sneaky. What the fuck kind of mother you think you're going to be? You don't even know who the fucking father of your baby is."

All of his words hit me below the belt, but I refused to let him see my pain. "I'll be a better fucking parent than you ever were to me."

SMACK! I instantly felt a burning sensation as my father smacked me across the face. I grabbed the lamp from next to my bed and held it over my head, ready to strike if he came at me again. My mother was holding him back against the wall.

"I TOLD YOU NOT TO PUT YOUR FUCKING HANDS ON HER!" she screamed.

"SHE SHOULDN'T HAVE BEEN RUNNING HER FUCKING MOUTH!"

"You will NEVER put your FUCKING hands on me again!" I screamed. "NEVER FUCKING AGAIN!" I hurled the lamp against the wall, shattering it into a million pieces, and my parents jumped in shock.

"GET THE FUCK OUT OF MY HOUSE!" my father bellowed. "You have disrespected me for the last time."

"You're really going to kick me out?" My mind was swimming and I felt nauseous, but I ignored it.

"Yes, you have to leave. We have given you chance after chance, but you refuse to listen to us. You have snuck behind our backs and disobeyed us at every turn. Now is the time for you to get out. You don't want to follow my rules, then you can get the fuck out of my house. You're not the parent here, we are."

I couldn't believe my ears. "So you're just going to kick your pregnant daughter out on the streets with nowhere to go because she won't get an abortion?"

"My pregnant daughter can figure this shit out since she thinks she's so fucking grown that she doesn't have to follow my rules."

"Mom…" I pleaded, turning to my mother with desperation in my eyes.

My dad didn't let her speak. He took control as usual. "No, you can pack your bags right now and get the fuck out of my house. There's no need to try to discuss it further."

My mom just stood there.

"Mom…" I said again, hoping I could at least reason with her.

"I'm sorry, Shaneece," she said, with tears in her eyes.

"So you're just going to let him kick me out?" Tears rushed to my own eyes as the weight of the situation hit me.

"I'm sorry."

"You have until six o'clock," my father said, his tone cold. "A minute after that, and I'm calling the police to escort you out." He turned toward the door, ushered my mother out, and slammed the door behind him.

***

My mind was reeling as I packed my bags. I had no idea where to go, but I knew that my father meant it when he said he was kicking me out. I had four hours to figure my life out.

I was in the middle of putting all of my shoes in a suitcase when I heard the front door slam. I went over to my window to look outside and saw my father getting into his car and peeling out of the driveway.

I went to my parents' room and saw my mother sitting on the bed, sniffling. It was evident that she had been crying.

"Where is he going?" I said, my tone accusatory.

"I don't know, Shaneece." She sounded defeated.

"Is he still kicking me out?"

"Yes."

"Well, can I have my prepaid phone back? I need to make some calls."

She wordlessly reached into her nightstand drawer, got my phone and charger, and handed them to me.

I took them from her, my hands shaking from anger and pent-up aggression.

"And you're not even going to do anything at all to try to help me, huh?"

She barely looked at me. "I'm sorry."

"Yeah, you're damn right you are." I stalked out of their room, slamming the door behind me.

***

I packed about three suitcases full of clothes and shoes. After that, I still had two hours left before I had to get out, but I had no idea where I was going.

I didn't want to bother Shanelle with all of this, because I knew it would put her in an uncomfortable position, but I had no choice. I called her, praying that she wasn't at work and could pick up.

"Hey, Shaneece." She answered breathlessly, as if she was in a hurry. "I've only got ten minutes left on my break. How did it go?"

"Dad kicked me out."

"He did what?"

"He kicked me out." I told her what happened. "So, now I have two hours left, nowhere to go, and I don't know what to do."

"Wow. God. Let me talk to him."

"I don't think he'll budge, Shanelle, and I don't know what else to do."

"Well, I can come and get you after I get out…" Her voice trailed off.

"What time do you get out?"

"I get out tonight at eleven, then I work tomorrow morning at six."

"Well, that won't work because he wants me out by six."

"Damn it! I don't think I can get off early today. Why the hell did he have to do this today?" She sounded really stressed out, not like herself at all. Usually Shanelle was the more level-headed one. I hoped I wasn't overburdening her.

"Listen, Shanelle, I don't want to stress you out. I'll think of something else—"

"No, no, it's not you, Shaneece. I've just been going through a lot with Steve."

"What's going on?" I demanded, and immediately felt angry. Steve had already put my sister through so much with his cheating and his bullshit. I wanted to punch him in the face the next time I saw him.

"It's nothing."

118

"No, Shanelle, you can talk to me."

"Okay." She sounded depressed. "I found out a couple of hours ago that he got somebody pregnant."

"What??? Who?" I was fuming. This had to be the last straw. The next time I saw Steve, it was on.

"One of my coworkers—this stupid skank bitch that I have to work with every day."

"That motherf—"

"Listen, they're paging me, Shaneece. I have to pull myself together and get back to work. I'll come get you at eleven, okay?"

"No, no . . . don't worry about it."

"What do you mean, don't worry about it? Where else are you going to go?"

"I'll stay at a friend's house. We'll talk tomorrow."

"What friend? Shaneece—"

"Shanelle, don't worry about me tonight, okay? I'll be okay. I will talk to you tomorrow."

"Are you sure?"

"Yes, I'm sure. I'll call you tomorrow, or we can just talk when you get out of work."

"Okay, but only if you're sure."

"I am. I'll be okay."

"Okay, I love you."

"I love you too, and stay strong."

"You too."

After we hung up, I shed a few tears for my sister. She really loved Steve, but he just couldn't seem to get his shit together.

***

I sat around for another half an hour, contemplating options. I was literally wracking my brain when it dawned on me that I actually had some money saved. I had totally forgotten that I had been saving up for a car when I worked at Sports Locker with Twon.

119

I finally felt a sense of relief. I had a couple thousand in the bank. That would surely be enough to at least get me into an apartment. I just needed to find a job to maintain it. Now I just needed to figure out a plan for the night…

"Okay, it's five-thirty, and you haven't left yet. I hope you don't think I was playing with you, Shaneece. I want you out of my house by six p.m."

My father was standing in my doorway again. I looked up at him in disgust.

"Don't you see all of my bags packed? I'm on my way out."

"Where are you going to go? Huh? Twon's house?"

"No. Twon's not even at Twon's house."

"What's that supposed to mean?"

"Nothing. It doesn't have anything to do with you, so you don't need to know."

He sighed. "Just get the fuck out of my house, Shaneece."

"Contacting Uber now." I shot him a sarcastic glance.

On the outside I was trying to look and act strong, but on the inside, it was tearing me up that my father could just throw me away like this. The Uber app said my ride should be here to pick me up within fifteen minutes.

I wordlessly picked up my suitcases and took them outside. By the time I got the last bag outside the door, my ride was there.

"Shaneece." My father looked uneasy now that he saw that I was actually leaving.

"Save it," I said. "Bastard," I muttered under my breath, loud enough for him to hear.

I loaded up my suitcases in the trunk and got in the back seat. I looked back at the house as we drove off. My father had already closed the front door, but I saw my mother in their upstairs window looking out at me.

I rolled my eyes in annoyance, then almost instantly, they were filled with tears as it hit me that I was leaving my parents' house with nowhere to go.

I was on my way to G-Ma's house. I prayed the whole way there that she would allow me to stay for just one night 'til my sister could come get me after work the next day.

Twon

Me and G-Ma was eating dinner in my room, kicking it. She is mad funny, yo. I think that's where Hype gets it from, because I can see a lot of her in him the more I get to know her. That lady is full of so much wisdom, it's crazy. Damn, all this time, I could have been getting to know her, but I never really thought of it that way. I guess it's because I was so used to trying to chase after my mother for her affection.

Even now, I'm still thinking about my mother, feeling guilty about chopping it up and getting close with G-Ma, while I still don't even know what my mother is up to. I mean, yeah, she kicked me out of her house, but still, that's my mother…

Hype left almost immediately after G-Ma got home. I wonder what's up with that. Now that I think of it, he always either shows up when he knows she's not home, or leaves as soon as she gets here. I'm kind of puzzled about it, because usually Hype and G-Ma are kicking it. They've been close for as long as I can remember.

The only thing I can think of is that Hype must be into some shit. That has to be the only reason that he's dodging her like this. I'm gonna have to talk to him about whatever it is he's doing the next time I see him. I hope it's not nothing too bad…

"So how are things going with you and Trav?" said G-Ma. We had just finished watching *Family Feud*, playing along with the contestants to see who guessed the most answers.

"We've been doing good. I'm so glad that you told me about him. It feels so unreal that I actually have a brother."

"That's good," she said. "It's good to see you smiling."

My heart slightly panged at those words, then we heard a knock at the front door.

"I wonder who that is?" said G-Ma, getting up from her seat. She went over to the door and opened it. "Girl, what you doing here? And what's all this?" She sounded surprised, and that piqued my curiosity, so I put the TV on mute.

"I . . . um . . . I don't know what to do!" Whoever it was broke down and started crying. G-Ma immediately stepped out and grabbed her into a hug.

"Shhhh, it's okay, girl. Twon, come here, boy!" G-Ma called over to me.

I got up and walked over to the door, and my heart dropped when I saw that it was Shaneece. She looked like a little girl, holding on to G-Ma for dear life and crying her eyes out.

"What's wrong?" I said, noticing that she had brought three big suitcases with her. She looked up at me, her entire face red, with tears streaming down her cheeks.

"My dad kicked me out…" Her voice trembled.

G-Ma was shocked to hear this. "He kicked you out? Why?"

"He tried to make me get an abortion, but I said no. He hit me, and I threw a lamp against the wall. Then he said I had to get out of his house by six p.m."

"He hit you?" I said, feeling myself getting hot. I been wanting to hook off on her father for a long time from all the things she told me about him, but I didn't know he had been hitting her too.

"Yes." She wiped her tears and sniffled. "And now I have nowhere to go." She looked at G-Ma. "I was wondering . . . I mean, I know we don't know each other very well, but I have no friends and nowhere to go for the night. I was wondering . . . my sister said she can come get me tomorrow after work, so if it's okay, can I . . . ?"

"Oh . . ." said G-Ma. She paused for a moment, assessing the situation. "Well, first, let's get you out of this doorway. Twon, bring this girl's suitcases into the living room please. Let's sit down and talk about this."

G-Ma walked Shaneece into the living room and they sat on the couch. I grabbed her suitcases and brought them into the living room.

"You hungry? When's the last time you ate?" G-Ma said to Shaneece.

"I haven't even thought about food all day." Shaneece let out a shaky breath. She seemed calmer now. She wiped her face with the Kleenex that G-Ma handed her.

I wanted to hold her, but it felt kind of awkward with G-Ma in the room.

"Listen, Shaneece," said G-Ma. "I can let you stay here for the rest of the week so you can go to school, but I don't feel too easy about this. It's not because I don't want you here, but it's because I know that you and Twon have a little relationship going on, and I don't allow no fornication in my house."

"Fornication?" said Shaneece.

"Sex, honey. I'm being blunt about this because there is no other way to say it. You both know that I am a Christian. I don't allow those types of activities in my house."

"We understand," I said, and glanced at Shaneece. She nodded.

"You sure now?" said G-Ma, looking back and forth at the two of us.

"Yes," said Shaneece in a small voice. "Thank you for allowing me to stay here."

"No problem, baby. But I want you both to know that I'm serious about what I said. I'm willing to trust both of you with this, but I am looking for you two to respect me as well."

"We understand," I said.

"Okay," said G-Ma. "Shaneece, I have a guest room that you can sleep in and store all of your things in. You hungry? You want me to warm up a plate for you?"

"Yes, if that's okay," she said, looking kind of uneasy.

"Twon, can you please go warm up a plate for her?"

"Yes, ma'am." I said, walking to the kitchen. I fixed Shaneece a plate and something to drink and brought it to the living room.

"Thank you," said Shaneece.

"Okay, so I'm going to go to my room because I'm sure you two want some privacy so you can talk. If you need anything, just let me know. But I do want to reiterate what I said. I need you two to know that I am very serious about this."

"We understand," I said.

"Okay now." With that settled, G-Ma went to her room.

I went over and sat next to Shaneece on the couch.

"So, what are your plans? Do you think your pops is really kicking you out for good?" I said, watching her eat. She looked like she was really hungry. She was almost done with the plate.

"This is good!" she said through a mouthful. When she was able to speak again, she sounded more serious. "I honestly don't know, Twon. I mean, I have some money saved from when I was working at Sports Locker. That's probably enough to put down on an apartment, but I need a job to maintain the rent."

"True." I thought for a moment, then I had an idea of my own. "Well, what if we got a place together?"

Her head whipped toward me. "Huh?"

"I'm saying . . . my legs are healed now. Maybe I can get my job back at the factory, and we can get an apartment together. Maybe we can work things out between us."

There were tears in her eyes. "Are you serious?"

"Yeah. I mean, if we are about to have a child together, why not try to make it work?"

Her eyes lit up. "Yes! I mean, I'm sure it will probably take some adjusting, but I'm willing to try to work it out if you are."

"Okay then," I said, feeling a little excited myself. "I'll go up there tomorrow and try to talk to my boss and see if he can give me my job back. I'll see if he can give me more hours during the week. I don't know how I'm going to keep up with classes now that I'll be working more, but I guess I'll figure out a way."

Shaneece looked at me for several long moments then offered a small, grateful smile. "Thank you, Twon."

* * *

I went to talk to my boss the next day. He wasn't there, but the big boss was. I explained to him my situation with the baby and everything, and he decided to give me another chance. He said he would schedule me around my school hours so I could work during the week. By the time I left that office I was full of excitement.

I'm happy that things are starting to look up for me, but I still have some unresolved issues. I'm not sure if everything is gonna be gravy with Shaneece because she still got some sneaky ways. That's another thing that we gonna have to talk about, because if we gonna be together, I can't have her lying to me. She's gonna have to be straight up with me if she really wants our relationship to work.

Another thing that's still kind of stressing me is my mother. It's really bothering me that I have not seen or talked to her at all since that day at the hospital when she told me she was kicking me out. I gotta go see her to see if we can reconcile our relationship. Regardless of everything that has happened, she's the only parent I got left.

Yet another thing that's really starting to hit me is that I may not be able to go to college like I originally planned. I always saw myself going straight through school, getting my Bachelor's and maybe even a Master's. I always wanted to make something of myself, but now it seems like I may not be able to do that because I have a baby on the way. Not to say that I blame my kid. I mean, he or she didn't ask to be here, and I'm the one that laid down with Shaneece. But still, it kind of hurts to have your whole life change because of one thing you did that can't be undone.

I don't know how this situation is going to work out, but I'm just going to take the hand that I'm dealt, and deal with it.

Shaneece

I just got off the phone with Shanelle, and I'm really starting to have peace about this whole situation. Twon and I are moving in together, and Shanelle agreed to give me some money to help us buy furniture and household items so we can get started. She set up a three-way phone call between her, me, and one of her friends who's a manager at a clothing store in the mall, and I was offered a job!

I'll be able to start Monday after school. I really feel like this is going to work out. Twon and I went to school together the morning after we talked. It was kind of weird and a little surreal to sleep in the same house as him, and then go together to school. Only a couple of months ago, Twon was cussing me out in the hallway and saying he wanted nothing to do with me.

I stared down at my stomach and smiled. I could not wait to meet our little bundle of joy. *I wonder if Twon will want him to be a junior if it's a boy* . . . . My smile widened at that thought. But what if it was a girl? What could we name her?

I almost tripped when Twon stopped short as we were walking down the hallway toward the senior lockers.

"What's going on?" I said.

"I asked you if you were going to be okay going to all your classes. I know you mentioned before about people trying to bully you." I looked up at him. Twon's expression was full of concern. That warmed my heart. My eyes welled up with tears—probably hormones.

"I'll be fine. Thank you for asking."

Twon smiled at me. "Of course."

We continued to walk, and people were staring at us as we passed them, but I didn't care. They talked all that shit about me being a THOT, but here I was, right with Twon. What would they have to say about that?

I got to my locker and yet again, someone had marked it up, but it wasn't lipstick this time. MAURY ASS BITCH was spray-painted across my locker along with the phone number to the television show.

"Who the fuck did this?" Twon glanced around at everyone lingering nearby, ready to take them on.

"Just let it go," I said. It upset me too, but I did not want to cause more drama.

"If I find out who did this, it's on."

"Just let it go, Twon." We left our lockers and went in separate directions to go to class.

Hype

G-Ma been getting real damn generous lately. I mean, Twon is family, but damn — Shaneece too? I guess I can't be too mad about it because of the circumstances that caused it. Shaneece's abusive ass pops kicked his pregnant daughter out on the streets. What the hell kind of parents do Twon and Shaneece got???

Anyway, G-Ma, my mom, and my two aunts decided to throw a baby shower for Shaneece when they found out what her dad did to her. Although the situation is still awkward, I do appreciate them looking out for her. Ain't none of us got no money for no baby anyway, so we need all the help we can get, regardless of who the father is.

Me, Quaid, Twon, Trav, and Charles was all sitting around in G-Ma's backyard. It was a nice day despite it still being a little cold outside, so G-Ma decided to hold the shower outdoors.

"So now that we all chilling together, there's some things that need to be made clear," Charles said.

"Wassup?" I said, wondering where he was going with this.

"Hype and Twon pretty much is back where they need to be, but what about Twon and Quaid?"

Twon looked kind of uneasy. He and Quaid hadn't really hung too heavy since what happened with Tierra.

"I'm willing to squash it," said Quaid. "I'm sorry for how everything went down."

"You mean you sneaking behind my back and stealing my girl?" said Twon, looking kind of salty.

"Look, Twon, I wasn't trying to be sneaky—"

"Oh yeah? Could've fooled me."

"Look, this ain't the time to bicker like a bunch of bitches." Charles interjected. "Quaid fucked with Tierra, and Twon fucked Shaneece. Both of y'all was at least partially in the wrong for what y'all did. Aside from all that, we supposed to be brothers. We can't let no silly shit like this get between us."

Charles was actually on it today!

I backed him up. "That's true. I mean, if I can forgive you, Twon, I think you should be able to forgive Quaid, especially since you basically stole Tierra from him in the first place."

Twon looked at me. "But I didn't know—"

I held my hand up. "I know you say you didn't know he was feeling her like that, but regardless, he was, and it still happened. So I think y'all should squash it."

Twon sat back and let it sink in before he responded. He looked at Quaid. "I mean . . . so are y'all officially together now? I been hearing shit around school."

"Yes," said Quaid, without hesitation. "Like I said, I'm sorry for how everything went down, and I apologize for my part in it, but you can't forget that you started this."

Twon looked like he wanted to protest, but he looked at me and then at Shaneece, who was sitting at a table with my mom and Aunt Gina. G-Ma was on the grill, and Auntie Shameka was in the house.

Twon looked back at Quaid. "A'ight man, whatever. I'm moving on, so I guess I can't expect Tierra to hold back for me. Y'all go ahead."

"Finally!" said Charles. "Hey, Ma!" he said to his mother, my Auntie Shameka, who was walking by G-Ma holding a beer. "Bring me one of those drinks! I'm ready to celebrate for real!"

Auntie Shameka grabbed one of the beers from the cooler and handed it to Charles. G-Ma's facial expression completely changed as she watched the interaction. The whole day she had been in a pleasant mood, but as soon as she saw Auntie Shameka give Charles a beer, her whole demeanor changed.

"So how long has this been going on?" she said, her hand on her hip, glaring at Auntie Shameka.

Auntie Shameka sucked her teeth. "Ma, come on. The boy is grown!"

"That boy is NOT grown," said G-Ma. "He is only seventeen years old, and you giving him alcohol. What is wrong with you, girl?"

"Look, don't tell me how to raise my son!" Auntie Shameka looked like she was getting heated.

"Aw, shit," I said. It was about to go down. I looked over at the other table. Shaneece, my mom, and my Aunt Gina were all staring at the drama that was unfolding. Then my mother decided to stand up and jump in the altercation.

"Rose, you don't need to get in the middle of this," said G-Ma to her.

"Oh yes I do!" Rose shot back. She glared at Shameka and pointed one long fingernail at her. "Don't talk to my mother like that!"

"Shit, Ma," I said under my breath.

Shameka stepped closer to Rose. "She's my mother too, and I can talk to her how I want to."

"Both of you calm down," said Auntie Gina, who was always the voice of reason in the family outside of G-Ma. "Remember, this is about the kids. This is their baby shower."

"Right," Auntie Shameka snorted. "She wanna talk so bad about what I'm doing with MY son, but look at what Hype is doing, running around getting girls pregnant. At least Charles knows how to wrap it up!"

"That's the last time you about to talk about my son!" said my mom.

"Well, neither one of y'all got a problem talking about MY son!" said Auntie Shameka. Now they were in each other's faces.

"Look, both of you need to calm down at *my* house," said G-Ma. "I'm not about to have no neighbors calling the police on me."

"Well, if you would have kept your mouth shut about my son, there wouldn't have been a problem," Auntie Shameka retorted.

At those words, G-Ma slammed her spatula down on the table next to the grill. She bumped my mom out of the way and got in Auntie Shameka's face. Her expression was livid. "Girl, who in the HELL do you think you are talking to? I am YOUR mother, not the other way around. You are NOT going to come up in my house disrespecting me."

"You're right, this is YOUR house," said Auntie Shameka. "I don't have to be here."

"Well, if you don't know how to respect me as your mother, you're right. You DON'T have to be here." G-Ma looked her straight in the eyes to let her know she wasn't playing.

Auntie Shameka turned to Charles. "Let's go." She grabbed her purse and stormed off toward the front of the house. Charles looked at us then got up.

"Guess I'm leaving," he said with a shrug of his shoulders. "I'll catch y'all later." He left with his mom.

"I'm sorry, y'all," G-Ma said to the rest of the group. "This is supposed to be about this baby."

"It's alright, Ma," said my mom. "She had no business talking to you like that."

Auntie Gina piped up. "Well, if you want to know what I think, Rose, you should butt out of it."

"What do you mean, butt out of it? Did you hear how she was talking to our mother?"

"Well, she is her mom too. It's between them. Plus, you know Ma has no problem defending herself."

"That's true, but I really can't stand her sometimes."

"I get that, but . . . look, this is not the time or the place. All of our kids are here. It never should have gone that far."

"You're right," she said. "But she's not about to keep disrespecting my mother."

Tierra

Me and Quaid are in a little groove now that we're together, but I still feel guilty because I don't think Twon knows about it. I am dying to ask Quaid if he told Twon, but he seems to get upset with me whenever I wonder how Twon feels about us being together. He is supposed to be coming over today, so hopefully I can bring the topic up without it causing friction between us.

"Hey," said Quaid. He kissed me softly on the lips, then we went into the kitchen to sit down. I could immediately tell that something was bothering him.

"What's going on?" I said.

He shook his head. "Just a lot on my mind." He took his hat off and ran his hand over his head. His waves were looking so sexy, I almost got distracted, but I forced myself to stay focused on his need to be heard.

"What is it? Let's talk."

"It's just . . . a lot of family issues. My aunts are always fighting, Charles is always up to no good, and now Hype…" He looked out the window.

"What's going on with Hype?"

"I don't really want to get into it, but it's bad." Quaid looked so stressed out, and it was making me nervous. What could Hype be doing that was so bad?

"Hype and I are very close, Quaid. I'm sure he wouldn't mind if you told me, especially if it was something he needed help with. Is it about the baby or something?"

"No, it's not about the baby, it's . . . listen, it's really not my place to say it. I really don't want to cause any more drama for anyone than I already have. Can we just pray for him?"

I wanted to protest, but I could see that Quaid was not going to budge. Whatever was going on with Hype, if I wanted to know about it, I would have to ask him myself. "Yes, let's pray." I said, standing up and holding out my hands. Quaid stood up as well, and he held my hands in his. His hands were so gentle yet firm and strong at the same time. My heart fluttered, and I struggled to stay focused.

I scolded myself inwardly. *You're supposed to be paying attention to the prayer, girl!*

Quaid prayed, and once again, his voice was so strong and so full of conviction that I was amazed. He prayed for Charles, Hype, and the women in his family. He also prayed for me and my mom. He prayed for everyone except himself.

When the prayer was over, we both said amen, but we continued to hold hands and gaze into each other's eyes.

"Thank you," Quaid said.

"No problem." I smiled.

He leaned forward to kiss me, but in that moment, the key turned in the front door, and my mom walked in. She had just gotten home from work.

"Hoo-wee!" she said, kicking off her shoes. She looked in the kitchen at us. "Oh, hey Quaid! What are you guys doing?"

"We just finished praying," I said.

"Hi, how are you?" said Quaid, letting go of my hands.

"Good. Glad to be home from work. Well, I'll let you two keep your privacy. I'll be upstairs if you need anything."

"Talk to you later, Ma."

"Mm hm." She went upstairs.

Quaid looked down at me when we were alone again. "Well, that was a fail." He grinned and looked so cute I just melted.

I smiled. "What, the kiss?"

He nodded.

"Well, how about we try it again?"

He leaned in and gave me a long, languid kiss, and this time it was definitely *not* a fail.

Twon

Me, Trav, Slink, and Wolf was all hanging over Trav's house. His mom had cooked us some fried chicken and mac and cheese, so we was going in.

I truly appreciate G-Ma for telling me about my brother. The more I get to know him, the more I can see we have in common. This makes me think about how my dad must have been like that too. My heart still hurts over the fact that I never got to meet him, but at least I got Trav.

Slink and Wolf are really starting to get to me though. Although I love the fact that I have cousins, I can low key see what Hype was talking about. I'm trying to stick through it and just try to get along with them because we are family, but these niggas is really starting to irk me.

"So what's that bitch ass nigga Hype up to?" said Slink, taking a sip of his Kool-Aid.

"Yo, don't talk about my boy like that. We brothers."

"Fuck that nigga," said Wolf, chiming in like he had something to say that everybody wanted to hear. "Trav is your brother. That nigga ain't got none of our blood flowing through his veins."

"I see him as my brother. We grew up together."

"Well, apparently, he don't see you the same way if he was willing to drop y'all friendship over some bitch."

I could feel my ears getting hot. "Yo, son, that's my girl you talking about."

Slink snorted and smirked. "Yeah, y'all might be trying to make it work for the baby, but Shorty a THOT, Twon. Point blank."

"Yo, we family and everything, but please keep y'all mouths off of Hype and Shaneece. What happened happened. We trying to push past it. Like I said, I see Hype as my brother, and Shaneece is my girl. I'm not about to have y'all disrespecting them in front of me."

"So you really gonna take them over your real family?"

Trav interjected. "I can see Twon's point."

"Of course you can, Passa," said Slink, laying it on thick with the mockery.

"Don't start with that, man."

"Well, you the one trying to be a peacemaker when we trying to make a point."

"There ain't no point to make. I said what I said. Y'all can either accept it, or don't. But either way, y'all not going to disrespect them in front of me."

"Man, whatever." Slink glanced at Wolf, and a look pissed between them that told me they were not going to listen to anything I had to say.

Hype

I went to G-Ma's house shortly after school on Monday because I wanted to link up with Twon to talk about Shaneece and the baby. I hope that Shaneece and G-Ma wouldn't be there. I really didn't feel like dealing with any drama today.

I let myself in with my key and went straight to Twon's room. He was in there on G-Ma's laptop. It looked like he was typing a paper or something. Shit, that reminds me. I got mad work to do too.

"What up?" I said, dapping him up. I pulled a chair from the corner of the room and settled into it.

"Nothing. Chillin'. Just finishing this paper for my English class." He saved his document then closed the laptop. "Wassup?" He turned toward me.

"Just came over to talk to you about Shaneece and the baby. She ain't here, right?"

"No, she started her new job today."

"Oh, where she working at?"

"Lacy's up at the mall."

"Oh, that's wassup. Is she planning on working the whole pregnancy?"

"She's gonna try to as long as she can. I won't expect her to work all the way 'til the baby drop, but hopefully she can at least work 'til summer when I can get fulltime hours. What about you? You planning to get a job in case the baby is yours?"

I opened my mouth to answer, but paused. I immediately felt guilty about how I was making money on the low. I avoided Twon's eyes.

"Yeah, I been doing what I can to make a little money."

"What's that supposed to mean?" Twon looked at me like he wasn't buying my vague answer.

I dodged his question. "What time is G-Ma supposed to be home?" I said, glancing around.

"She said she was running some errands then going over Auntie Gina's house. Why, what's up with you?" Twon eyed me suspiciously. Guilt consumed me as I thought about how close me and G-Ma had been all my life, and now Twon knew more about what she was up to than I did.

"Look, Twon, I'm into some shit." I explained to him how Charles said he needed me to help him while his mans was locked up, and he didn't have anybody else to trust. I didn't want to do it, but I figured I needed money for the baby, and I didn't want to leave Charles hanging. Twon sat back when I finished my story.

"Damn, Hype."

"I know."

We stared at each other for a few moments, but I already knew the direction Twon was going with this. Like I said before, Quaid reminds me of my conscience, Charles brings out my reckless side, and Twon is always the logical one.

"Look, Hype, I don't want you to think I'm trying to tell you what to do, but what if you get caught? What if you get locked up? Charles been doing this shit for years, and not saying it's good for him either, but you ain't never been no drug dealer, bruh. I honestly don't think this is a good look for you."

"I understand that, but what was I supposed to do? Just leave him hanging?"

"I understand you didn't want to leave him hanging, but on some real shit, neither you or Charles needs to be selling drugs. Ain't neither one of y'all homeless or starving. When does Charles' boy get out?"

"I don't know." I shifted in my seat. "He was supposed to have a court date, but it got pushed back."

"Damn." Twon paused. "Like I said, I'm not trying to tell you what to do, but I really don't have a good feeling about this, Hype. You gotta think about what's best for you. I understand trying to help Charles. I get that. But selling drugs is a dangerous game. Niggas get robbed, niggas get shot, and niggas get caught. Look what happened to Charles' boy. Do you want to get locked up?"

"No, but I don't want to leave him hanging either."

"I feel you, but . . . watch out, man. Be careful. That's all I can say at this point."

Damn. Twon just added to my negative feelings about this whole situation. I already been paranoid about getting caught, and been wanting to tell Charles I want out, but I just don't know how to do it. I hope Chief gets out soon.

Shaneece

Things are truly looking up for Twon and me. I started my new job, and I love it already! Also, I called around to a few places to try to find us an affordable apartment, and we just met with one of them yesterday. I just got off the phone with the landlord, and she said we were approved, so all we have to do is sign the lease and pay the deposit and first month's rent, then we can move in this weekend! I am so excited. I'm off today, so I'm waiting for Twon to get back to G-Ma's house from work so I can tell him the good news. I already told G-Ma, and she seemed really excited for us. She even offered to get us a gift card to a department store so we could get our utensils and stuff like that. God bless that woman. She has truly helped us both, taking us in when we aren't even family, feeding us, talking to us and encouraging us, and not even charging us for our stay. I am overwhelmed with gratitude for her. I've never known anyone like her, a true selfless giver.

Twon walked in the door, finally. I hopped up from the couch to walk over to him. "Guess what??" I said, practically jumping up and down.

"Hold on a second, girl!" Twon grinned and slipped off his shoes then went upstairs to give G-Ma her car keys. She let us use her car sometimes for work when she didn't need to go anywhere that day. I heard them upstairs laughing about something. My heart warmed. Twon came back down the stairs. "Hey," he said, walking over to me. He kissed me on the lips, first softly, then a little more firmly. "What's up?" he said, staring into my eyes.

I almost forgot what I had to tell him because I was lost in his lashes. Twon was SO fine! And he was all mine...

"Shaneece?"

"Oh, I'm sorry." I said. "I got a little lost in your gorgeous eyes, Mr. Fine." I smiled when he blushed. "So I heard from the landlord today, and—"

"What happened?" Twon looked like he didn't know whether to be nervous or excited.

"We got approved!"

His face broke out in a big smile and he lifted me up in his arms and spun me around in a circle.

"Boy, you are so silly!" I laughed as he put me down.

"When can we move in?" He looked even more excited than I felt.

"She said we just have to sign the lease and pay the money, and we can move in this weekend!"

"That's wassup!" He said. "My girl gets it *done*! I gotta tell everybody."

My heart panged at his words. At least he had people to be excited for him. I had no one except my sister Shanelle.

"What's wrong?" Twon said, noticing the change in my disposition.

"Nothing," I said, trying to brush it off. "So do you want to go tomorrow after school? I know we both have to work, but I figured we could squeeze it in right beforehand."

"Umm, that shouldn't be a problem. I'll ask G-Ma if we can use the whip, and if she says yes, I can drop you off to work after, and pick you up when your shift is over."

I smiled at that thought—my man bringing me to work and picking me up.

"Sounds like a plan." I said.

***

Later that night, I went outside on the porch to call Shanelle while Twon was in his room doing homework.

"So, we got the place!"

"That's great, Shaneece," Shanelle said half-heartedly. I was surprised that she didn't seem too enthusiastic. "Congratulations," she added, her voice flat and unemotional.

I could tell something was wrong with my sister. "What's going on, Shanelle? You know you can tell me anything."

"Just Steve."

"What did he do now?"

"It's nothing new that he did, it's just that I found out that he's been seeing my coworker much longer than I thought. Apparently, it's been over a year, and he told her he was planning to leave me for her."

"Wow, Shanelle." I shook my head. "That fucking bastard."

"I can't believe him! So all that stuff he was saying about how much he loved me, how he cared for me, how this was all a mistake and he would never do it again, it was only because he got caught. I mean nothing to him."

"You're going to have to let him go, Shanelle. He's no good for you."

"I know. It's just so hard because I've been honest and faithful to him. How can he not see that?"

"Because he's a selfish prick! He doesn't realize the value of a good woman like you."

"I guess so." I heard her fumbling around when her pager went off. "Listen, I gotta go. I've been on call today, and they're paging me nonstop."

"Oh, okay." I said. "Feel better, okay?"

"I'll try." She snorted in derision. "I just hope they don't have me working with *her*, or you might see me on the news."

I chuckled at that last remark, then we hung up.

I really felt bad for my sister and what she was going through with Steve. Why do guys do that? They have a good woman, and then they leave them for some whore!

As soon as I had that thought, I realized that I was basically the whore in my situation. My thoughts went back to the day my dad found out that I was pregnant. He called me a filthy fucking whore.

A tear slipped down my cheek as my heart filled with pain. Tierra was a really nice girl, and she never would have done anything like that to me. The only thing I had thought about was how much I wanted Twon, and it never occurred to me to consider her feelings.

Now I really felt guilty.

I never wanted to hurt anyone. I had just gotten caught up in my feelings and made some bad decisions.

Will everything ever be right again?

Tierra

I felt bad after that conversation with Quaid. Now I'm *really* worried about what Hype might be up to, and I feel guilty that I haven't been checking in with him like he did for me. Hype has been a really good friend to me through all of this. Before Quaid and I got together, Hype was the closest one to me out of all of Twon's friends.

I really need to call him. I'm calling him right now.

"Hello?" he said, after the third ring.

"Hey, stranger!" I said, wondering exactly how I was going to start this conversation, and also hoping he wasn't upset with me for not keeping up with him.

"Long time no see."

It was hard for me to get a read on his mood, so I just plunged in. "Yeah, I'm sorry about that. I've been really distant lately. What's been up with you, Hype? When are you coming over again to chill or do homework or something? Have you heard from any of the colleges or scholarships we applied to?"

"I haven't heard from any colleges yet, but I heard from a couple scholarships. I got two of the ones we applied for, they denied me for three other ones, and I'm still waiting to hear from the other ones. What about you?"

"Pretty much the same situation. I haven't heard from any colleges, but I've gotten three scholarships, two denials, and haven't heard from the others."

"I guess we even then."

We sat there for a few moments in silence.

"What else has been up, Hype?"

"What do you mean?" He sounded uneasy.

"Listen, I talked to Quaid today, and he said you were in some kind of trouble. What's going on?"

"What you mean, you talked to Quaid? That nigga been spreading my business?"

"No, no. Calm down, Hype. First of all, Quaid is my man now, remember? Secondly, he is your cousin and he cares about you deeply. Lastly, you are one of my best friends. I would never gossip about you behind your back. I'm calling you because I care about you. I'm sorry I've been distant lately, but it really sounds like we need to catch up."

"True," Hype said after a brief silence. "My bad, because I been distant too."

"So what's going on with you? Spit it out."

"I don't know, Tierra . . . I don't even know if I should tell you all this."

"Tell me all what?"

"Look, I been into some shit with Charles." By the time he was finished telling his story, I was deeply worried for him.

"Hype . . . this is not good."

"I know, but don't judge me, Tierra. I'm just trying to do right by my cousin and the baby."

"By selling drugs? What if you get caught?"

"We keep it on the low."

"I'm sure all people who sell drugs feel that way, but people get caught all the time, Hype. That's really dangerous. I'm worried for you."

"I'm trying to get out of it, but I don't know how to tell Charles without sounding fucked up."

"What about college? If you end up going to jail, you'll have a criminal record and lose your chances for school and your scholarships!"

"I know, Tierra! Are you even hearing me?"

I decided to back down a little bit. "I'm sorry if that came across the wrong way. It's just that I'm really worried about you, Hype. We have literally spent hours together filling out scholarship applications and typing college essays. I don't want all of your hard work to go down the drain."

"Me either, but what if that whole college thing ain't for me anyway?"

"What do you mean?"

"I'm not really no A and B student like you and Twon. I basically do enough just to get by. I'm not sure if I could even succeed in college like that. Y'all the ones with the brains. I'm just a regular nigga."

"You don't have to be a rocket scientist to go to college, Hype."

"I know, but shit, I just got a lot going on right now. I can't even really think about college. What if the baby is mine? What if something happens with Charles? What am I gonna do then? How am I supposed to go to college with all this going on?"

I paused. "I know it's a lot. Have you talked to G-Ma about all this?"

"Girl, you crazy? G-Ma would kill me if she found out what I was doing. I been laying low from her too."

"Wow, Hype." I reflected on the gravity of his words. If Hype was hiding from G-Ma of all people, I knew he was in way over his head. Hype and G-Ma were very, very close. This was not good at all. "Well, I don't want you to think I'm trying to pressure you or that you can't talk to me, but I really am worried for you, and I really hope this situation works out for you, from the bottom of my heart."

"Thank you, Tierra. That means a lot."

When Hype and I hung up the phone, I felt so unsettled. My heart was heavy, and my mind was consumed with thoughts of how Hype could get out of the situation he was in. I briefly considered telling my mom, but I think she would end up telling G-Ma, and I know Hype would hate me for that. I didn't know what else to do, so I decided to pray.

I felt really, really awkward at first, because I usually prayed with my mom or Quaid. I never really prayed by myself. But I pushed past my awkwardness and said a prayer for Hype, and asked God to help him get out of this situation, and that Charles would be okay too.

I felt a little better after praying, but I still went to sleep that night feeling worried for my friend.

Twon

Me and Shaneece's new spot is tight! Her sister came through with the furniture, and G-Ma came through with all the little extra stuff for the kitchen and bathroom and shit. I can't believe I got my own place. This shit is lit.

I invited all my boys over. Trav, Slink, and Wolf is already here, and Hype, Charles, and Quaid is pulling up now.

"Wassup, niggas?" I said, cheesing as I dapped up Hype, Quaid, and Charles.

"Wassup," said Hype.

I led them to the kitchen, where the other guys were already sitting around the table eating pizza. Hype gave me a look when he saw Slink and Wolf.

"What's up?" he said, trying to be cordial.

"Hey, brotha!" said Trav, getting up to dap him, Charles, and Quaid.

Slink and Wolf just sat in their seats, but they nodded in Hype, Charles, and Quaid's direction.

"Y'all want some pizza?" I said, grabbing some paper plates. Hype, Charles, and Quaid situated themselves around the table to eat.

A few moments later, Hype reached forward to grab one of the sodas to pour himself a cup, but Slink grabbed the soda before he could get to it and poured the last of it into his cup.

Hype was annoyed, but he just shook his head and chuckled.

Charles wasn't about to let that slide. "What the fuck was that?" he said, his eyes narrowed at Slink.

"The fuck was what?" said Wolf, shooting Charles the same look.

"Look, I see this shit ain't gonna work." Charles hopped up from his seat. He looked at Hype and Quaid. "Let's be out."

Hype and Quaid stood up as well, but so did Slink and Wolf.

"Where y'all niggas going?" said Slink. "I thought we was here to party."

Hype finally spoke. "Well, y'all niggas don't know how to have a good time, so we out."

Wolf took him on. "It seemed like everything was going fine 'til you and your lil' cousin over here started acting like a couple of bitches."

"Chill, everybody, chill!" said Trav, standing up. "Let's all just relax. This was supposed to be about Twon's new place."

"I just don't see why Twon feels the need to associate with niggas like this when he got us," said Slink, dismissing Hype, Charles, and Quaid with a wave of his arm.

Hype looked at me. "Look, we 'bout to be out anyway. I told you before I didn't want to associate with these niggas. Don't invite me to no more shit where these niggas is gonna be unless you want shit to get poppin'."

"Well, let's get shit poppin' now then, lil' nigga!" said Wolf.

Quaid couldn't take it anymore. He'd sat there long enough listening to their foolishness. "Look, there's no need for all of this drama. This was supposed to be a celebration. Can't we just eat some pizza, drink some soda, play some video games...?"

"Look at this soft ass nigga," said Slink, nudging Wolf.

"That's the last time you gonna come at any of my family like that," said Charles.

Hype leveled a steady gaze at Wolf. "Look, nigga, let's just be out. We not trying to fuck up Twon's place."

Wolf was ready for this. "Then let's take it outside."

"Come on, y'all. Chill!" I said.

"So you gonna take up for these niggas instead of your family?" said Slink.

"Nigga, we IS his family!" said Hype. "Fuck y'all niggas."

Quaid set down his cup and stood up. "Guys, let's go." He practically pushed Hype and Charles toward the door.

After they left, I turned to Slink and Wolf. I was furious.

"I told y'all niggas about disrespecting them in front of me."

Wolf smirked. "They had it coming."

"No, you two started that," said Trav.

"What, you taking up for them niggas too?" said Slink.

"What's right is right."

"Yeah, a'ight, Preacher Man."

Suddenly, I knew exactly what was going on here. Slink and Wolf were trying to force me to choose between them and my boys Hype and Charles and Quaid. It was time I showed them that shit was fucked up, and it ain't gonna happen on my watch.

I looked at Slink then Wolf then back at Slink again. "I said it before, and this is the last time I'm gonna say it: Don't disrespect them in front of me ever again."

"Yeah whatever, nigga. We was just playing. Them niggas don't know how to take a joke."

"I meant what I said."

They snorted and laughed like it was no big thing. All I can say is, I hope these niggas take heed.

Hype

After me and Charles dropped Quaid off at home, we headed to my house to talk about what just went down at Twon's.

"Man, we should have hooked off on those niggas," said Charles.

"I know," I said. "I was just trying to have respect for Twon's apartment. I'm not trying to get the nigga evicted when he just moved in."

"He should have known not to invite us and those niggas when he know we got beef."

"I know. He probably wasn't thinking."

"Damn right he wasn't thinking!" Charles was steamed. "The next time I see them niggas, it's on sight. Plain and simple. Fuck Twon's feelings."

I nodded my agreement. "Can't argue with that."

Just then, the front door opened, and G-Ma walked in. My heart dropped and I immediately felt nervous. I had been laying low from G-Ma, and now she'd popped up on me. G-Ma walked over, pulled up a chair, and sat directly across from Charles and me on the couch.

Charles looked a little nervous too. He didn't have much respect for his own mother, but G-Ma put fear in his heart.

G-Ma was all business. "Hello, Hype. Charles."

"Hey, G-Ma," we said in unison.

"Hype, what's been up with you?"

"Nothing, just school and stuff."

"School and what stuff?"

"Huh?"

"Don't play with me, boy. What stuff besides school have you been into?"

"What do you mean?"

"Hype, I know you. You've been hiding from me. I was trying to wait for you to come around, but you are taking too long, so I decided to come and see you."

"Nothing, G-Ma. Just school."

"Don't lie to me."

"Why does he have to answer you anyway?" Charles said, jumping in. "His mother don't question him like that."

G-Ma pinned Charles with a steady gaze. "Well, she needs to. Yours does too."

"What goes on with me and my mother is really none of your business."

I was getting offended with him now. "Charles, you wilin'."

"How am I wilin'? She's our grandmother, not our mother."

"Which means we should have even more respect for her!" I spat.

"Enough," said G-Ma. "No need for you two to get into it." She stood up. "But I will say this: Both of you need to stop what you are doing. Charles, I know about you, and have known for years. You need to stop, seriously. And Hype, boy, you know way better than this."

"Why you all in our business?" said Charles.

"Because I love you, and I care."

Charles shrugged his shoulders. "We good. I understand your concern, but we good."

"No, you're not good. You need to stop, and you need to stop now." She turned to me. "We'll talk later."

After she left, Charles kept trying to talk shit about G-Ma, and he was getting real disrespectful, so I started to get heated.

But then when he left, the truth of what G-Ma said began to sink in. This was like the fifth warning I'd had lately: first Quaid, then Twon, then Tierra, and now G-Ma and my own guilty conscience.

I gotta find a way out. I feel like something bad will happen if I don't.

Shaneece

Twon told me about the incident that occurred with Slink and Wolf. I've only seen those two a few times, but I have a bad feeling about both of them. Twon's brother Trav is a sweetheart, but I really don't want Slink and Wolf over our apartment anymore. I would never tell Twon this, but I caught Slink checking me out when Twon wasn't looking. I don't trust them, and I hate the fact that they could have made us lose our apartment if they had fought with Hype and his cousins and made enough noise for the neighbors to complain.

Twon and I already have enough stress with everything else we're dealing with. We don't need more drama from his family.

My pre-paid phone rang, and I saw that it was my mom's cell phone number. My ears immediately started to get hot.

What does SHE want?

I quickly answered. "What is it?"

"That's how you greet your mother after not speaking for almost a month, Shaneece?"

"It's not like you picked up a phone to call me any sooner."

"Look, I'm not calling to argue with you. Shanelle told me you got a new place. Are you living with Twon?"

I snorted in disgust. "What's it to you?"

"What do you mean, what's it to me? I'm your mother. I care about you!"

"Yeah, Mom, you care about me *so much* that you let my father kick me out when I'm pregnant and have nowhere else to go, and now when you find out I'm living with a boy, suddenly that's a big deal. Really? You call that caring?"

There was a long silence. "I'm sorry about what happened with your father."

"You weren't sorry enough to stop him."

"Look, Shaneece, I didn't call you to fight. I just want to see how you're doing."

"Well, I'm fine. Anything else?"

"How is school?"

"I'm dropping out."

"What do you mean you're dropping out? Shaneece, you can't just throw away your future for some boy!"

"I'm not throwing away my future. School is too stressful. I have a child on the way. I'm doing what's best for him or her."

"What's best for him or her is you getting your education."

"Oh, now *you* want to tell *me* how to be a good parent?"

She sighed. "I'm sorry about what happened with your father, Shaneece."

"Well, if you really mean that, prove it to me."

"How am I supposed to do that?"

"Sign the papers for me to drop out so I can get my GED."

"Shaneece, no. I can't do that."

"You can, but you won't."

"That's not a good decision."

"And kicking your pregnant daughter out on the streets is?"

"Look, let's not talk about this over the phone. Where are you living? I can come over and we can talk."

"I don't want to see you right now."

"Shaneece, we can't just let this situation continue."

"Well, sign the paper then."

"I told you I can't do that."

"Why, because Dad won't let you? Why do you let him control you so much—even to the point of hurting your own children!"

"Shaneece . . . listen, this was a bad idea. I'll talk to you later."

"Yup, bye."

After we hung up, I felt very guilty for how I talked to my mother, but I was so angry at her for letting my father treat me the way he did.

She had her hand in it too. All my life, both of them made it seem like the only thing they cared about when it came to their kids was whether or not we made straight A's. It was like our entire worth as their daughters was tied to a report card. I don't know how this situation is ever going to work itself out.

Tierra

Me and Quaid were in my living room watching movies and eating pizza and popcorn. My mom went upstairs to give us privacy, and we were having a great time. It was good to see Quaid smiling and laughing. He had been so stressed lately about Hype's situation and the situation with his family.

"You want to watch another one?" I said after our third movie.

Quaid looked at the clock. It was 11:00 p.m. "No, I think it's about time we call it a night. I have to work early in the morning."

"Oh yeah, that's right. Well, that sucks. I was having so much fun with you."

"Me too." He smiled.

"Quaid…"

"What's up?"

"So . . . have you talked to Twon lately?" I didn't know if this was the right time or not, but I had been dying to know if Twon knew about us. From the look on Quaid's face, I could tell that this was definitely *not* the right time.

"Tierra, why are you so concerned about what Twon thinks of us being together?"

"Because, I just . . . I want to make sure you guys are still cool."

"But even if we weren't, that's between Twon and me. It would have nothing to do with you. Why are you so worried about him? He's not worried about you!"

"What's that supposed to mean?" I could feel my ears getting hot.

"Twon has moved on, Tierra. He's with Shaneece now."

I rolled my eyes at that statement. "Can't say I didn't see that coming."

"Let me ask you a question."

"What?"

"Do you still have feelings for Twon?"

"Why would you ask that?"

"Well, you keep asking me about him and how he feels about us, so I'm beginning to think you're using me as a rebound."

"A rebound? Quaid, I would never do th—"

"Are you sure? Because that's what it feels like."

"Quaid, no. You're not a rebound. I told you I had feelings for you just like you had feelings for me."

"So why do you keep asking me about Twon?"

"Because, I just want to be reassured that you and him are cool!"

"Well we are, okay? We talked about it, and now we're back to where we were before. You happy now?"

"I don't understand where all this attitude is coming from."

"I don't understand why you are so concerned about Twon."

"You must have forgotten that Twon and I were together for two years, Quaid! Plus, one of the reasons we broke up was because he thought I was cheating with you."

"Weren't you?"

"What do you mean by that? You and I were not fooling around while I was with Twon."

"Look, I'd rather not discuss Twon's feelings about our relationship anymore. What's done is done. Twon says he's okay with it, so why aren't you?"

"I am. Okay, then. I'm glad to hear that."

"You're glad to hear it? What's with the formal reply, Miss Proper? Are you glad to hear that I'm not so sure about you and me?" He stood up and grabbed his keys and phone.

"Quaid! Where is all this coming from?"

"We'll have to discuss it later. I have to get home."

Twon

Me and Shaneece was in our bedroom discussing our plans for the baby and our future.

"So," said Shaneece, "my plan is to rack up as many hours as I can until I can't work anymore. Hopefully by that time I will have enough saved to help keep our financial situation afloat."

I just sat there, kind of lost in my thoughts. This was really happening. I got a girl, a place of my own, and now we got a baby on the way . . . My mind drifted to where I thought my life would be at this point, and where it's actually at right now. Two totally different scenarios. I never would have guessed this.

"Twon?" said Shaneece. She waved her hand in front of my face.

"What's good?" I said, snapping out of it.

"Did you hear anything I just said? What's wrong?"

"Yeah, I heard you. But my question is, how do we plan to manage school around all of this? What about college?"

"Well, I'm honestly not too concerned about school right now. I plan to drop out and get my GED. I'll figure out what I want to do later."

I looked at her in surprise. "You're dropping out?"

"Yes, Twon. I can't stand that school and all those people bullying me every day. I get called all kinds of sluts and whores on the regular. I can take it most of the time, but now that I'm going to be a mother, and I got my baby to think about, it's starting to feel overwhelming."

I felt for her. "I really wish you would tell me who is doing this to you, and when it happens."

"Why? Are you going to fight the whole school, Twon? I'm the common denominator here. I'm the one who slept with two guys who were best friends. I'm the one who doesn't know who the father of her baby is." Shaneece had tears in her eyes.

My heart panged to see her hurting like this. I pulled her to me and held her close.

"Look, you made a mistake. We all did in this situation. You didn't lay down by yourself."

"I know, but society always blames the female."

"Man, fuck society!" I said, but at the same time, I felt kind of guilty because I had previously felt the exact same way that Shaneece just described, and part of me still did.

"Yeah, you say that, but if it wasn't me and you in this situation, would you still feel the same?"

I deflected. "So you really don't want to go to college?"

"Not right now. I never had a chance to really think about what I wanted to do with my life. My parents always shoved grades down my throat, and I was so focused on getting straight A's that I never really thought about what I wanted to do with those grades. I know for sure that I don't want to go into the medical field like Shanelle, but beyond that . . . I just don't know."

"Maybe you should try management, like a business degree."

She looked at me kind of sideways. "What do you mean?"

"You were really good with the customers at Sports Locker, and you say you love your job at Lacy's. Maybe business is a good field for you."

She thought about this for a moment. A tear slipped down her cheek. "I don't know, Twon."

"What do you mean? Why are you crying?"

"Because they never . . . I mean, what you just said shows me that you actually see *me*. I know this is not what our conversation was about, but this is the whole point! My parents never saw me for who I am. They never even noticed my talents and abilities, or encouraged me to grow in any of those ways. They only saw my grades, they saw me being sneaky, they saw all the trouble I got into, but they never saw *me*. And I guess it kind of hurts that I have to go outside of my family, far away from the people who are supposed to know me and love me the most, to find a person who actually sees me for me. Does that make sense?"

Damn. Shaneece just told my whole life story. My mother never saw me either, and I never met my father. My mother basically just wanted me around to do things for her and pay bills. I don't feel like she ever saw me either—she was too busy hating me for my father's death or ordering me around. Damn.

"That makes a lot of sense," I said, getting a little choked up myself. "Seems like we got a whole lot in common, Shaneece. For real."

"But at least we got each other, though." She smiled.

I smiled too. "Yeah, you right about that."

Hype

I hopped in the shower after school because I'm supposed to be meeting up with Charles later on today. I'm still trying to find a way to tell him that I want out of this drug shit. I stood there under the water letting the steam rise. I was totally in the zone when I heard a thump coming from the living room. That immediately put me on guard because I was the only one at home. My mom was at work, and nobody was supposed to be coming by today.

I quickly turned the shower off, got out, and wrapped a towel around my waist.

I left the bathroom and crept toward the living room. When I got there, the cold air was wafting in. I saw that the front door was wide open.

The fuck? I thought, as I heard tires screeching in front of my house. I quickly ran to the front door just in time to see Slink and Wolf peeling around the corner in Slink's car.

"I know these niggas. . ." I turned and quickly scanned my eyes around the living room. My gaming system and all my games was gone! *Fuck that shit. This means war.*

I called Twon's number a few times, but it kept going to voicemail. Then I remembered he said he had to work today.

I was growing more and more heated by the moment. I could not believe these niggas just robbed me.

Feeling dazed, I went back to the bathroom when I realized I still had only a towel on. After I finished changing, I got on the phone with Charles.

"Wassup, nigga?" he said. "We still on for five?"

"These niggas just robbed me."

"*Who* just robbed you? What the fuck you mean? Where you at?" Charles sounded even more heated than I felt.

"It was those niggas Slink and Wolf. They came up in the crib while I was in the shower and took my system and all my games. I seen them driving around the corner cuz they left the front door wide open."

"Wow . . . those niggas is really bold. They just waltzed up in your house and stole all your shit. Time to get the strap, nigga."

"Nah, I ain't trying to do all that. But I'm definitely ready to fuck these niggas up though."

"Did you talk to Twon?"

"I tried to call that nigga, but he at work, so he probably can't see his phone."

"Well, his fucking cousins 'bout to have a rude awakening. Hold on, let me see where those niggas be. I'm-a call you right back."

"Bet."

After Charles and I hung up the phone, I could feel myself getting more and more heated by the second. I really wanted to kill these niggas. It wasn't about the stuff they stole, though I certainly wanted to fuck them up and get my shit back. It was more about the fact that they was trying to treat me like I was some kind of pussy nigga. These niggas was comfortable enough to just walk up in my house and steal my shit. Fuck that. Nigga, it's on.

Shaneece

Twon and I went to school together in the morning. It was becoming
kind of a routine for him to walk me to my locker before first period to
make sure that I was safe. Whenever I was with Twon, no one
bothered me, but as soon as he was gone, that's when all hell broke
loose. It's pathetic that I need a bodyguard when I'm only in high
school.

When I got to first period, they were already starting in on me.
As I walked toward the back of the room to find a seat, a guy stood up
and blocked my way. I sighed, already annoyed.

"Excuse me," I said, trying to go around him, but he kept
stepping in my way. "Move!" I said, pushing him forcefully, and he
bumped into a girl's desk and knocked her books to the floor in the
process.

It was Shatina, a real nasty bitch if ever there was one. She
looked up at me with a fierce expression. "Unh uh, pick that up,
bitch."

"It was *his* fault!" I said. "He wouldn't get out of my way!"

"You pushed me," said the boy, looking innocent.

I rolled my eyes because I really did not have time for this today. I bent down and picked up the books.

"Yeah, yeah, you know that's what you like to do anyway. Don't try to act like you have a problem bending over now!" said the boy.

I quickly stood up straight and put the books on the girl's desk. "Fuck you!" I said. "You're disgusting."

"No, you're disgusting."

"Are you a virgin?" I said, stepping around the desk impatiently. I had to go on the other side because he was still in my way.

"What do you mean?" He looked embarrassed. "No, I ain't no virgin."

"Alright, shut the fuck up then." I headed to my seat in the back of the room.

I made it through that class, but when I got to second period, I was feeling kind of nauseous, so I had went to the bathroom. By the time I got to my class, I was late, so I had to get a hall pass from the front office. When I finally got to my class, the only empty seats were in front, so of course I could hear everyone talking about me under their breath the entire period.

When class was over, I rushed to the door, but the teacher stopped me.

"Shaneece, can I talk to you for a moment?"

I didn't have any choice but to say yes. I stayed behind and waited for the rest of the students to leave the class.

"I wanted to talk to you about your grades. You started off very strong this year, but now it seems like you're slipping. You missed three assignments, and the ones you turned in were all a C or lower. This is not like you, Shaneece. What's going on?"

"I got a lot on my plate." I felt terrible that my grades were slipping like this, even though I did want to leave school.

"I understand that this may be a busy time for you. But I do have to remind you that this is your senior year, and this is a required class. If you don't start pulling your grades up, you might not graduate."

I wanted to explain to her my situation, but I decided against it. She seemed like she genuinely cared, but I didn't feel like there was anything she could do to help the situation, so I just kept it to myself. "I understand." I said. "I will try to do better."

"Great." She looked relieved. "Let me know if there is any way I can help."

"I will."

I left her classroom and went to my next class, which I had with Twon. I got there in the nick of time because it was only a few doors down the hall. That class felt like a safe haven because no one talked to me or about me with Twon there. People were so phony, it was pathetic. When Twon was there, everything was cool. But the moment he left, they all started in on me.

I could not wait to get out of here so I could go home, change, and head to work. Work was so much better to deal with than school. I thought about what Twon said to me the other night about going to school for management. *I wonder if I actually could do well in business?*

I was so lost in my thoughts that I accidentally bumped into someone standing in the hallway. When I regained my balance, I saw that it was Shatina.

"Watch where you walking, bitch!" she said, pushing me.

"Don't put your hands on me!"

"Shut the fuck up before I beat your THOT ass."

"You won't be beating shit!"

"Oh really?" She stepped toward me. "If you think you got hands, why don't we find out?"

"I don't have time to deal with your ignorant ass."

"Who you calling ignorant, bitch?" Shatina pushed my head, and that did it. I swung at her, but someone stepped between us and pushed us apart.

"Chill, chill!" he said. "Both of y'all is pregnant!"

I immediately felt guilty. I had completely forgotten about my baby because I was so mad at that girl. That was about the third time she put her hands on me, and I was ready to fight. If that boy hadn't broken us up, something could have happened to my baby, and I never would have forgiven myself.

My last class for the day was no better than any of the others. I was so sick of all the name-calling and snide remarks. Apparently, I was now a meme. I didn't even want to look at social media to see what people had come up with.

I remember when my father called me a filthy fucking whore. Those words replay in my mind every day. If he knew the pain they caused me, I wonder if he would have said them.

Probably, I thought. I sucked my teeth and slammed my locker shut.

Tierra

After the mini argument with Quaid, I felt so conflicted that I reached out to my mom to see what she thought about the whole situation.

"Ma, I really need to talk to you about something," I said to her as soon as she walked in the door from work. She gave me a strange look.

"Sure. Hold on, let me get settled," she said, slipping off her shoes. She went upstairs for about ten minutes then came back downstairs dressed in her house clothes.

"I made some spaghetti. You want me to fix you a plate?" I said.

"Did you use that spicy sausage again?" she said, wrinkling her nose. "You know I don't like spicy food."

I rolled my eyes playfully. "No, Ma. I made sure *not* to use my spicy sausage, though I definitely think you are crazy for not liking it."

"Girl, you know my motto: If it ain't broke, don't fix it. Regular sausage and hamburger is fine for me."

"Ma, I'm-a need you to expand your horizons."

"My horizons are set exactly how I like them, thank you very much."

We both chuckled.

"So, what's up? Why did you look so worried when I came home? Did something happen with Quaid?"

I had opened my mouth to answer her, but I paused when she said her last sentence. My mother knew me so well it was scary.

"How you always know what's going on with me before I even tell you?" I asked.

"Girl, I keep telling you: I birthed you and I raised you. I watch you even when you don't know I'm watching. That's all part of being your mother. So what happened with Quaid?"

"Well, apparently, he thinks I'm using him as a rebound." I went on to explain how Quaid kept getting upset whenever I asked about Twon's feelings about us getting together, then about the argument we had when he accused me of using him as a rebound. My mom just sat there and listened to my story as she always did. When I finished, she was ready with a response.

"Well, Tierra, even though you think Quaid is way off base with his accusations, I can kind of see his point. If you and Twon are truly over each other, and Twon has already moved on with Shaneece, why do you feel the need to keep asking how he feels about you and Quaid? Do you still have feelings for him? Are you jealous that he's with Shaneece? All of these feelings are normal, but in order to move past them, you have to confront them."

It never really occurred to me that I might be jealous of Twon and Shaneece's relationship. I mean, sure, I was mad as hell that he ended up sleeping with her and that she might be pregnant with his baby, but I never really thought about the fact that I might have been so against them being together because I was jealous. I mean, both of them definitely did me wrong, but if things were over between Twon and me, I really had no hold over him or who he chose to be with.

"I never really thought about jealousy," I said after a long pause.

"Girl, if you are, that is perfectly normal. That girl did you dirty. She went behind your back and slept with your man after claiming to be your best friend. Any woman would feel some type of way after that. But my concern is not necessarily that you are feeling these feelings, but that they might be affecting your relationship with Quaid and even your other relationships. Do you truly believe you gave yourself enough time to get over Twon before you and Quaid got together?"

There was another long pause after that statement. This was beginning to look more and more like Quaid was a rebound for me. I felt terrible that I was possibly using him, but that was definitely not my intention. I sincerely did have feelings for Quaid, and though I just recently admitted it, I always had.

"I don't think I gave myself enough time," I admitted. I was starting to get a little choked up. This whole situation was so confusing and painful for me.

"Girl, there is no need to be upset with yourself. This is all new to you. You were hurt, and you're probably still hurting. You and Twon were in a relationship for two years. All those feelings are not going to go away with the snap of a finger."

"That makes sense." I already felt a little better. "So what do you think I should do? I don't want to hurt Quaid, and I don't want to break up with him, but I also don't want to use him either."

"Listen, I know you don't want to hear this, but it might be best for you to take a break from Quaid. Give yourself time to heal and regroup. Focus on God and school like we discussed before. Didn't you say that you felt like God was calling you to be saved?"

That was another touchy subject for me. All of a sudden, I felt like I was in the hot seat. I had basically been putting my thoughts and feelings about God and salvation on a back burner, focusing instead on Twon and Quaid.

"I mean, yeah, I have been feeling like He is calling me, but I'm not sure I'm ready for all that just yet."

"So your relationships with Quaid and Twon are more important to you than building a relationship with God?"

I knew that my mother didn't mean those words in a judgmental or condescending way, but they still made me feel extremely guilty.

174

"I mean, I don't see you bending over backward to go to church either." As soon as those words left my mouth, I knew that I was in trouble.

"Look, Tierra," said my mom, giving me a stern look. "I know you are just going through a lot with this situation, so that's why you're lashing out at me, but I will not tolerate disrespect. Do you hear me?" She looked me straight in the eyes as she spoke to let me know that she meant business.

"I'm sorry, Ma." I really wasn't trying to pick a fight with her.

"It's fine, but I want you to know that I meant what I said." Her expression softened slightly.

"I know, but can you at least tell me why you won't go to church?"

"We will have to talk about that later."

And just like that, she shut down the conversation.

She stood up. "I'm going upstairs to relax."

Twon

Me, Hype, Quaid, and Trav was all chilling at my house after school. Shaneece was at work, and today was one of my off days. I didn't invite Slink and Wolf because it was clear that it would only add more beef between them and Hype and his family.

"I honestly don't know the best way to handle all these situations, yo," I said.

"With Shaneece and the baby?" said Hype.

"Yeah, and college and the future and shit. This is not how I thought my life was gonna turn out at eighteen."

"Shit, who you tellin'?" Hype said, then he glanced at Charles.

"Wassup?" said Charles.

"Nothing. Just mad stress."

"Don't worry about that shit, nigga," Charles shot back at Hype. "I told you we gonna get shit poppin."

That statement puzzled me. *What could they be talking about?* That didn't sound like it fit in with what Hype told me about how he wanted to stop with the drug shit. I made a mental note to hit Hype up later and talk to him one on one.

Quaid had been staring intently at Hype and Charles, but he shifted his focus to me. Me and Quaid were starting to get back to normal, though I must admit I still feel low key salty about the whole situation with Tierra. But at the same time, I can't really hold nothing over either of them if I'm with Shaneece. I really just wished this whole shit hadn't happened. I wish I never fucked with Shaneece.

As soon as I had that thought, I felt guilty because me and Shaneece were supposed to be building toward the future now, and Shaneece was supposed to be my girl.

Quaid spoke up like he'd read my mind. "So, what do you think you should do with all these big life decisions?"

"I don't even know, Quaid. I mean, I always wanted to go to college. That was my plan: Go to college, play some ball, get out, find a job, settle down, then find me a girl and start a family. But this shit happened all backwards. This whole situation is fucked up. Even though there's a chance the baby ain't mine, I can't deny that I already feel connected to it, like it's my kid. And I would never want my son or daughter to grow up like I did, with one parent gone and another who don't even like them."

"This is heavy, lil' bro," said Trav, chiming in for the first time. Trav has really been a strong support system for me, even though we literally just met this year. I'm still amazed at the fact that I have a brother now. This shit is surreal.

"I know," I said.

"Hype, how do you feel about the situation?" said Trav. "What if the baby is yours? Do you have a plan?"

Hype shot me a glance before he answered Trav.

"I been just, you know, trying to save money and shit."

Charles snickered. "Nigga, you sound like a fuck boy!" he said. "*Trying to save money and shit,*" he mocked. Charles looked at Trav. "Hype is good. If the kid is his, it will be well taken care of."

"Not if he continues taking care of the situation the way he is now," Quaid shot at Charles. I knew that shit was coming. Hype told me how Quaid and Charles got into it when Quaid found out he was selling drugs with Charles.

"Nigga, money is money," said Charles. "As long as he getting it, it don't matter where it comes from."

Trav was looking back and forth between Quaid, Hype, and Charles, taking in their dynamic. He shot me a look but didn't say anything. I knew just from his look that he had pretty much figured out what was going on with these three. Trav was a sharp dude aside from being goofy at times.

"Yes, it does matter how you earn your money," Quaid said, but I held my hand up.

"Quaid, let's not get into all that today. We got other shit to worry about."

Hype shot me a grateful look, but Charles looked like he wasn't quite done yet.

"Yeah, you right about that." He chuckled. "We sure do got other shit to worry about."

***

Later on that night, I called Hype to see what was up with him and Charles.

"Hello?" said Hype, answering on the fourth or fifth ring.

"Yo, what was up with you and Charles earlier?"

"What you mean?"

"Charles kept talking shit like something is 'bout to go down or something."

Hype was silent for a moment. "Look, Twon, I know you getting acquainted with your new fam and all, but Slink and Wolf 'bout to get this work."

That put me on alert. "I thought yall niggas was over that shit."

"Nah, nigga. Some new shit happened." Hype told me that Slink and Wolf broke into his house while he was in the shower and robbed him. They got in easily because Hype and them never locked their front door. I found myself getting more and more heated as Hype spoke. *Why would they do some shit like this?* I already told them that Hype and his family were like family to me.

"You sure it was them, Hype?" I said, but I already knew the truth.

"Yes, nigga. I saw them pulling off in Slink's car when I went to the front door, which they left wide open like they didn't care if I saw them or not."

"Shit!" I said, wanting to throw my phone. I knew this shit was 'bout to go down whether I liked it or not. I just didn't know how to handle it. *Should I warn Slink and Wolf?* They were my cousins, despite the fact that they had done some grimy shit like this.

Hype and Charles were not about to let this shit ride. Shit, I probably wouldn't either. That was like the ultimate disrespect, to walk up in a man's house and rob him. There was really no turning back from this, and now I felt like I was in the middle, with one side of my family beefing against the other.

I was starting to regret letting Slink and Wolf into my life.

Hype

I was riding in the passenger seat as me and Charles were on our way to Twon's house to pull up on Slink and Wolf. Someone who knew them tipped us off that they would be there.

"Yo, you think this is a good idea?" I said to Charles. I wanted to beat the shit out of Slink and Wolf, but a part of me felt guilty because they were Twon's family.

"Hell, yeah!" said Charles. "Them niggas ain't 'bout to make you out to be no pussy."

Those words kind of settled it for me.

We pulled up to the house just as Twon, Slink, and Wolf stepped outside. Trav was behind them closing the door. It looked like they were in the middle of some kind of argument. Twon was yelling and gesturing at them, and Slink and Wolf were shaking their heads and dismissing him like what he said didn't matter.

Charles parked the car in the middle of the street, and we both hopped out and swiftly made our way toward Slink and Wolf, ready for action.

"So y'all think y'all can just rob a nigga and get away with it?" I said as we got to the porch.

Slink and Wolf stood at the top of the stairs with smug expressions on their faces.

"Yeah, we did it. And?" said Wolf.

Slink chimed in all sure of himself. "Wasn't like y'all niggas was gonna do shit about it no way cuz you're a bunch of—" Before he could finish his sentence, Charles yanked him by his shirt off the porch, and they went at it.

Wolf looked excited as he came at me. These niggas was crazy, I could see that. Me and Wolf squared off and began fighting. Trav and Twon looked conflicted, then they both tried to break us up—Twon went for me and Wolf, and Trav went for Charles and Slink.

Things were moving so fast. Trav pulled Charles off of Slink—he had been stomping him out after pulling him off the porch—while Twon was still trying to break me and Wolf apart. Wolf was a pretty good fighter, but that nigga's hands was no match for mine. Something glinted in the distance, and I quickly turned to see that Slink had something in his hand while Trav was still trying to hold Charles back. At first I thought it was a knife, but then he hit Charles with it, and I realized it was a crowbar.

"Charles!" I yelled as soon as I saw it, but I was too late. He hadn't seen Slink coming because he was too busy going back and forth with Trav. Blood was all over Charles' face. Wolf tagged me with multiple blows because I lost focus, but I didn't care about that. All I saw was blood dripping down my cousin's face as I went for Slink. I got the crowbar from Slink as Trav and Twon tried to hold me back. Charles was dazed because he had been hit in the head and was bleeding.

I got out of Twon and Trav's grip and began wailing on Slink with the crowbar. "Nigga, that's my fucking cousin!" I screamed. I felt Wolf raining blows on me from behind as I sat on top of Slink hitting him over and over with the crowbar. His face was bloodier than Charles' now, but I didn't care. I didn't even know if he was still conscious—I was running on pure adrenaline. Finally, Trav and Twon managed to get Wolf off of me and me off of Slink, and then we heard sirens.

We all made a mad dash toward our cars. I drag-walked Charles with me, shoved him in the front passenger seat, hopped in the driver's seat, and took off for the hospital.

Slink and Wolf sped off in Slink's whip.

Twon and Trav were left standing in the middle of the street.

***

When I got to the emergency room, they had me wait outside the door while they took Charles into a room to clean him up. He needed stitches. Luckily, the cut wasn't too deep.

Once Charles got his stitches, the cops came in and questioned both of us to find out what happened. They thought the fight must have been gang related. After they realized that they weren't getting any information out of either of us, they gave up and left.

"Fucking kids," one of them sneered in my direction as he walked off. I didn't care. The only thing I cared about was that Charles was okay.

Shaneece

The Uber driver dropped me off at me and Twon's apartment just as two police cars were driving off. When I saw the cars, I immediately felt anxious. Had something happened to Twon?

I jumped out of the car and ran toward the house feeling nauseas the whole way. I let myself in and practically ran Twon over because he was standing near the door. Trav was sitting on the couch.

"Twon, what happened? Are you guys okay? Why were the police just here?"

Twon held his hands up. "Hold on, Shaneece. I just need a minute." He looked over at Trav. "Hey bro…" He didn't need to say anymore. Trav nodded in understanding and got up from the couch.

"I'm about to head out anyway," he said. "See you Shaneece. Catch you later, bro."

I said bye to Trav and watched him drive off in his car before I turned back to Twon.

"What the hell happened, Twon?"

"It was like this—" He sucked his teeth in annoyance when his phone rang. He looked at the caller ID. "Hold on, I need to take this."

He answered the call. "Yeah . . . Is he okay?" A look of concern flickered across his face, then relief. "Good. A'ight. I gotta talk to you later. Shaneece just got home."

"Okay, what happened?" I said as soon as he ended the call. My hand was on my hip. I needed answers.

"Some stupid shit went down."

"What stupid shit?"

He opened his mouth to answer, but his phone rang again. He answered quickly.

"Yo, I can't even talk to either one of y'all niggas right now!" He practically growled he was so angry.

Whoever was on the other line must have been arguing back at him because he cut the conversation short. "Look, I said I can't talk right now. We'll have to get up later." He ended the call before the other person had a chance to respond.

"Who was that?" I demanded. "And what is going on?"

"Look, Shaneece, Hype and Charles got into it with Slink and Wolf. Slink hit Charles with a crowbar, then Hype grabbed it from him and pounded on Slink like I've never seen him do before. It was crazy. There was blood everywhere." He went on to explain to me everything that led up to the fight. By the time his story was over, my head was spinning, and I was furious.

"How DARE they bring that to our house?"

"I know. I'm sorry, baby. It won't happen again."

"They could get us evicted, Twon! We just got this apartment! What if I had been home? What if something happened to the baby? What if someone died? What if they brought weapons? They have no respect for us or our house, Twon."

I was truly freaking out. So many things could have gone wrong tonight, and so many things still could go wrong. I had a sick feeling that this wasn't over. If our landlord found out that the police were here, we could get in huge trouble. If we end up getting evicted from our first apartment, where were we going to go? Neither one of us had parents to rely on. We couldn't put that burden back on G-Ma. This situation was getting way out of hand.

Twon just stood there looking at me. "I'm sorry, Shaneece."

"This wasn't your fault, Twon. But as for your cousins . . . Wait, what happened with the police? What did they say?"

"They just asked a few questions, that's all. Everyone had already left before they got here. A neighbor called the cops. I told them a fight broke out in front of the house, but I didn't know who it was or what it was about."

My mouth dropped open in shock. "You lied to the police?"

"What else was I supposed to do, Shaneece!" Twon threw his hands up in exasperation. "I didn't know what else to do. I didn't want to cause any more drama than what already happened. Plus I didn't want this to get back to the landlord."

I assessed the situation based on everything he said. "Look, I know you probably don't want to hear this, but I don't want your cousins back over this house. It's too risky. It honestly seems like they have been nothing but trouble since you met them. I don't even believe you should continue to associate with them. I definitely wouldn't want our child around them with them acting like that."

Twon just looked at me. "I understand. I have to figure this whole situation out."

"I just hope we don't get evicted."

Tierra

After my conversation with my mother, I thought a lot about my relationship with Quaid. I know it seems like I've been using him as a rebound, but that was never my intention. I called him after a few days, and he agreed to come over.

I waited anxiously for him to get to my house. Finally, he pulled up in the driveway and made his way to the door. I opened it to greet him.

His eyes widened in surprise. "Wow," he said. "You must have been looking out the window or something."

"I just want us to talk about this situation."

"Understood." We made our way to the kitchen to sit down. My mom was at work, so we would have full privacy, not that she had anything to worry about with Quaid anyway.

"So, where should we start?" he said, taking his seat.

"Do you want some cookies?" I said. "I just finished baking some."

"I thought it smelled good in here. Let's see what you got." He smiled, and I smiled too, but then my heart panged because that was one of the reasons Twon and I had broken up: I had baked Quaid some cookies, and Twon had found out about it and assumed that we were messing around.

I grabbed two plates and put some cookies on one for Quaid and the other for myself, then I poured us both some milk. I couldn't cook much outside of spaghetti and cookies, which my mother often made fun of me for, but hey, at least I knew something.

"Mm-MM! Girl, these is good!" Quaid said, around a mouth full of cookie.

"Stop talking with food in your mouth, you nasty boy." I pushed his shoulder playfully.

"I can't help it. These cookies so good, make me wanna smack my momma!"

"Boy, you crazy!" I said, but I had to laugh a little at his silliness.

He took a swig of milk and set down the glass. "Tierra…"

"What's up?"

"I'm sorry for the other day. I don't want you to think I'm trying to accuse you of anything with Twon. It's just that I really want us to have a good relationship, but it seemed like you were more concerned about Twon's feelings than you were about mine."

"I understand." I said. "I'm sorry for making you feel that way. I really am not trying to use you as a rebound, Quaid. I really do like you. I guess since we got together so quick, I didn't really take the time to process my breakup with Twon. Even though we were no longer a couple, some feelings were still there about the situation."

He nodded. "I can definitely understand that. I guess that's a fault on my part. I was so excited about the idea of us being together that I didn't give you enough time to breathe. I'm sorry, Tierra. I didn't mean to be a source of confusion for you."

My heart panged once again. Quaid was so sweet and so mature. I couldn't help but compare him to Twon. Whenever Twon and I got into it, Twon always ended up yelling and cussing at me then storming out.

"Thank you for being so understanding," I said.

"It's no problem at all. So where do you think we should go from here? Do you think we should take a break?"

I looked at him in surprise. I hadn't expected him to suggest something like that. My mom kept saying it, but I didn't feel like a break was something I wanted. I was sure that Quaid would agree with me.

"You want to take a break?" I asked.

"Not that I *want* to, but if it will help you sort out your feelings for Twon and be ready to move on, I don't think it would be fair to try to hold you to this relationship. I would never want to stress you like that."

Again, Quaid was touching my heart like no other guy had ever done. He was so sweet and so understanding. I just couldn't bear the thought of being without him right now.

"How about we talk about a break later? I don't want to make a quick decision before really thinking about it."

"I can definitely understand that." He smiled.

"So what else is new with you? You seemed upset over the phone. Did something new happen with your aunts, or with Hype and Charles?"

He gave me a look I couldn't quite figure out. "Did Hype tell you what happened?"

"I called him on the phone after we prayed about his situation, and he told me that he was selling drugs with Charles. I tried to get him to stop, and he said he wants to, but he doesn't know how."

Quaid looked upset at the mention of Charles. "I really can't stand the fact that he allowed Charles to talk him into that in the first place. I mean, can't he see that no good is going to come from this? Charles has been arrested more times than I can count! He keeps getting into trouble—he was just shot by the police a few months ago! When is it going to end? And why is Hype following behind him?"

Quaid looked extremely worried.

"Well, he did say he doesn't want to do it anymore." I tried, but it sounded lame even to my ears.

"Well, that's news to me. Every time I talk to him, he's always saying that he's just doing what he can to save money, as if that's the only way to make money. This situation is way out of control, not to mention what just happened…" He stopped himself like he didn't want to say anything more, and took a big bite of a cookie for something to do.

"Quaid, what are you not telling me? What else happened?"

"Nothing. I don't really want to get into it."

"Was it something else with Hype and Charles?"

"Yeah, but it's better if Hype tells you himself."

"Oh, Lord." I sighed. "So much is going on in our senior year!"

"Tell me about it. We're supposed to be graduating, and hell is breaking loose on all sides."

"It must be the devil, right?" I hoped he would say something to reassure me.

Quaid looked at me. "Sometimes it's the devil, and sometimes it's our own decisions."

***

Quaid's words stayed with me long into the night. Even though he was talking about Hype and Charles, it felt like he'd said something I needed to hear.

For a while now, I've been feeling like God is calling me—but what if something bad happens, and I'm not able to make the decision before my life is over? I mean, I don't plan on dying any time soon, but you also can't predict the future. I don't know if it's paranoia or if I'm just overly anxious for no reason, but I really feel like I need to make a decision soon about God.

Twon

This entire situation is fucked up. I feel like no matter what I do, I have to take somebody's side. Charles had to get stitches, and Hype fucked up Slink's whole face. He gave him a concussion from hitting him so many times in the head with that crowbar.

Me and Trav went over Slink's house and got Hype's game system and games, so that was one good thing, but I feel like that's an insignificant detail when it comes to the real problems we're facing.

Slink and Wolf was even talking shit when me and Trav went over to get Hypes' games back. This was all a big joke to them. I hate to say it, but it looks like I'm gonna have to cut off my cousins that I just met. So there goes another relationship down the drain.

I can't seem to hold on to shit in my life. I lost my two year relationship with Tierra, I lost my dad, I lost Hype for a little while, I don't know what the hell is going on with my mom, and I'm about to lose my two cousins. Seems like a nigga can't win for losing. Every time I try to move forward, I get pushed two steps back. What did I do to deserve all this? I mean, I know I ain't perfect, but I ain't never tried to hurt nobody intentionally.

I really, really need to talk to my mom. I tried calling her phone back to back earlier today, and at first it rang, but then it started going straight to voicemail. I left a few messages, but she probably ain't even gonna listen to them.

The only other option I can think of is to pop up on her at the house. Maybe I can catch her while she's going in or leaving out or something. I really just need to hear her voice or see her face. Even though she wants nothing to do with me, she's still my mother.

Nobody seems to understand why I try to hold on to her, but I can't just let her go. Despite all the bad things she's done to me, she's the only mother I got. And besides, she might be 'bout to be a grandmother. Maybe when I have a kid she'll want to build a relationship with me. Maybe that will help her snap out of her hatred for me.

Hype

I feel like what I'm about to do is real fucked up, but I gotta do it anyway. I gotta tell Charles I'm done with this drug shit. All these warnings and shit got me spooked—Twon, Tierra, Quaid, G-Ma, hell, even my own conscience be warning me that this situation is not going to end well if I don't get out.

The only thing I really gotta figure out is how the hell I'm gonna tell him. I feel mad grimy leaving him hanging, especially after he just rode for me with that Slink and Wolf situation. Nigga got stitches on the side of his head because of me. But at the same time, I don't know what else to do.

I was jolted out of my thoughts when I heard a loud knock on the door. Before that shit happened with Slink and Wolf, we never kept our door locked, but now I guess shit got to change.

"Who is it?" I said, irritated that somebody was interrupting me.

"It's me, nigga! Open up!" said Charles.

"Shit!" I said under my breath. This was the last nigga I wanted to see right now.

I opened the door to let Charles in.

"What's wrong with you?" said Charles, noticing my expression.

I decided to just come right out with it. "Yo, Charles, I gotta talk to you."

"What's up?"

"It's about this shit we been doing. I don't know if I can keep doing this drug shit, Charles."

Charles looked taken aback, like I had surprised him. "What— did you have another conversation with Quaid or something? That nigga need to stay out our business."

"No, it's not even Quaid. It's…" I stopped myself from telling him that everybody had been warning me lately, but I didn't want to get into all that. I needed to own this myself. "Look man, I want to hold you down like you hold me down, but this drug shit just ain't me. I ain't never been that type of nigga, feel me?"

Charles took in my words. "Look, Hype, I understand you don't want to do this. But right now, my back is really against the wall. I don't have nobody I can really trust but you. Niggas try to rob me all the time, snitches got the police on my back, and Chief ain't getting out for another two weeks. If he was out, I could handle it, but they kept pushing his date back, and it's only a hope that he actually gets out this time. Can you just do it for two more weeks?"

I could see that he understood where I was coming from, but he needed me to understand him too. Although everything inside of me did not want to do this, I felt like I had no choice. I couldn't just leave him out there like that with nobody to hold him down. Charles has had my back and been like a brother to me since day one. I couldn't just leave him now when shit was hot.

"A'ight man, I gotchu." I said finally.

Shaneece

I wiped tears from my eyes with a Kleenex after reading the letters that had been stuffed in my locker by my classmates. I was truly sick of this bullying shit. I was done with that school. I had enough going on in my personal life without having to deal with this bullshit. It was time for me to go.

Twon was at work, so he didn't see the letters or my tears. I didn't want to show them to him anyway, because they said some really filthy foul shit. I knew he would be furious and want to fight whoever sent them, but to me, it was no use. Twon had enough going on right now anyway, plus the letters were anonymous (of course), so he would have to literally pick a fight with the whole school. In my mind, the only option was for me to remove myself from the situation.

I was time to drop out, get my GED, and focus on earning money and preparing for my baby.

I decided to call my mom. Maybe I could explain the situation and get through to her. She picked up on the second ring.

"Mom?"

"So she *did* give you your phone back," my dad responded. I rolled my eyes, annoyed that he had my mom's phone.

"Look, I really just need to talk to Mom. Can you give her the phone?"

"She's in the shower. Besides, whatever you have to say to her, you can say to me."

"I don't want to say it to you. I need to talk to mom."

"What do you want, Shaneece? Do you and your little boyfriend need rent money or something? I heard you were living with him."

"No, we don't need any money from you. We both have jobs."

"Bravo." His sarcasm was too obvious. "So where are you working?"

"You mean you haven't been tracking me? I figured you would have found that out by now."

"No, you're not my problem anymore, so no need to track you."

Those words kind of hurt, but I held it in.

"Can I please speak to Mom?"

"I told you, she's in the shower. If you don't need money, what do you want?"

"It's none of your business."

"Well, if it involves my wife, it is my business. That's how things go in the real world, honey. You'd know that if you'd waited to get married before getting pregnant. But wait, who would you marry?" He snorted what barely passed as a chuckle. "You don't even know who the father is!" I could practically feel the venom in his tone.

I blinked back tears and put on a brave front. "Look, Dad, like you said, I'm not your problem anymore. I should be of no concern to you. Can you please just tell Mom to call me when she gets out of the shower?"

"For what?"

"Why do you need to know?"

"She's going to tell me anyway."

"I need to drop out of school, okay?"

"Why are you dropping out of school? Are those kids bullying you again?"

The worst part about it was that he actually sounded concerned. I literally could not deal with my father. One moment he was spewing hurtful, hateful words at me like I was a piece of scum he needed to wipe off of the bottom of his shoe, and the next he was super concerned about my future. I was so tired of his mind games.

"Look, Dad, I don't want to get into it, but I need to drop out. Can you have her call me please?"

"She's not doing it. I don't agree with that decision."

"Well, it's either drop out or fail out, because I'm not going back."

"Well it looks like you're going to have to add failing in your senior year to your list of fuck-ups in life, because there is no way I'm letting her give you permission to drop out."

"You know what? FUCK you! And I mean that from the bottom of my heart."

"Fuck you too. Goodbye." He hung up the phone.

Tears streamed down my face after that phone call with my father. Why couldn't I just catch a break?

***

I took the next day off of school. I told Twon I was sick, but I was really just trying to come up with a way to get my mom to sign the papers for me to drop out of school. He offered to stay home and take care of me, but I declined, urging him to go to school. He must have sensed that I wanted to be alone, so he left.

About an hour later, when I was still sitting there trying to figure out what to do, I heard a knock on my door.

I went to answer it, and it was my mom!

"What are you doing here?" I said, letting her in.

"Shanelle gave me your address."

"Why would she do that?" I felt myself heating up. I could not believe Shanelle had betrayed me like this!

"Calm down. I'm going to sign the papers."

"You are?"

"Yes. Shanelle told your father and me about the bullying at school, and I decided to do this for you. But Shaneece, you have to promise me you are going to get your GED. I realize that the only thing you care about right now is the baby, and I certainly understand, but you are not going to get much further in life without at least a diploma or a GED."

I was taken aback by all of this.

"What did Dad say?" I finally managed in a small voice.

"He didn't agree with this decision, but I decided that it needed to be done. I want what's best for you, even if it's not what I want for you. It's not healthy for you or the baby to be in an unsafe environment. Do you promise to get your GED?"

"Yes!" I snatched the study book from the end table next to the sofa. "I've already been studying for it."

She looked at the book and smiled. "You've always been resourceful."

My heart warmed at those words. That was the nicest thing I could remember either of my parents ever saying to me. I blinked back tears.

"Well, let me get dressed," I said, suddenly feeling brisk and efficient. I wanted to get this thing done now.

"Nice place," she remarked, taking a seat on the sofa as I went into the bedroom to throw on some clothes. I could not believe I was finally getting out of that horrible school.

Tierra

I was walking down the hallway after school to go to my locker before meeting Quaid at his car. We were supposed to be going on a date before he went to work, so I was kind of pressed for time. On my way out of the school building, I saw Shaneece exiting the guidance office with a large folder in her hands. Wow, she was really showing now. Seeing her reminded me that Twon possibly had a child on the way with her, and now they were living in an apartment together, according to Quaid and Hype.

Fuck that bitch. I will never forgive her for stealing my man.

I know, I'm terrible, but it still hurts. Anyway, there was no way to avoid the guidance office when exiting the school, so I held my head high as I approached the front doors of the school. She must've felt my eyes on her because she looked up and saw me. When our eyes connected, she almost dropped her folder.

I smirked at her. "No need to be scared. I don't hit pregnant bitches."

Fierce protectiveness glinted in her eyes. "I'm not afraid of you, girl."

I stopped walking. "You should be. The only thing holding me back is that baby in your stomach. You better thank it when it's born. That child just saved they momma's life."

She rolled her eyes at that statement. "You are so wack. Get over yourself."

"At least I ain't a THOT who doesn't know who the father of her baby is."

"I'm about ninety-nine percent sure it's your man's." She gave a smug little smile and waited for my reaction.

Those last words cut my heart, but I acted like I didn't care.

"It might be. But you'll get yours. What goes around comes around, honey. You don't do people like you did me and just get away with it."

"Are you threatening me?"

"I don't need to threaten you. That's just the way life works."

I quickly walked away from her before she could say anything else, because I didn't have too many more comebacks for her biting words. I shot a quick backward glance at her before I walked out the doors, and saw her standing there looking unsure of herself, like my last statement bothered her.

I rolled my eyes. "Good. I want it to hurt."

Twon

I was up in bed half watching TV and half consumed by thoughts of everything that was going on. I was waiting for Shaneece to get home from work. She had called to tell me that her mom had signed the papers for her to drop out and get her GED. I was kind of disappointed that she was dropping out so close to graduation, but at the same time, I understood why she wanted to. The bullying at the school was really stressing her, and I low key feel like she is still very ashamed that she is pregnant and doesn't know whether I'm the father or Hype is.

I mean . . . she was definitely wrong for what she did. She destroyed my relationship with Tierra and almost caused me to lose my best friend in the process. There was no getting around that, but at the same time, there had to be an expiration date on holding grudges.

An idea popped into my mind a few minutes later. *Maybe I could run her a bubble bath to help ease the stress!* I was so proud of myself for thinking of something romantic to do for her, not my usual jam. I jumped up from the bed to get everything ready before she got home. I only had like fifteen minutes because she would be home any minute. I turned the hot water on full blast in the tub and poured in the bubble bath so it was nice and foamy for her. I dimmed the lights and lit some candles, being careful to position them so they wouldn't fall over. Couldn't afford to burn down the apartment trying to be romantic!

When I heard her key turn in the lock, I admired my handiwork before going downstairs to greet her.

She opened the door, and I greeted her with a big smile. "Hey, girl," I said, pulling her in for a hug. She hugged me half-heartedly. "What's wrong?" I said.

"I got into it with your ex earlier."

My heart dropped. "Tierra?"

"Yes. She saw me when I was leaving the guidance office to get my records. We had a little argument."

I shrugged. "Don't even worry about that, Shaneece. You done with that school, so you won't have to run into her anymore."

She sighed. "I know, but this whole situation is just so hard, Twon." A tear slid down her cheek. I wiped it away. Her voice trembled. "I try to be strong for the baby, but . . . I feel so dirty."

My heart filled with compassion for her. It hurt me to see her hurt. "Shaneece, you doing the best you can. You made some mistakes, but you can't live the whole rest of your life with regret."

She stared at me for a few moments then asked a question. "Do you regret meeting me?"

I paused at that statement, because I had had that very same thought a couple of weeks ago. I decided not to answer. "Oh, I almost forgot! I got a surprise for you. Come with me." I grabbed her hand and gently led her upstairs to the bathroom.

When she saw the candles and the bubble bath, she looked at me with tears glistening in her eyes. "Thank you, Twon, but remember, I can't really be in hot water with the baby." She put her hand in the tub to feel the temperature of the water. "Yeah, this is probably too hot." My heart sank. I forgot about that. She must have seen my expression change because she tried to make me feel better. She smiled. "But I really, really appreciate it though. This was really sweet."

She hugged me and gave me a kiss on the cheek. I let the water out the bath and blew out the candles I'd set on the ledge so she could take a cool shower. While I was clearing out the bathroom, I reflected once again on everything that was going on. Was I really thinking straight with this whole couple thing between me and Shaneece? I mean, I definitely didn't want to just leave her hanging with the baby and all, but I had always wanted to go to college, and I couldn't foresee that happening with me being a fulltime worker and a fulltime dad. Was this really for me?

I let that thought linger, but then I squashed it when I thought about the fact that I really didn't have a choice. I had a kid on the way. I wanted to give him or her a better life than I ever had. Maybe I only have to wait a few years to attend college when our child is in kindergarten and doesn't need a parent in the home for most of the day.

That thought made me feel more positive. I definitely want to provide the best life for our child so that he or she has more opportunities in life than I ever had.

I resolved in my mind that I was going to focus on my child and my family, and put college on the back burner for now.

Hype

Today was the day. I breathed a sigh of relief that it was finally over. Charles' boy Chief had finally gotten out of jail, so now he could pick up the slack and hold him down, which means I can get the hell out of this drug shit. I felt like a huge weight was being lifted off my shoulders. I don't care what nobody say—if you not really that type of nigga, you gonna be paranoid as hell trying to sell drugs.

Speaking of Charles, he just hit my line. I answered the phone with a smile on my face, glad things could finally get back to normal.

"Wassup?" I said.

"Yo, Hype. You home?" Charles sounded kind of anxious.

Aw shit. Here we go. What happened now? "Yeah. Why? What's up?"

"I'm 'bout to come through."

"A'ight." I said, and we hung up. I sighed as I waited for him to get to my house, my heart sinking by the minute. I just knew that whatever he had to tell me was not gonna be good. He wouldn't have sounded so worried.

When Charles walked in the door, he got right to it.

"Yo, I know we talked about you being out when Chief came back, but we got a problem."

"What?" I said, my hands in my pockets. I was getting sick of this shit.

"Chief said he's out, man."

I looked at him in shock. "What you mean?"

"He said shit is too hot in the streets, and he don't want to get locked up again. He said he wanna go legit cuz his girl is pregnant, so he got a baby on the way."

"Fuck, man! I thought y'all already talked about him getting back on?"

"We did, but I guess he changed his mind."

"Shit, Charles."

"I know."

"Look, Charles, I know shit is heavy right now, but I can't do this shit no more, man. I want out too."

"Hype, man, I understand that, but I ain't got nobody else, man."

"I understand, but . . . look nigga, I know you trying to make money, but why don't you stop this shit too? Maybe Chief getting out is a sign or something. Do something different. Ain't shit really out in these streets anyway unless you a kingpin or some shit like that. It's a dead-end life."

Charles looked like he was almost with me 'til that last line. I regretted saying it as soon as the words came out.

"So that's how you really feel? You think I'm a low-life?"

"Nah, nigga, you know what I mean. It came out the wrong way. What I mean is, you're better than this. Why don't you just stop this shit and go legit? Maybe you could use your stash to start your own business or something. Leave that drug shit behind."

"There really ain't shit else out there for me to do, Hype."

"Yes there is, nigga! You made it all the way to your senior year, so you must be smart in some kind of way. I bet if you applied yourself, you could find out what you're good at and go into business."

"Nigga, you sound like G-Ma or Aunt Gina. You must have been hanging around Quaid's ass or something."

"This is not from none of them, Charles. This is from me. I'm trying to get out of these streets. You could get out too. Take this as a sign. Do something different."

"Like I said, ain't shit else for me to do, Hype."

Charles sounded like he was getting heated, so I decided to back off a little. But I wasn't going back to this drug shit.

"A'ight, man, I ain't gonna try to convince you to do something you don't want to do. But you gotta understand that I got goals too. I might really have a chance at this college shit, and I don't want to risk getting locked up before I even graduate high school."

Charles sucked his teeth. "Nigga whatever. Do what you gotta do."

Charles stalked off, slamming the door behind him as he left. I watched as he drove off and had a sick feeling that I might regret this decision.

Shaneece

I was off school and work for the day, so I decided to just relax at home. I was going through some online catalogues for baby stuff when Shanelle called my cell phone. We still needed some of the major items like a crib, a car seat, and a stroller, even after the baby shower that G-Ma and Hype's family had thrown for us. I smiled at that thought. We really needed to get her a thank-you card and some flowers. She had done so much for us.

I was so lost in my thoughts about the baby that I almost forgot Shanelle was calling me. I quickly answered on the last ring.

"Hello?"

"You're not at work, are you?"

"Oh, no. I'm just looking up some stuff online that we still need for the baby."

"Oh. If you're busy, I can call you back…"

"Girl, I always have time for you. What's up?" Shanelle sounded kind of stressed, as she had been a lot lately. This was not like my sister at all. She was always strong, even under pressure, so I knew that what was bothering her had to be something big, probably some mess with Steve as usual. I rolled my eyes. He got on my last nerve.

Shanelle deflected. "Well, first tell me how everything went with Mom and dropping out to get your GED."

"Oh, it went fine. She signed the papers, and they accepted it without a hitch. I got all my records and stuff from the school, and I am set to take the GED test next week."

"That's great. I know you are going to ace it."

"I hope so. I've been studying since before I even left school. It seems like the stuff is not too difficult. Definitely better than studying for the SATs."

"Tell me about it. The SATs were a killer."

"Girl, stop! You got a perfect score, remember? It was me that basically failed."

"You did not fail, Shaneece. You were in the ninetieth percentile."

"Yeah, but ninetieth is not hundredth, like you."

I said that with way too much bitterness in my voice. My father had really fucked my head up with school. Even if I did well on grades or assignments, I always felt like I failed if it wasn't perfect, because that's what he drilled in our heads all of our lives. Shanelle just had it slightly easier because her grades were always perfect. She went through her entire high school and college career with nothing less than an A. She never even made an A minus. Needless to say, she was always the golden child in my parents' eyes.

"Grades don't mean anything when it comes to *life*, Shaneece." She sniffled at those last words, and it hurt me to hear her hurt. All my bitterness went straight out the window as I tried to comfort my sister.

"What did he do this time?" I almost didn't want to ask, but I knew she needed to talk.

"It turns out she's not the only one he got pregnant."

My mouth dropped open in shock, but actually, nothing surprised me about Steve. He was a real piece of work.

"What do you mean?"

"He has a fucking two-year-old child, Shaneece!"

"Are you sure?"

"Yes, and I found out in the worst way. We were supposed to be making up, so I stayed over his house a few days ago. He told me the same lies he always does about how much he loved me, and how this was just one little mistake he made, and how he would never do it again. But then when he went in the shower, I snooped through his nightstand and found DNA results that he got only a week ago for yet another bitch and another kid. The DNA proved he's the father."

"That fucking bastard," I said through gritted teeth.

"I left his house right after I saw that, but I could barely drive because I was so upset. He got not one but TWO women pregnant during our relationship! I have never once so much as even KISSED another guy, and this is how he treats me!? What, do I have a big sign on my head that says 'Fuck me over'? What have I done to deserve this? You can be as faithful as they want you to be and still get treated like shit. I'm sick of it, Shaneece!"

I could hear the anguish in her voice, and it brought me to tears. "I hope you are leaving him, Shanelle." I said as gently as I could. "This relationship is not healthy for you. He keeps hurting you. You don't deserve this."

"Thank you." She sniffled again.

"Hey, aren't you on vacation next week? Why don't you come visit Twon and me? Maybe getting away will help take your mind off Steve."

"That actually sounds like a good idea," she said. "Are you sure Twon won't mind?"

"No, I'm sure it will be fine. Girl, we haven't seen each other in ages. We can hang out like old times."

She chuckled. "Yeah, except Dad won't be breathing down our backs, checking the living room every five seconds for hidden boys."

I burst out laughing at that last remark. It sounded like my sister was almost back to her usual happy self.

Tierra

After my run-in with Shaneece, I started feeling bad for kicking the girl while she was down. I found out that she had dropped out of school due to all the bullying she was facing. I had seen people say and do things, and I even said a few things myself, but she always acted like it didn't bother her, so I didn't think she cared.

I should've known she had feelings like everyone else...

I had been so caught up in trying to make her feel the same pain I felt that I never thought about the fact that she was getting hit on every side. I mean, the whole school was in on it – even freshmen, and we were seniors! She had become the target for everyone's mockery. There were memes made about her, videos, everything. I had heard she was not on social media, but what if she saw the stuff people were saying about her anyway? I was consumed with guilt when I thought about how many of those memes and videos I had laughed at, liked, and shared. This was starting to get real.

I didn't know what else to do, so I decided to call Twon on my bus ride home. Quaid was at work, so he couldn't give me a ride.

"Tierra?" said Twon when he answered, sounding surprised.

"Hey . . . how are you?"

"Um . . . I'm good. On my way to work. What's up?"

"Um, I'm actually calling about Shaneece. I heard that she dropped out due to all the bullying. Is she okay?"

"Um . . . yeah, she's fine. Why are you asking?"

"I don't know, I just . . . look, I know bullying affects some people in really serious ways, and I wanted to make sure that she was not going to . . . go the wrong route."

"She's good, Tierra." He sighed. "She actually is happy now that she's out of the school. Her sister is coming to visit us next week, and she is really excited about that. She's good. Don't worry about it. I'll watch out for her."

I suddenly felt awkward. "Oh . . . okay. Well, thanks. I guess I'll talk to you later."

"A'ight." He hung up.

That was so abrupt, I thought, and it made me angry, but I reminded myself that I was with Quaid now, and things were going well with him. I was in a new relationship, and so was Twon, so I needed to just move on. I slipped on my headphones and lost myself in music the rest of the way home.

***

When I got home, my mom was already there. I had forgot she was getting off early today. I should have asked her for a ride home. Maybe that would have saved me from the awkward conversation with Twon.

"Hey, what's up with you?" she said casually as I took off my shoes at the door. She was sitting in the kitchen eating a salad.

"Ooh, that looks good! Is there any left?" I walked into the kitchen and headed toward the fridge.

"Yup, I saved you some."

I fixed myself a plate. My mom could make anything taste good. I would literally eat boiled water from her. I chuckled at that thought.

"What you laughing at?" she said.

"Nothing. I just know I'm 'bout to go HAM on this salad."

She chuckled at that statement. "Girl, stop. Didn't you eat at school?"

"Yeah, but you know those people can't cook!"

We both laughed as I took a bite of my salad.

"So what's up?" she said again after a few moments.

"Nothing. Just had an awkward conversation with Twon." I went on to tell her about our conversation and everything going on with Shaneece. "So you probably think I'm stupid for calling him, huh?" I said.

"Girl, there is nothing wrong with following up on whatever you feel convicted about in your heart. That is the work of the Lord. Bullying is wrong, period. I know she did you wrong, but you really should not have participated in bullying that girl. I know you know better than that."

"I know, but I guess I was so caught up in all the drama that I didn't really think about how it affected her. Then when I heard that she dropped out because of it, that was what really made me snap out of it, and I started feeling guilty. You really think that was God?"

"I'm sure it was," she said. "God gives us a conscience from birth. We have it all our lives, but it gets even stronger when He calls us to salvation. We start to see things a different way than we used to. Things we did before with little or no remorse suddenly seem more significant. We realize how small we are compared to Him, and how much we need Him to forgive us and be with us."

"Do you get convicted?"

"Oh girl, yes! All the time." She nervously toyed with her fork as she pushed her salad around on her place. "He even uses you to convict me."

My mouth dropped open. "*Me*? How?"

She sighed. "With the whole not going to church thing. I know I should go, but sometimes I feel like I lost my way."

I sensed that my mom was about to finally tell me why she stopped going to church, so I kept my mouth shut.

"You see, Tierra, when I first got saved, I went to the wrong kind of church. There was a lot of good, but also a lot of bad. The preachers made us feel paranoid, like if we made one wrong move, we were going to hell. I lived my early years trying so hard to do everything right that I made mistake after mistake. Every time I felt like I was moving forward, I ended up taking two steps back. All I thought about was how God was gonna give up on me one day, and every time I sinned, I wondered if this was my last chance. Then when I got pregnant with you, out of wedlock, of course, I stopped going to church because I knew that I had gone too far with sinning and pushed the limits of God's grace.

"It was then that I spent some alone time with just me, you, God, and the Bible. I read scriptures to you while you were growing in my belly. During that time, I learned about God's grace, and He began to show me that the church I was at was teaching us wrong.

"I realized that God isn't waiting with a baseball bat so that He can blast us into hell when we sin. Not at all! On the contrary, He loves us, and He is always with us. There are definitely consequences to our behavior after we get saved, both good and bad, but God is not going to send us to hell for every little mistake.

"Since that time, I feel like I lost my way with the church because I lost trust in pastors and preachers. I wanted you to grow up in the Lord because I knew it was right, but I just didn't want to go wrong again, and it seemed like being in the church was a guarantee that I would because of what I went through before. I guess I've just been confused."

I took in my mother's words, not really knowing how to respond. I had never known all this about her. She had always instilled in me to go to church and listen to the pastors and preachers, but after hearing her story, I wasn't sure what to think.

Twon

I haven't really been talking to Slink and Wolf since that whole fight with them and Hype and Charles. I feel like they disrespected us one too many times, and I ain't with that shit. They claim to be so much about family, but when I try to set some boundaries and tell them that certain things is not cool, they take me for a joke. I really don't like the idea of cutting them off because they are blood, but I might have to do it if they don't make some changes.

Another thing that's been heavy on my mind lately is my mom. I've tried calling her multiple times, and she refuses to answer the phone or just turns it off so it goes straight to voicemail. This is killing me. Why won't she talk to me? Am I really dead to her that quickly? How can she go from seeing me every day for almost eighteen years to completely cutting me off? We haven't seen or spoken to each other since I left the hospital. She doesn't know my legs are healed, she doesn't know that I've met my brothers and cousins, hell, she doesn't even know if I'm going to school or graduating. She doesn't know about the baby either!

This is the time I need her the most, and she just refuses to answer. I know everyone thinks I should just cut her off, but she's the only mother and the only parent I got.

I decided to pop up on her at the crib. I borrowed G-Ma's car and told her I had to run some errands. She said she didn't have anywhere to go today, so she let me use it. Me and Shaneece really gotta get her a nice card or some roses or something for all she has done for us. I will never forget it yo, straight up.

I pulled up to my mother's house and immediately noticed that things looked different. Something seemed off. The grass wasn't mowed like usual. My mom always had me do it before, but I guess since I ain't been there, she ain't have nobody to do it for her. Her car was parked outside, so that was a good sign—at least she was home.

I walked up to the front porch to knock on the door. I stood there nervously at first, because I wasn't sure what I was gonna say to her, but I decided to push past that and just knock. I knocked several times and waited. I was about to leave when I heard footsteps coming toward the door.

"Who is it?" my mother yelled from the inside.

My heart started beating faster when I heard her voice. "Ma, it's me, Twon. Can I come in for a second?"

"No, get away from my house!"

"Ma, I just want to talk to you!"

"I don't give a fuck what you want!" She screamed that last sentence, and her voice cracked.

I didn't know what else to say. I stood there for a few moments, but it was clear that she wasn't going to open the door. I didn't have a key, so there was nothing I could do. I turned around and went back to G-Ma's car. I sat there staring at the house then put the key in the ignition and drove off down the street and around the corner, but for some reason, I felt like I needed to go back. I needed to talk to my mom. I needed to see her. I turned around and drove back to her house.

When I pulled up in front of it, my mom was walking toward her car, but she looked totally different. She had lost weight, and not in a good way. She was wearing a wig, and my mom never wore wigs. *What the hell is going on with her? Is she on drugs?*

I know my mom always smoked cigarettes, but I never knew her to try anything harder than that. She didn't see me until I got out the car and started walking toward her.

"Ma," I said, and she turned around, one hand on the handle of her car door and the other holding her purse.

"Didn't I tell you to get away from my house?"

"Ma, I just want to talk to you."

"Well, I thought I made myself clear. I'm done with you. You seem to have been doing fine without me anyway. You can go back to wherever the hell you came from. I see you got a new car."

"That's not mine. Hype's grandmother let me use it."

"Well good for her."

"Can we just talk for a minute?"

"No! Get away from me. I don't want to talk to you."

"Ma, what's going on with you? Why you wearing a wig?"

"None of your business!" she spat. "Now leave my house and don't come back, or I'll call the police!"

She wrenched open the car door, flung herself inside, turned the key in the ignition, and sped off.

I was left standing on her front lawn wondering what the hell was going on with my mother.

Hype

I been feeling kind of guilty since I let Charles down. I know it was the right decision for me, but I don't know if it was good to just leave him hanging like that. I needed to talk to somebody, but I knew Quaid's ass would start rejoicing, so I decided to talk to Twon. I hit him up and told him I needed to talk to him. He said he had something to talk about too, so we agreed to meet up at his crib.

When I got there, some chick I never seen answered the door.

I stared at her for a second, trying to register what was going on when she spoke up.

"Hey, you must be Hype, right?"

"Yeah," I said, shaking her hand.

"I'm Shanelle, Shaneece's older sister."

"Damn," I said, taking in her beauty. "I mean, hey, how you doing?"

She chuckled. "I'm fine. Come on in. Twon and Shaneece should be back soon."

I walked in feeling kind of awkward. Shaneece's sister was fine as hell, and I appreciated the view even more as she walked in front of me toward the couch.

"Do you want something to drink?" she said, turning to face me.

"Huh? Oh yeah, thanks." I definitely needed to snap out of it. This chick gonna think I'm weird as fuck.

"So, Shaneece never told me how sexy you were."

That statement caught me off guard. I chuckled nervously. *I mean, was she feeling me too?*

"I'm just joking," she said. "Relax."

Something told me she wasn't, though, but I sat there and sipped my juice without saying anything more. She turned on the TV and found some kind of romantic chick-flick movie. When they got to this lovey-dovey scene, I rolled my eyes, but then I heard Shanelle sniffle. I looked at her.

"You a'ight?" I said.

"Yeah," she said. "It just sucks that love like that only happens in movies."

Damn, she must be going through something. I took a wild guess. "Your man cheated or something?"

"Shaneece told you?" she said, looking surprised.

"Nah, I just figured that's what happened based on what you said."

"Oh, well yeah. He cheated on me in the worst possible way."

"I wouldn't even worry about him." I gave her my sweetest smile. "I'm sure you got plenty of other guys lined up to take his spot."

She snorted. "Not really. Life is so busy, it's hard to even meet anyone anymore. All I do is work, work, work. I mean, I love my job, don't get me wrong, but it's really demanding, and then to deal with his cheating on top of that . . . sometimes it just feels like too much."

"Hm." I paused. "Well, maybe you should try to take more time to just do you."

"But that's hard to do when you work at a hospital. I'm a nurse."

"Damn, that's rough. I heard nurses be working crazy hours."

"Tell me about it."

"But hey, at least you getting money though."

"Yeah, but money doesn't buy love."

"Shit, you right about that."

"So, what's your deal? Did you really love my sister, or were you just like all these other guys?"

I was caught off guard by her question, but I decided to answer honestly. "Real talk? Yeah, I liked your sister. A lot. But then she fucked me over by fucking my best friend. After that, I was like 'fuck her'."

"Ouch."

"Well, you asked."

"I did. I should probably keep my mouth shut sometimes."

"You good."

"So are you single now?"

"Why? You know somebody who's looking?"

"Well . . . I know I've been wanting to blow off some steam for a while."

Shit. This conversation just took an unexpected turn. I got kind of nervous again. "Blow off some steam, huh?"

"Yeah. What about you?"

Damn! This chick was bold. *Older chicks is where it's at!* She kind of made me nervous but turned me on at the same time.

"I mean, I'm always ready to blow off some steam, but I'm not sure if you would be ready for all I have to offer."

"All you have to offer?" She chuckled. "And what exactly is that?"

"I could show you better than I could tell you."

"Okay, well let's see what you got."

Before I knew it, she had crawled across the couch and was all up against me kissing me. I had a fleeting thought of Twon and Shaneece, but all that was forgotten as she led me to their bedroom.

***

About fifteen minutes later, I was lying next to Shanelle in the bed wondering what the hell I just did. I mean, it happened so fast that I didn't have time to think, but I guess it was over now. *I really just fucked Shaneece's sister.* In a strange way, I felt vindicated, but kind of guilty too. I didn't have too much time to reflect because I heard the key turning as Twon and Shaneece opened their front door.

"Shit!" I exclaimed in a loud whisper as Shanelle and I scrambled out of their bed to put our clothes on.

"Shanelle!" I heard Shaneece saying from the front of the apartment. "Where are you?"

"I'm coming!" said Shanelle, practically tumbling over herself as she left the bedroom to go meet Twon and Shaneece in the living room.

"What were you doing in there?" said Shaneece. "Did you take a nap or something?"

I stood there awkwardly, wondering whether I should just walk out there too, or try to play it off like I was coming from the bathroom or something.

"Oh, I um . . ." Shanelle's voice trailed off as she tried to cover up what we just did.

"Shit, they gonna find out sooner or later anyway," I said under my breath.

Both Twon and Shaneece's mouths dropped open when they saw me.

Twon caught on first. "Nigga!" he exclaimed, looking at me, then at Shanelle.

Shaneece put two and two together after that as her sister's face reddened with embarrassment.

"You filthy bastard!" she said. "You took advantage of my sister?"

"More like she took advantage of me." I smirked, all my guilt gone out the window.

"I can't believe you!" she said. "Get out! Now!"

219

I chuckled. "A'ight, but I guess we could say we even now."

"Even? What the hell are you talking about?"

"You fucked my brother. I fucked your sister. We even."

Shaneece looked at me in disgust. "Just get the hell out of my house, Hype."

Me and Twon walked out to go talk.

"So you want to go back to G-Ma's house?"

"Nah, we can hit my crib," I said, grabbing G-Ma's car keys from Twon. We drove in silence almost the whole way.

Once we pulled up, I looked at Twon. He stared back at me, his grin growing wider and wider. Then he busted out laughing.

I started laughing too. "What, nigga?" I said.

"You dirty dog," Twon gasped. "You dirty fucking dog!"

"Nigga, she came at me! What was I supposed to do?"

When we got inside my house, we had finally finished laughing over the Shaneece and Shanelle situation.

"I'm probably about to have to hear about this shit for the next three days," said Twon.

"Shit, like I said, she came at me. I mean, she came crawling across the couch like a wildcat and was on me before I knew what was happening. You wouldn't have said no either if it was you."

"Nigga…"

"You ain't say no to Shaneece, did you?"

"Point taken."

We chuckled for a few more moments, then I spoke up.

"So what was on your mind?"

Twon's expression turned serious. "I don't know, man. I think my mom might be on drugs or something. She lost mad weight, Hype. I ain't never seen her that skinny."

"Damn."

He explained to me what happened when he went by her house to try to talk to her.

"You really sure it's drugs though?" I said.

"That's the only thing I can think of. She was always asking me for money when I was there. The amount kept getting bigger and bigger before I left. I was giving her enough to cover the whole rent, plus some. I don't know what else it could be."

I had another idea of what it could be, with the weight loss and the wig, but I didn't say anything. I didn't think Twon was ready for that possibility.

"What you want to talk about? Something new with Charles?"

"Yeah. Man . . . I told Charles I wanted out." I explained to Twon how we had been waiting for Charles' boy Chief to get out so he could pick up where I left off, but how Chief had changed his mind. "Once it got to that point, I couldn't take no more, Twon. I had to go."

"Damn." He said this to me the same way I had just said it to him a few minutes ago. "Seem like shit getting real for everybody."

Shaneece

I stood there staring at Shanelle in shock after Twon and Hype left. I really could not believe what just happened.

"So you really just slept with my ex?" I was flabbergasted.

Shanelle was totally red with embarrassment. "Shaneece, I am so sorry. It literally just happened."

"Just happened, huh? With my *ex* though?"

"I swear, I didn't mean to hurt you in any way. I've just been so emotional lately, and then I came here to visit, and you and Twon seem so happy together, and then Hype comes over and he's so freaking hot, and all I could think about was everything Steve did to me. All this time, I've been faithful to him, and look what he does to me."

"So you had revenge sex with my ex?"

"Look, I'm really sorry. It will never happen again. I promise. It was just a weak moment, I swear. I am so sorry, Shaneece."

She looked thoroughly embarrassed, and I could tell she was sincere in her apology. I knew she was vulnerable. I just didn't think her vulnerability would express itself in this way. Although I never truly had feelings for Hype, it was still awkward as hell to think of him sleeping with my older sister. *I wonder if he planned this?* I thought, but then I quickly pushed it out of my mind. Hype didn't even know Shanelle was here. I sighed. Twon and I were in for a very awkward conversation tonight.

"Well, do you feel accomplished now? Was it even good for you?" I felt totally lame and weird for even asking that question, but I didn't know what else to say. This situation had truly caught me off guard.

"Yes! I mean, no. I mean . . . I'm just confused. While it was happening, I felt like I was getting back at Steve, but now I just feel terrible that I probably hurt you in the process."

"Well, no, I'm not hurt. Shocked, definitely, but I'm not hurt. I really just hope you're okay. I really don't think this is a healthy way to get over Steve. Sleeping with random guys is not going to heal you." As soon as those words left my mouth, I felt like a total hypocrite and a bitch. "Wait, I didn't mean it that way. I meant..."

"I get it, Shaneece. I understand."

We stood there awkwardly for a few more moments.

"You better not be pregnant." I chuckled, trying to make light of the situation.

"Oh no, I wasn't that crazy. I'm on the pill, and we used a condom."

"Great." I breathed a sigh of relief, but I felt a pang of guilt when I thought of my own situation. I had never used birth control, and I barely used protection with either Twon or Hype. Maybe if I had, I wouldn't be in the predicament I'm in now.

"What's wrong?" said Shanelle, sensing that my demeanor had changed.

A tear slipped down my cheek. "It's just crazy how one mistake can literally change your whole life."

Tierra

I was in the middle of trying to finish a major paper for my English class when I got a call from Quaid. We hadn't really talked much since that conversation I had with Twon, and then with my mom. I guess I was low key avoiding him, but I didn't fully understand why.

"Hello?" I said.

"Hey. How are you?"

"I'm good. Just trying to finish this stupid paper for English."

"What's it about?"

"We had to read this stupid, boring book and write a five-page essay on it. I am so through with school. I can't wait to graduate."

"Have you thought about where you want to go to college yet?"

"Yeah. I'm considering State. My mom wants me to go there because it's only a couple of hours away, but I don't know. So far, I've been accepted to five schools, and they all have given me some kind of scholarship, but I just have to figure out which one is giving the best deal, I guess. What about you?"

"I'm pretty much in the same boat. I was actually offered a hefty scholarship at one of my reach schools, but I'm not sure if I'm ready to move so far away from my family."

"Wow." I shivered with nervousness all of a sudden. We were really about to graduate and potentially change our entire lives. What if we all moved away from each other? Would we still be friends? What about me and Quaid? If we went to colleges in different states, could we survive a long-distance relationship? It seemed like a thousand questions literally just opened up in my mind. Fuck that paper—what was I going to do about college??? And what would that decision mean for the rest of my situations?

"Tierra?" Quaid was saying.

"Huh?" I said, trying to shake from my thoughts.

"Are you okay? I noticed you got really silent."

"Yeah, I'm just thinking about college. Like, when I was younger, I dreamed about going somewhere far away and living in the dorms, going to parties, joining organizations, all of that, but now, it's like . . . really about to happen. Like, Quaid, we are graduating! We're about to be legit adults! What does that even mean? Aren't you scared?"

He paused. "I guess I'm a little nervous, but I figure that thousands of people go to college every year. It will probably take some adjusting, but I know I can make it."

Quaid sounded so confident. I wished I could be as grounded as him.

"So . . . if you do decide to go away to your reach school, what would that mean for us?"

"What do you mean?"

"Like, are we supposed to do the long distance thing? How are we ever gonna see each other?"

"Wow. I never thought about that." He was silent for a moment. "Maybe we could visit on breaks or something."

I suddenly felt trapped. My relationship with Quaid was great while we both could see each other any time we wanted, but I didn't know how I felt about a long distance relationship.

I decided to answer truthfully. "I don't know how I would feel about that."

"How you would feel about what? Us being away from each other at college?"

"Yes. I feel like that would be too much pressure."

"How so? We could video chat, and talk and text, and we could still see each other on breaks."

"I don't know about that, Quaid. I don't want to feel tied down."

"How would that make you feel tied down?"

"Because! I'm barely eighteen years old! I don't want to feel like a married woman or something while I'm just getting into my freshman year of college."

"Tierra, I don't understand where all of this is coming from. Do you feel like I try to control you or something? How would you feel like a married woman just by being in a relationship with me?"

Quaid sounded hurt, confused, and offended. This conversation was going way left.

"It's not you—it's the idea of being held down in a relationship while I'm entering a new chapter in my life. I feel like that would be too much stress and pressure."

"So, you're saying you want to break up with me."

"No, that's not what I said."

"That's exactly what you said. You feel like I'm holding you down, like I'm some kind of ball and chain or something. But you know what? I never put a gun to your head and forced you to be with me, Tierra. You said you had feelings for me just like I have feelings for you. But if that's not what you want, I'll let you go, so you can go ahead and be free."

"Quaid…"

CLICK.

I stared at the phone, confused. What in the world had just happened? Did Quaid just break up with me? How did the conversation even go in that direction?

I put my phone down on my desk and sighed. I never knew life could be so complicated.

Twon

I stared at my acceptance letter from State until my eyes blurred. I had only applied to three schools, despite my guidance counselor's protests. I really only wanted to apply to State, but I let her convince me to try two other schools as well. I got accepted to one of the other ones, but it was so far away, there was no way I could go there. I had only applied to appease my counselor anyway. I sighed. Life was so fucking heavy.

I'm happy I got into the school I wanted, and they even offered me a good scholarship because of my grades, but State is over two hours away. I don't know how that would work with Shaneece and the baby. I can't just leave them here so I can go to school. That would make me extremely selfish, plus it would take food out of my kid's mouth. I wouldn't be able to work fulltime and go to school fulltime, so how was we supposed to survive? And even if I did work and go to school, who was supposed to help Shaneece raise the baby? I wanted to be there in my kid's life, and I couldn't do that two hours away.

I was stressed and depressed at the same time. I looked at my phone thinking maybe I could call Hype or Trav, or even Quaid about this situation, but I shook my head, deciding against it. No matter what they said, they couldn't change anything anyway. Nobody had a magic wand or a reset button for me, plus Hype was basically in the same situation.

I was so lost in my thoughts that I barely noticed Shaneece come into the kitchen. She had just gotten home from work.

"Hey," I said.

"Hey." She leaned over and kissed me. "What's that?" she said, looking at the letter.

"My dreams—all gone down the drain."

"Oh, don't be so dramatic, Twon. Your entire life is not going down the drain because you can't go to college right now. You can always go later."

"That's easy for you to say," I shot back. "You don't even give a damn about school."

"I do, but our child is my number one priority."

"And how the fuck are we supposed to raise a kid working minimum wage, Shaneece? Ain't shit out there if a nigga don't have a degree." I was way heated, way fast.

"First of all, lower your voice when you talk to me. I understand you are angry, but this is not the end of the world. Plenty of people have kids and go to school too."

"Plenty of people ain't us though. If I go to school two hours away, who's gonna help you with the baby? Huh? Your parents? My mom? Shanelle? We ain't got nobody, Shaneece. We ain't got shit."

I ran my hand over my head. I couldn't think straight. Everything was weighing me down, and I seriously just wanted it all to be over. This shit was getting too real for me. Too much was happening at the same time.

"We may not have much, Twon, but we have each other. I can be here for you, and you can be here for me. We can make this work. You can still have your dreams, just maybe not in the way you wanted to."

Her eyes were full of sincerity. When I saw that, my mood changed. I guess I was just going overboard.

"You right," I said. "We can make it work. I guess I just feel like I'm taking a huge L with this, because I had my heart set on State since freshman year, but there are other schools. Maybe I can go somewhere closer."

She smiled. "We're gonna be okay, Twon."

***

The next day, me and Shaneece had fully made up, so we decided to finally do something that was long overdue. We got G-Ma a beautiful card, gift cards to a spa and a nice restaurant, and some flowers. It wasn't much, but we wanted to show her our appreciation for everything she was doing for us. That woman took us into her home when we wasn't even blood, and she never charged us a dime or made us feel any different from her own family.

She even let us use her car when she wasn't using it to help us get on our feet. We had just got approved for our own car loan a few days ago—well, Shaneece did. Her parents made sure she had good credit by putting her name on one of their credit cards when she became a teenager, so she had almost a perfect score at age eighteen. We got a really good deal for the car, low interest rate and everything.

We went over to G-Ma's house to surprise her with the gifts and show her our new whip.

When we got there, she was happy to see us. "Well, look who's here!" she said, giving us both a hug. Quaid was there. I dapped him up, and he and Shaneece exchanged hello's.

"This is for you," I said, handing her the card and the flowers.

"Oh, thank you so much! You two did not have to do this!" There were tears in her eyes, and that touched my heart.

"Oh yes we did," I said. "You been like a mother to me when…" My voice got kind of choked up. I ran my hand over my head as G-Ma stepped in to give me another hug. It was really hitting me that G-Ma had basically been a mother to me when my mother rejected and abandoned me. That shit was so real, and I will never forget it.

Shaneece was in tears too when she saw me get choked up. The three of us shared a group hug while Quaid stood to the side looking like he felt awkward.

"You better not tell nobody about this, man," I joked.

He laughed too. "Your secret's safe with me." He looked kind of like something was on his mind, but I would have to talk to him later. Shaneece had to go to work, so we was only stopping by for a few.

We all went outside to the porch to say our goodbyes. I had to drop Shaneece off at work, and Quaid was about to head out too.

Our heads all whipped in the same direction when we heard tires screeching as a car swerved into G-Ma's front yard, stopping about fifty feet from her porch. It was Charles' car.

"What the hell is going on?" said G-Ma.

All of us watched in shock as Charles stumbled out of the car and onto the ground, his entire shirt covered in blood.

Shaneece started screaming. I stood there, frozen in place. Quaid immediately got on his phone to call 911. G-Ma ran over to Charles. I left Shaneece standing on the porch and walked over to Charles. I could hear my heart pounding in my head as I made my way over, my legs wobbling and my mouth completely dry.

"I got shot," Charles was saying to G-Ma as she bent over him, trying to apply pressure to his wound.

I swallowed. *What the hell was happening?* This shit was too much for me. This was the second time I'd seen Charles laid out on the ground covered in blood. I'm still not over the first time.

"I'm sorry. I'm sorry," Charles kept saying.

"Shhh, I know. It's okay, baby," said G-Ma.

"What happened, Charles?" I finally croaked.

"Some niggas set me up." He started spitting out blood.

"Shit," I said. I looked at Shaneece then Quaid. Quaid was still on the phone with the 911 operator. Shaneece looked as scared as I felt. I wanted to reach out to her, but I couldn't move.

"I'm sorry," Charles said, looking at Quaid. Then he looked at me. "Tell Hype I'm sorry too."

"Baby, they are not upset with you," said G-Ma.

"Am I gonna be alright, G-Ma?" Charles sounded like a little boy. He was losing a lot of blood. His voice was weak.

G-Ma looked down at his wound, then into his eyes. "You gonna be okay," she said. "I want you to do something for me, okay? Can you repeat these words after me?"

A tear rolled down Charles' cheek. "Okay," he said.

"Lord Jesus..." she started, and then I lost it. I felt like I was blacking out. My legs gave out on me, and I ended up on the ground. Shaneece rushed over to me as Charles repeated a prayer with G-Ma, asking God for salvation and forgiveness.

After the prayer, his eyes kept rolling back. I didn't want to see it, but I couldn't look away.

The ambulance finally came, and the EMTs rushed in to take over. They got Charles on the stretcher and took off for the hospital. I felt numb all over. I was completely out of it. Shaneece got the keys and led me to the car. G-Ma drove Quaid to the hospital in her car, while Shaneece and I followed.

Hype

I can't shake my guilt over leaving Charles hanging like that. I know I ain't no drug dealer at heart, but shit. That's my cousin. He been like a brother to me since birth. Even though I know it's the wrong decision, I gotta go back in and help him. I know he would do it for me.

I decided to call Charles to tell him I was back in. I would just have to hold him down 'til somebody could take my place. I hit his cell, but he didn't answer. I called him again, but still no response.

Damn. He must be taking it hard. I considered dropping by his crib to see if he was there, but right when I was walking to the front door to leave the house, my phone rang. It was Tierra.

"Yo," I said.

"Hype, did Quaid tell you he broke up with me?"

"Um . . . nah. Why, what happened?"

"We got into a huge argument about college and…" Before she could finish her sentence, Quaid started beeping in.

"Oh, hold on T. That's Quaid beeping in now. You want me to talk to him for you?"

"Yes, if you could please just convince him to call me, that would be great. He's not answering my calls."

"I gotchu."

I quickly hung up with Tierra to catch Quaid's call.

"Hey," I said.

"Hype!" Quaid sounded frantic. "Hype, you gotta come now. You gotta come to the hospital!" Quaid's voice ratcheted up an octave as he choked back tears.

My entire body went on alert. Something went down. I knew it. "What happened, Quaid?"

"It's Charles. You gotta come, Hype!"

"I'm on my way."

***

When I got to the hospital, I went to the front desk to ask where my family was, and they led me to the same room we was in last time Charles was in the hospital. As I made my way down the hall, an eerie feeling swept over me like something wasn't right. When I stopped in front of the door, I almost didn't want to go in, but I knew I had to. I could only imagine what was on the other side.

I took a deep breath and opened the door. My eyes weren't prepared for the scene that awaited me. Everyone in the entire room was silent. You could hear a pin drop. Twon sat on the floor, his elbows on his knees, staring straight ahead and seeing nothing. His face was stained with tears. He didn't look up when I came in the door. Shaneece was next to him. Quaid was pacing the floor with tears streaming from his eyes. My heart ached to see him like that, because I knew it could only be bad news. Charles' mother, my Auntie Shameka, was sitting there with the wide-eyed gaze of complete shock while my Auntie Gina, Quaid's mom, held her. My mom was probably still at work. G-Ma looked distraught. That scared me. I never seen her look like this.

I was almost too scared to speak, because I knew I didn't want to hear whatever they had to say, but I had to know.

"What happened, G-Ma?"

She looked up at me. "Charles was shot, baby." Her voice was gentle, like she was trying to soften the blow.

I felt like I knew what she was trying to tell me, but I didn't want to hear it. This was all wrong.

"He's gonna be okay, right, G-Ma?"

She just looked at me.

"G-Ma, we can pray, right? Like last time?" I held out my hands. I looked at Quaid. "Come on, Quaid." I looked back at G-Ma. "We can pray like last time, right? Then Charles will be okay?"

G-Ma stood up to face me. "Baby . . . Charles is gone."

Gone.

When she said that word, I felt like all the breath in my body left me.

"What do you mean, gone? What do you mean, G-Ma? Where is Charles?" Shivers ran all through me. It felt like the room was spinning, but my head was going in the opposite direction.

A tear streamed down G-Ma's face. Her expression was filled with pain. "He . . . he accepted Christ . . . before he went."

My entire world turned black. I don't even remember hitting the floor.

Shaneece

Twon is not doing good at all. Neither am I, for that matter, but I have to stay strong for him. The image of Charles covered in blood keeps coming back to me, but I try to shake it off for Twon's sake. He has been mostly silent since we got home. We stayed with the family until they were ready to go. I feel so heartbroken for all of them. Hype, Quaid, and Twon were like brothers because they grew up together, but now that one of them was gone, none of them knew how to take it.

I wouldn't know how to take it either. If something ever happened to Shanelle, I don't know what I would do. I've been trying to comfort Twon by talking to him, but he barely speaks, and he won't eat. I hate to see him this way.

"Shanelle, how do you help someone with grief?" I called my sister because I didn't know what else to do. I explained to her what happened with Charles and how Twon, G-Ma, Quaid, and I all saw him after he got shot.

"Oh my gosh, Shaneece, are you okay?"

"I'm really shaken up because I can't get the image out of my head, but I have to stay strong for Twon. How do I help him? He doesn't want to talk, and he won't eat."

"Shaneece, there really isn't a whole lot you can do for a person during a time like this. You can be a shoulder to cry on when he is ready to talk, and if he still hasn't eaten by tomorrow, you can try to force him to eat something, but other than that, there really isn't much you can do. He has to work through his grief in his own way and in his own time. I'm so sorry to hear all of this. I can't imagine how horrible it was."

"Yeah, we're all feeling traumatized right now."

"Do you want me to come down? I can try to use some personal time."

"No, I don't want you getting in trouble asking for more time off when you just came back from vacation."

"Are you sure? Maybe I can convince Twon to eat."

"No, we'll be okay. I'll keep an eye on him, and if something else happens, I will definitely call you."

"Okay. Keep me posted."

Thank God I have my sister to talk to about what's going on. I briefly considered calling my parents, or at least my mom, but I couldn't afford for her to tell my dad and then have him call me with some bullshit. Things were too fragile right now, so we would have to handle this alone.

Tierra

Hype never called me back that day, and Quaid didn't call either, so I figured he was still mad at me.

I decided to give it a couple more days so he could cool down and then we could talk, but surprisingly, Quaid called me the next day.

"Hello?" I said, picking up on the first ring.

"Tierra..." He sounded weary and worn out.

"Quaid? What's wrong?"

"Tierra...."

I felt panic rising. "Quaid, what's wrong? Why do you sound like that? Are you okay?"

"Charles died."

I sat up completely in my bed. "*WHAT?*"

"He's gone. He got shot yesterday." His voice sounded so empty and lost that it broke my heart. My eyes filled with tears.

"Oh my God, Quaid. I'm so sorry. Where are you?"

"Can I come over?"

"Yes. Are you okay to drive?"

"Yes."

"Are you sure?"

"Yeah, I can make it. I just need to see you."

"Come on. I'm here."

I hung up the phone and immediately rushed downstairs to the living room where my mom was watching TV.

"Ma," I said, feeling shaky.

"What's wrong?" she said. She put the TV on mute when she saw my face.

"Charles died."

"Charles who?" She looked concerned.

"Charles—Hype and Quaid's cousin."

"The one I met at the hospital when Twon was there?"

"Yes."

"What happened?"

"Quaid said he got shot."

"Oh my gosh. Where is Quaid?"

"He's on his way over."

"Wow." She said. "I am so sorry to hear this."

I stood there, numb, until Quaid pulled up in the driveway a few moments later. He looked devastated, confused, lost—there's not a single word to describe the conflicting emotions on his face.

"Quaid…" I wrapped him in a full body hug. I felt him trembling, and then I started crying. My mom came over and rubbed Quaid's back.

"It's okay, honey." She said. "You can let it out."

There were tears streaming down his cheeks. He looked like he was in so much pain.

"He was my brother!" he cried out, and then he broke down into a wailing sob like I had never heard come out of another human being before. We held him as he cried, and my mother prayed.

Twon

I can't take this shit. Everything just keeps replaying over and over again in my head. The day Charles died started off so good, but then it took such a tragic turn. Life just keeps getting worse and worse and worse. It's been three days since Charles been gone. Tomorrow is his funeral. I can't even say that fucking word. It don't even sound right.

Me, Hype, Quaid, and Trav is over my crib, and me and Hype is sipping on some Henny. We offered some to Quaid and Trav, but they declined.

Trav's mom cooked us some food, so we was eating that. I know Shaneece was happy, cuz she been hounding me to eat something since the day it happened. I don't know what it is . . . I just lost my appetite. My job gave me a few days off because I told them my brother died. There was no way I could go in there like this. All I can think about is Charles and how I don't want to see him lying in a casket.

I looked over at Hype. His eyes were low. He looked tired too. We both was kind of drunk because the bottle was almost gone, and we had already finished one prior to this.

"You ready for this, man?" I said, referring to tomorrow.

"Nope. You?"

I shook my head. We both looked at Quaid. He was staring into space.

"I wish we could have come to some kind of agreement before this happened," he finally said. "We left on bad terms."

"Y'all was good," I said. "You didn't hear him, but he was saying y'all was good when you was on the phone with 911." I turned to Hype. "He said y'all was good too."

Hype just looked at me. "I left him out there, man."

"This wasn't your fault, bro. He said some niggas set him up."

"Yeah, but if I had been there, I could have stopped it."

"You don't know that. Nobody can foresee something like this."

I could tell Hype wasn't hearing what I was saying. He really felt like it was his fault that this happened because he left Charles hanging. I guess it would take time for him to process it. Hell, we all needed time.

I reached for the bottle again, but Trav gently blocked my hand.

"That's enough, bro. I know you hurting, but that's enough."

I didn't protest. The alcohol was doing a little to ease the pain, but it wasn't enough anyway. Nothing could make it go away.

We spent the rest of the night talking about old memories of Charles when we was growing up. Shaneece stayed in the bedroom to give us privacy. Trav tried to crack a few jokes to lighten the mood, but I don't think anything could prepare us for what we would have to face the next day.

Hype

I sat next to Twon and Quaid in the front pew. I couldn't take my eyes off of Charles. He was laying a few feet away from us in a fucking casket.

I could barely pay attention to anything the preacher was saying. The only thing that kept coming to me was that this was all a bad dream, and I hoped I would wake up soon. That didn't even look like Charles in the casket. It looked like somebody else. My cousin had to be out there somewhere still. This was all just a big fucking mistake.

I feel like it's my fault he's gone. If I had just stayed on a little while longer, maybe niggas wouldn't have felt like it was so easy to set him up. I'm-a find the niggas that did this shit, straight up. They not gonna get away with it.

Some lady was singing a gospel song to try to comfort everybody, but that shit wasn't working for me. From the looks of Twon and Quaid, the shit wasn't working for them either. No song in this world could bring my cousin back.

I shot a glance in my Auntie Shameka's direction. She was sitting between Auntie Gina and G-Ma in the pew across the aisle from us. She looked how I felt. Guilty.

I guess all of us feel a little guilty, because we wish we would have said more or done more to stop Charles before all this went down. I take the most blame, though, because I could have been there with him.

After the singing, the preacher showed a slideshow my mom made of all of us when we were kids. It was painful to see all those pictures of me, Twon, Charles, and Quaid. All those birthdays, cookouts, and parties, and now my nigga laying in a casket. He was barely even eighteen.

After the funeral, we was all supposed to go to the cemetery to see them put him in the ground, but I couldn't see that shit. I was one of the pallbearers to help put Charles in the limo and then to take him out at the cemetery, but I couldn't take seeing them lower him into the ground. I left.

My mom called after me, but I acted like I couldn't hear her. I just kept walking.

I don't know what I'm supposed to do now. I feel like there is no coming back from this.

Shaneece

It hurts me to see Twon hurt like this. That funeral was so sad. Twon told me how close he, Hype, Charles, and Quaid were when they were kids, but I didn't really get the full effect until I saw that slideshow that Hype's mom made of the four of them. They had the song by Boyz II Men playing in the background "It's so Hard to Say Goodbye to Yesterday." There wasn't a dry eye in the room by the time that song was over. There were so many pictures – baby pictures, birthday pictures, random party pictures, school pictures . . . You could tell that these boys had formed true, lifelong bonds with each other. Now that one of them is gone, I don't know how the others are going to function.

I'm glad that Twon at least started eating again. He just went back to work today. I hope he makes it through the shift because he is still very distraught, and understandably so. So much has happened this year, for all of us. Life is not supposed to be like this. This is our senior year of high school, for crying out loud!

We're supposed to be consumed with college, SAT scores, graduation, and prom – not death, pregnancy, and trying to figure out how to make ends meet as a young couple who got thrown together by life's circumstances.

I know this probably sounds selfish, but I keep thinking about my parents and Shanelle. If anything happened to any of them, I don't know how I would take it. My relationship with my mom has gotten a little better. She tries to send me encouraging quotes every day and information about pregnancy and childbirth. My dad is a different story. I haven't heard a word from him since our last argument. I guess he really meant it when he said he was finished with me.

It's funny how you spend your whole life trying to please someone, and then when they determine that nothing you do will ever be good enough, they throw you away. I am going to do everything in my power to make sure my child never feels rejected. I don't want my kid to feel like his or her whole life is tied to a grade on a paper at the end of a marking period. I want my child to grow up happy, healthy, and surrounded by love and support. Furthermore, if I have more kids, I will never treat one child better than the other because of their performance in school. Parents don't realize how much they can fuck up their kids' heads by the things they do. Maybe I can break the cycle of abuse by starting fresh with my child. At least that will be one good thing that comes out of all this.

Tierra

Charles' funeral was so sad. I feel so bad for Hype, Twon, Quaid, and their whole family. They may have had their issues with each other, but the family always was close and tried to stick together from what I saw. My mom went with me to the funeral. We sat a couple of rows behind the boys. This is impacting all three of them so deeply that I don't know who to reach out to first.

Twon has Shaneece, but he and I have history too. When Charles got shot the first time, Twon was really messed up about it. I could only imagine what was going through his mind now, after seeing Charles bleeding and dying then buried in the ground.

And Hype, he was like my best friend out of all of Twon's friends. He had been there for me when I was going through my situation with Twon, and I know he was actually the closest one to Charles. This has to be hitting him heavy, especially after all that stuff he was telling me about him and Charles selling drugs.

And then the situation with Quaid . . . I keep thinking about how we had an argument and broke up right before this happened, but before our breakup, he kept telling me he was deeply worried about

Hype and Charles. He and Charles never really got along, even though they still were close. Quaid feels guilty that he and Charles never had a chance to resolve their drama. I try to find different ways to comfort him, and I believe it helps, but nothing can really take the pain away.

My mother and I spoke with G-Ma, Hype's mother Rose, Charles' mother Shameka, and Quaid's mother Gina after the funeral to pay our respects, and they are not doing too good either. It seems like there is some friction between Shameka and the rest of the women, especially her and Rose. Twon told me Rose and Shameka had been beefing for as long as he could remember, but I guess the funeral must have opened up old wounds and sparked some raw emotions in them.

G-Ma kept saying that she was holding on to the fact that Charles accepted Christ before he died. That was her source of comfort during the grieving process.

That made me think of my own life. I remember telling Hype a while back that I wanted to go to heaven when I died. I wonder if Charles is in heaven? He must be, since G-Ma said he accepted Christ before he slipped from this life to the next.

God has been calling me for a long time, and I've basically been ignoring Him and running in the opposite direction. But now, I wonder if it's time to stop running. Charles was barely eighteen, and now his life was over. You never expect this to happen to somebody you know, even though you see it on the news every day. What if my life ends early like Charles? We feel like we are going to live forever, but life is really not promised to us. I just don't know anymore. I guess it's something to think about.

Twon

I sat alone in the living room thinking about Charles. It still hasn't really hit me what happened. I been trying to hold on and manage, going to work and school, turning in papers and shit, but in reality, I feel like I'm not even here. I'm just going through all the motions—smiling when expected, laughing when necessary—but on the inside, I feel detached. Charles is really gone, yo. Gone. That shit sounds so final, but he was just here a couple of weeks ago.

I was lost in my thoughts when I heard the doorbell ring.

I opened the door and immediately tensed when I saw Trav, Slink, and Wolf.

"What y'all niggas doing here?"

"Damn, nigga, can we pay our respects?" said Slink.

"He died over two weeks ago."

"We was trying to give you some space," said Wolf.

I opened the door to let them in, but I really wasn't trying to deal with no bullshit today. Slink and Wolf both had terrible attitudes. They had no respect for anybody, and I wasn't up for it today.

"So how you been holding up, Twon?" Trav said, concern in his eyes. He had been holding me down since it happened, stopping by, making sure I ate, listening when I needed to talk, everything. It was crazy how close me and Trav had become after knowing each other only a couple of months. He was truly a brother to me now.

"I just been trying to maintain," I said.

"Yeah, well . . . you still could have called somebody or something." That was Slink's "helpful" contribution, like he showed up just to get on my case. I tried to tune him out but he went on. "We your real blood, but you stopped talking to us after that situation we had with Hype and Charles."

"That's cuz y'all did some grimy ass, disrespectful ass shit!" I barked.

"Whoa, hold up lil' nigga," said Wolf, as if I were a child. "We understand you in your feelings and all, but niggas die every day. Nigga should have kept the strap."

"Fuck you!" I said, jumping to my feet. "That was my fucking brother, yo!"

Slink stepped closer, too close. "Them niggas ain't your family, Twon. We is."

"Y'all ain't no fucking family to me."

"Oh, so it's like that?" Wolf was standing now too, and suddenly it felt like I was being ganged up on.

Trav sensed that we were about to go off. "Let's not get too deep into it today," he said, standing up and placing himself between us.

I had to get my last word in so I could be done with Slink and Wolf for good. "It's exactly like I said. Y'all ain't family to me." I waited for them to get a clue, but they didn't.

"Yall can leave," I said. "Now."

"So you really gonna cut off your real family for some other niggas that don't even share your blood?" Wolf shook his head. He turned to Slink. "Come on."

He and Slink left without another word.

"I don't want to be around those niggas ever again, Trav," I said to my brother.

"I understand." His expression was grave. "I'm sorry for popping up on you like that. I didn't know they would be like that even in this type of situation."

"Yeah, well now you know. How the hell did you deal with them your whole life?"

Trav chuckled. "I just learned to block them out, I guess."

"Well that's a whole lot of fucking blocking."

He chuckled again. "But I'm glad I got a chance to meet you, though."

"Me too."

"I always wanted a brother."

Hype

Nobody seems to want to fucking tell me who set up my cousin. I keep calling around to niggas who knew Charles, but nobody wants to talk. The last nigga I talked to, this nigga named Reg, I know he knew something, but just didn't want to snitch. Fuck that nigga. If it was his family, he would want to know too. I just cussed that nigga clean out, and he ain't say shit. I know he knows something. I don't care. I'm gonna find out who killed my cousin, and I'm-a fucking end that nigga, yo. Word up.

I called another nigga on the phone, this nigga named Slim.

"Yo," said Slim when he answered.

"Yo, Slim, you gotta tell me who did that to Charles, yo. Nobody wants to talk, but I know somebody knows something."

He sighed. "Hype, I know that's your cousin and everything, but I really don't want to get into that. Just know that that nigga got what's coming to him."

"Oh, I know he's gonna get what's coming, cuz it's coming from me!" I hung up and threw my phone.

"What's coming from you?"

G-Ma startled me.

"G-Ma, what you doing here?"

"Your momma gave me a key. Who was that on the phone?"

"Nobody."

"It wasn't nobody, boy. Who was you talking to?"

"Look, G-Ma, I know you don't want to hear this, but I'm gonna find out who did this to Charles."

"And do what?" Her words hit me like a punch in the chest.

"I'm-a do to them what they did to him."

"No, you're not, Hype. Don't go out there in all that foolishness."

"I gotta do something, G-Ma."

"You don't have to do anything."

"I'm gonna kill him, G-Ma."

"No, you're not. Don't go out there, Hype. I already lost one grandchild to these streets. I'm not trying to lose another one. So many young lives keep getting lost every day to these senseless killings. I can't afford to lose another one of you."

She had been strong for so long, and suddenly she just crumpled into a chair and started sobbing.

I knelt on the floor next to her chair and hugged her. I know she's hurting like I'm hurting, but she don't understand. I got to make this shit right.

Shaneece

Today is the day that Twon and I are supposed to find out whether we're having a boy or a girl. We tried to find out during the last ultrasound, but they couldn't tell because of the baby's position. We're both kind of excited, though Twon is still depressed over Charles. I hope he is able to get through it soon, because we still have a child on the way.

We went out to the stores to stock up on diapers and clothes and things for the baby's room. Our appointment was today at 3:00 p.m. We called Hype to ask if he wanted to come, but he declined.

I feel like that was kind of messed up to miss out on an appointment to find out what the sex of your own child is, but I kept my mouth shut. I *so* hoped that Hype was not the father. I didn't even know how we were going to deal with it if he was. At least Twon and I are trying to be responsible by working fulltime and saving money. Hype hasn't done anything! He hasn't gone to one appointment since he found out about the pregnancy, and now he is blowing us off yet again. I can't wait 'til this is over so I can be through with him as far as the baby is concerned. I know I'll still have to deal with him because he and Twon are friends, but I just want closure on who the father of my baby is so Twon and I can move forward.

"Isn't this exciting?" I said, smiling as I looked over at Twon.

Twon gave me a restrained smile. "Yeah, I kind of want to know too."

We were in the examination room waiting for the technician to come start the ultrasound. My heart was pounding. I hoped it was a girl. Twon said he didn't care what it was.

Just then, the door opened and the doctor walked in.

"And look at this happy couple over here!" she said, smiling at us. "How has everything been going?"

Twon and I looked at each other. We definitely were not going into a long history of everything that had happened in the past few weeks, so we decided to keep it simple. "We're good," I said.

"That's great," said the doctor. "Well, I know you've been waiting for this moment, so let's get started!"

I looked at Twon with excitement in my eyes and got on the table. An ultrasound technician came in the room to assist the doctor. I shivered a little when they applied the cold gel to my belly. The doctor moved the wand around a little then stopped. "Well, looky here!" she said. "You are having . . . drum roll, please . . . a boy!"

My mouth dropped open in surprise, and I looked at Twon.

"We're having a boy?" I asked of no one in particular.

"Yep. Check it out." She pointed to an image on the screen. It was clear that we had a little boy. At that moment, I felt him kick and saw it on the screen at the same time.

Tears filled my eyes. I gazed at Twon. "I hope he's just like his dad."

***

Twon and I were elated after that visit. We wanted to go out to celebrate. He seemed like his spirits were really lifted. He kept staring at the ultrasound photos when we got in the car.

"Hey, do you think we should call Hype?" I said.

"Huh?" he said, distracted. Then he looked at me. "Oh, yeah, he probably wants to know." He got his cell phone out and called Hype's cell.

"Yo," he said after Hype answered. He put him on speaker.

"What's up?" said Hype, with zero enthusiasm.

"We found out what we're having!" I tried to sound excited to cheer him up.

"What is it?" he said, but his flat tone gave the impression that he didn't want to be bothered.

"*He* is a boy," I shot back at him, offended that he didn't seem to care.

"Good." His tone was emotionless.

"A'ight, man, I'll get up with you later," Twon said, then he ended the call.

I rolled my eyes. "He is such a fucking asshole."

"You gotta be easy, Shaneece. This is not easy for any of us."

"Yes, I know, but we still have other priorities. He can't just shut his whole life down because of this. He still has to live."

"I know that life is supposed to go on, but I really don't think you understand. Me, Hype, Charles, and Quaid was more than just friends and cousins. We was brothers. I can't even explain to you how this feels."

At that point, I shut my mouth. I wasn't trying to get into it with Twon today. I understood where he was coming from, but I don't think he understood me. We drove home in silence, my mind on the baby, his probably on Charles.

Tierra

I got up on Sunday morning thinking about Quaid. He was really going through it over Charles. I kept trying to remind him that he didn't have to feel guilty because it wasn't his fault, but it didn't make a difference. It hurt me to see him hurt like this.

I made my way downstairs to see if there was anything in the fridge to eat. While I was looking through the shelves preparing to warm up some leftover Chinese, I heard my mom walking down the stairs. When she walked into the kitchen, I looked over at her and almost bumped my head as I straightened up in surprise. She was all dressed up with heels, a nice dress and everything.

"Where are you going?" I said.

"Church."

My mouth dropped open. "Really?"

"Yes. I believe it's time."

I closed the refrigerator door, forgetting all about my hunger.

"What made you decide to go today?"

She sighed. "Tierra, this has been a long time coming. The Lord has been speaking to me for a while, but I was afraid to take that first step back into the building. I was scared for so long, but what happened with your friend Charles really shook me out of those feelings. Life is too short to dwell on the past. It's time to move forward to the future. I know God is with me, so I just have to follow."

Her words inspired me.

"Are you about to leave right not?"

"Why? Do you want to go?"

I smiled. "Yes, I think I want to go too."

I dashed upstairs and hopped in the shower. When I got out, I quickly found something to wear. My mom talked about how God had been calling her, and I knew that He had been calling me too, but like her, I had been afraid. I wasn't sure if I was ready to be saved just yet, but I knew that if my mom finally started going back after all these years, I had to go with her.

I threw on a dress and some flats and made my way downstairs. My mom smiled at me as we exited the house and made our way to the car to go to church together for the first time.

Twon

I got up with Hype later on after Shaneece went to bed. I drove over his house because I needed to check in on him after that phone conversation. It was hitting me what happened with Charles, but I knew it had to be hitting him more because he was the closest to Charles.

I made my way to his front door and twisted the knob, confused at first because it was locked, but then a brief feeling of anger flashed through me as I remembered why they were locking their door now. I knocked and waited. After what seemed like a full minute, Hype finally opened the door. He looked seriously depressed. He hadn't shaved or lined up his hair since the funeral.

"Wassup, man?" I said, dapping him up as he let me in.

"Ain't shit."

We went over to the couch and sat down.

"So how you been holding up?" I said, although the answer was obvious.

Hype shook his head. "I haven't been, man."

I tried to approach the subject as lightly as I could. I didn't want to get into an argument, but Hype needed to understand. "Look Hype," I started, and then I sighed. "I know you taking it hard. We all are. But you gotta believe this is not your fault. It wasn't your fault what happened."

"You don't understand, Twon. I left him out there. If I wouldn't have left him, I could have stopped this."

"How, Hype? If whoever did this had guns, was you gonna shoot them? Do you have a gun? Was you gonna jump in front of a bullet? If you did, you might be the one that got hit. Then Charles would be in the same spot you in now."

He looked like he was actually listening this time.

"I still feel like there's something I could have done."

"Hype, wasn't nothing you could do. Charles was out there, man. That's not to speak bad on him, but we had plenty of conversations where we told him to focus on school or get a job or learn a trade or something. He was a good dude, but he made his own decisions. We all do. He made his choice to be out there on the street."

Hype just sat and stared at nothing in particular. "I gotta find the nigga that did this shit, and when I do, I'm-a—"

"You'll do what?"

"I'm-a end that nigga."

"Hype, that's not the answer, yo. You ain't no killer. I know you hurting, but this shit ain't the way. We can't afford to lose you too."

"I don't care if I die, as long as that nigga die with me."

"Well, we care if you die. I care if you die. Me, you and Quaid is still here. And I know damn well Charles wouldn't want you dead."

"Ain't shit left for me on this earth, Twon."

"Stop talking like that, man. You still got family left. What about the baby? What if it's yours? Plus you applied to college. You still have a future."

"Fuck that baby, fuck college, and fuck the future."

What he said was harsh, but I knew he didn't mean it. I decided to just chill with him the rest of the night to try to take his mind off Charles.

Hype

I feel like I'm going crazy. I didn't know pain could run this deep. I keep calling Charles' phone then realizing that he's not gonna answer. I keep seeing him everywhere. I swear this all feels like a bad dream that I'm waiting to wake up from. I feel like don't nobody understand me.

I keep going back and forth between not believing that he's really gone, to seeing him and trying to call him on the phone, to feeling like I could have saved him, to wanting to find the nigga that did this and kill him, to wanting to die myself.

I think about the future, about the baby and college, but then I think about how it's not fair that my life gets to go on while Charles' life is over. This shit ain't never gonna be right.

I would've sat there all day with my thoughts circling through my brain if I hadn't heard a knock on the front door that jolted me back to reality. I went to open it thinking *who's bothering me now*, and there stood Quaid.

"What's up?" I said.

"Hey," he said, walking in. He looked exactly how I felt. Maybe somebody did understand.

He took in my appearance. I know I had fallen way off since the funeral. I didn't really give much of a fuck about anything. I barely even showered.

Teachers kept threatening me that I was gonna fail in school, so I turned in half-assed papers and assignments just to get them off my back. A part of me knew I had to keep living, but another part of me didn't want to.

"Have you been eating?" Quaid said. That's when I noticed that he was holding a brown paper bag in his hand. From what I gathered, it must have been food.

"Not really. Ma and G-Ma been on my back, but I ain't really been hungry."

Quaid nodded his head like he understood. "Me neither, man." He sniffed and blinked. I could see the tears in his eyes. "I see you've been feeling the same way I have," he said.

"Yeah," I said. "But you look like you got a fresh shave."

"That was just this morning. Up until today, I've been exactly the same as you."

"Is that why you brought the food?"

"Yeah. I had to learn it's okay to eat…" His voice kind of trailed off, and suddenly I realized how hungry I was. I took the bag, and me and Quaid sat down to eat.

"We gotta get you shaved, man," said Quaid between mouthfuls of the best barbeque sandwich we'd eaten in a long time. "Man, this is good," he added.

"I really just ain't been caring about none of that, Quaid."

"I know. Believe me, I know. I've been feeling so guilty since it happened. I feel like it's partially my fault, and then I keep seeing him over and over again."

My sandwich was halfway to my mouth, but what he said stopped me cold. Quaid was basically telling my life story right now.

"I feel guilty too," I said. "And I really want to find the nigga that did this, but nobody's talking."

Quaid looked at me. "Hype, I completely understand you wanting to go out and get the guy who did this. I've felt the same way myself. But honestly, despite how we feel, that's still not the answer."

"So what are we supposed to do? Just let him walk?"

"God will deal with him."

"And how is God gonna do that?" I jabbed some fries into a puddle of ketchup with more force than necessary and crammed them in my mouth.

"I don't know, but I just know that trying to go out and kill the guy is not gonna solve anything. If we kill him, yes, we've avenged Charles' death, but then what? One of his family kills us? Then we go back and kill another one of them? The cycle never stops."

Everything within me wanted to flip over the table and send the food flying, but in my heart, I knew Quaid was right. "I just don't feel like I can rest 'til that nigga is gone, whoever he is."

"I understand. I just wish Charles and I had ended on a good note."

"He didn't hate you, Quaid."

"And he didn't blame you, Hype."

We stared at each other. Neither of us wanted to accept what the other was saying, but we both knew the other was right.

Shaneece

Twon got letters in the mail about prom and graduation. Both are supposed to be held next week. I'm not sure if he wants to go, but I'm going to try to encourage him to participate. Even though I hated that school and most of the people in it, Twon needs some kind of relief. He's been functioning, barely, finishing up the semester's schoolwork, going to his job, and coming home to help prepare for the baby, but I can tell that he's not really there. It's like a piece of him is gone now, and I don't know if there is any way to help him get it back.

I'm really worried about how we're going to handle things once the baby is here. I'm seven months pregnant, and I'm already getting tired of going to work. I'm literally physically exhausted. I'm trying to hold out as long as I can to save money, but it's getting harder and harder to get out of bed in the morning. I can barely sleep at night because I can't find a good position. My back hurts, my feet hurt, and everything hurts, and Twon tries to help, but I know he's hurting too, just in a different way.

I really don't want to put the whole financial burden on him so soon, so I am going to try to make it to at least my eighth month.

"Twon, we need to talk about something," I said when he came home from work. I was laying in our bed propped up on some pillows.

"What's up?" He leaned over and gave me a kiss.

"Are you . . . do you want to go to prom and graduation?"

"What for?" he scoffed.

"Calm down. I'm not trying to upset you. I just think it might be good for you to go. You've worked so hard, and you finished school despite everything that you've been through. You deserve this, Twon." Tears filled my eyes. I wasn't trying to upset him. I hoped he understood.

He got choked up too. "I just don't even feel like I'm living anymore, Shaneece. Plus, who's even gonna come to graduation? My mom don't care about me. She won't even talk to me."

"You can go for yourself. I'll be there, and I'm sure Shanelle will come, and I'm sure Hype's family will be there. G-Ma will definitely be proud. And don't forget about Trav."

He stared at me, taking in my words.

"See, Twon? You have people who care about you."

"I just wish she would let me know what's going on with her."

He told me how he went to his mother's house that day, and she rejected him. I had my suspicions about what might be going on with her, but I didn't want to say anything because I didn't think Twon could handle such serious news right now. He had already been through too much.

"How about we just try it?" I said, trying to redirect the conversation. "If it turns out to be a bad idea, we can leave, but I wouldn't want you to not go to either one and then regret it later."

He stared at me for a few more moments, contemplating my words. Finally, he nodded.

"A'ight. I'll try it."

***

Prom was okay, at least at the beginning. We went, and Twon also convinced Hype to come. Quaid went with Tierra. I tried to stay away from her as much as I could. She shot a few dirty looks in my direction, but I ignored them.

It seemed like all the boys had a little bit of fun. Everything was going fine until all the girls kept trying to swarm around Hype to "comfort" him. These thirsty broads were really just fishing for information. Hype saw through it and left. Twon wanted to go after him, so we left too. Quaid stayed with Tierra because he didn't want to leave her by herself. She is such a fucking princess. I actually heard her mention that she had bought the perfect prom dress, and she didn't want to waste it by leaving early. I can't stand that bitch.

Twon

I keep looking at these college acceptance letters and wondering how my life went so far off track. They meant so much to me before, but they ain't nothing but pieces of paper now. My life ain't nowhere near what I imagined at this point. I'm seventeen years old, I survived an attempted suicide, which left me with two broken legs, I lost a brother, gained a brother, and got a baby on the way. This shit is crazy.

I keep trying to call my mom, though I know it's no use. She is clearly never gonna answer. I decided out of desperation to stop calling the house phone and to just call her at work. I know it was probably stupid, but I just wanted to hear her voice. I pretended to be somebody else so she would come to the phone.

"Hello?" she said in her professional voice.

"Ma, it's me, Twon. I really need to talk to you."

She sucked her teeth, but then she must have remembered she was at work. "Excuse me, but it's inappropriate for you to call me at work."

"Ma, I'm your son. A lot has been going on. I really need to talk to you."

"I'm sorry, but this isn't a good time. I will have to reach out to you later."

She hung up on me.

She is so fucking cold. I don't even know why I tried. I briefly contemplated calling her again, but I decided it was no use.

As much as it was obvious that I should just leave her alone, I felt like I couldn't. She was still my mother, and I still cared about her, even though she didn't care about me.

Hype

I played some basketball with Quaid and some other guys to blow off some steam. When I got home, G-Ma and my mother were both in the kitchen with happy smiles on their faces.

"What's going on with y'all?" I said, going straight to the refrigerator to grab a bottle of water.

"We're proud of you, that's what's going on!" said my mom. She was holding some opened mail in her hand.

"What's that?" I said.

"Your acceptance letter from State! Why didn't you tell me? And you got a scholarship too! Boy, why didn't you tell me? My baby boy is going to college."

G-Ma just stared at me, assessing me.

"No I ain't," I said, taking a swig of my water.

"What do you mean, you ain't? Yes you are. Boy, you have worked hard for this. You are going to college."

"You can't make me do it, so there's no point to this conversation."

"Boy, you better watch your mouth talking to your momma like that!" said G-Ma, shooting me a stern look.

"I don't care about college, G-Ma."

My mom said, "Look, we are all hurting over Charles, but you are not about to throw your whole life away."

"You didn't even fucking like him!" I slammed the water bottle down on the table. The anger rose up in me so fast, I didn't know how to handle it.

"You better lower your voice, boy!" said G-Ma.

"Or what?" I said boldly. I had never disrespected G-Ma before, but I was losing control.

My mother took over. "Hype, I don't know what's gotten into you, but you really need to calm down."

"Don't try to act like you Parent of the Year now." I stalked out of the house, slamming the door behind me.

I knew I was way out of line with my attitude, but my mother had really pissed me off by going in my room and finding my letters. She had to have been snooping through my shit. Then she had to go and call G-Ma and tell her. She couldn't just leave well enough a-fucking-lone.

I couldn't just go off to college somewhere, living the dream, while my fucking cousin's body was decomposing underground. I couldn't just move on like the shit didn't happen.

I was pacing on the sidewalk in front of our house when I got a call from a number that looked familiar, but I couldn't place it. I answered it anyway. "Hello?"

"Hello, is this Hype?"

"Yes. Who's this?"

"This is Dr. Chris Young from the Sociology department at State University."

"Oh." This caught me off guard. I didn't really know how to respond. "What's going on?"

"I just wanted to congratulate you on your acceptance and your scholarship. I know you must be excited about going to college."

My heart panged. "Well, truthfully, I'm not."

"Why? What's going on?"

Something about the way he said it made me feel like he actually cared. Every time I spoke to this dude, I felt like he was some type of father figure or something. I didn't even know the nigga, but just from my few interactions with him, I knew he was a real one. I didn't know how else to say it, so I broke down and told him everything. I sat on my front steps and told him about Charles, the baby, my doubts about the possibility of success, everything. I probably said way too much, but he didn't hang up on me or cut me off. He just listened.

"That's tough, Hype," he said when I was finally done. "I know you probably won't believe this, but I know almost exactly where you're coming from."

He went on to share with me that at my age he went through a similar experience, except he lost his brother while he was already in college during his freshman year. He told me how he felt guilty like I did, and wanted to go after the guys like I did, but he came to the realization that that wasn't the answer. He encouraged me to go to school and at least try. I told him I would think about it. He said if I ever needed to talk again, I had his number. He gave me his cell number too. I really appreciated that shit.

I didn't even know this nigga, but he talked to me for over two hours, trying to convince me to go to college and think about the future. He gave me hope when I didn't have no hope.

I guess I got a lot to think about. I honestly don't know what my decision is going to be. I know there is a possibility that the baby is mine, and if it is, I gotta do something to help support him. I meant what I said a while back about fathers not being in they kid's lives. I never had my father. None of us did—Quaid, Charles, Twon, none of us. Despite all the shit I'm going through, I wouldn't want to push that off on my kid.

I don't really want to live, but I guess I gotta keep living anyway.

Tierra

It feels so weird to have my mom going to church with me now. We went last Sunday, and afterwards, she said that she felt renewed. I feel great for her, but at the same time, bad about myself. Last Sunday, the preacher gave an altar call, and said if anyone wanted to be saved, to come down the aisle, but I felt like I couldn't go, despite the fact that I knew God was calling me.

We are supposed to be going to church together again today, and I've been praying the whole morning for enough boldness to get over my fear and just go down the aisle. I feel like I have been wrestling with this for way too long as it is. Today has to be the day.

***

The wait is finally over! Quaid helped me walk down the aisle. I was so scared at first, but then the preacher asked everyone to look at their neighbor and ask them if they have accepted Christ, and if not, were they ready to do it today?

When Quaid looked at me, my heart dropped because I had been praying all morning for boldness to go down the aisle, but when the preacher first made the alter call, I was too scared to go. I had no idea that he would do something like this. Quaid asked me if I was ready to accept Christ, and I said yes, but that I was too afraid to go down there by myself. I was totally shocked when he said he would walk with me. He took me by the hand and walked me down the aisle, and now I can finally say that I have accepted Christ into my life.

Shaneece

I was so proud to see Twon walk across the stage at graduation. I know he was sad that his mother didn't show up, but Hype's family was there to support him, and his brother Trav came with his girlfriend, Stephanie. We all definitely have to hang out more sometime soon. Those two are so cute together.

I also got my results a few days ago for my GED test. I passed all sections with top scores. For a second, I considered calling my father to tell him that I had done something right, to put it his way, but I decided against it. He would just find a way to ruin it anyway.

After the graduation, Hype's family held a cookout for Hype, Twon, and Quaid, and to my surprise, they also invited me as well as Tierra, so that was awkward for a few minutes. Tierra's mom was also there. Tierra and I tried to be cordial to each other, but there were a few times when I caught her staring at my baby bump.

The atmosphere was mostly pleasant at the cookout, except you could see that the women in the family had some serious issues with each other. Charles' mother, Shameka, mostly kept to herself, and when she did talk, she made it a point to exclude Hype's mother, Rose, from the conversation. I remember how those two got into it the last time they had a party. Twon told me they had always had problems, but I figured that with everything that happened with Charles, they would resolve their differences and move on past whatever it was, but unfortunately, that doesn't look like it happened. I felt bad for Charles' mom though. She kept looking at all of us and crying, then she ended up leaving early. Quaid's mother, Gina, went after her.

Twon

I decided to go to my mother's house one more time because I couldn't shake the feeling that I needed to talk to her. She needed to know everything that had been happening to me, and I needed to know what was going on with her. She couldn't just drop me after all these years. I refused to believe that she didn't care at all.

I drove up to her house and saw her car there. Instead of knocking at the door, I decided to wait outside, hoping that she would come out of the house soon. I waited for over two hours. It felt like I was at a stakeout or something. Finally, she came out of the house and headed toward her car. She had lost even more weight and was wearing a different wig from the last time I saw her. She was also walking more slowly than before.

I got out the car and crossed the street to go meet her before she got in her car.

"Ma," I said. She turned around, startled to see me, and almost fell. I reached out to steady her, but she drew back sharply, a venomous look in her eyes.

"What are you doing here?" she spat. "Didn't I tell you I wanted nothing to do with you?"

"Ma, you gotta talk to me sooner or later. What's going on with you? A lot is happening with me. I need to talk to you."

"Talk to G-Ma." Her voice was so cold.

"Ma, I found out about my brother, Trav." She froze. Once I said one thing, I couldn't stop talking. "And me and Shaneece have a son on the way. We got a new place. I finished school and graduated . . . and Charles died." I trembled at the last words.

"Charles died, huh?" she said.

"Yeah. He got shot." I looked at the ground.

"Well, you won't have to worry about me much longer either."

My head shot up in surprise. "What do you mean?!"

She opened her mouth like she was about to let me have it, then she paused. Her mouth closed, and she stared at me for a long time. From the look she was giving me, I was almost afraid to persist, but I needed to know what was going on.

"What is it, Ma?" I braced myself.

She stared me up and down. "Later." she replied.

"What do you mean, later?"

She pressed the button on her key fob to unlock her car door, then she opened it and got inside as I stared at her.

"What is it, Ma?" I repeated.

She looked up at me. "Later, Twon. Not right now."

I opened my mouth to protest, but something about her eyes made me stop. I continued to watch as she backed out of the driveway, and drove off, while I stood there, frozen in place.

Hype

I finally found out who killed my cousin . . . after the nigga was already dead. It was this nigga named Brick who lived a few blocks over. While he was still alive, nobody wanted to talk. Nobody wanted to say it was him that killed Charles. But after he was gone, all of a sudden everybody wanted to sing like a canary.

People are so full of shit.

When I heard the news, at first I felt a sense of relief because I felt like Charles' life was vindicated, but then I felt kind of guilty for being happy that somebody else had died. The whole time I was trying to find out who did it, I was focused on figuring out who it was so I could kill him, but now that he's gone, I feel like it doesn't even matter. It feels like everything is cheapened. One guy gets killed, then the guy who killed him gets killed, then life goes on and the cycle continues, just like Quaid said.

There has to be a way to put a stop to all this shit. Charles was barely even eighteen years old. Brick had four kids who are now left without a father. Charles didn't even get a chance to have kids. Shit really gotta change in these streets, yo. Deadass.

My auntie Shameka not doing too good. I keep trying to reach out to her, but it seems like she really hates everybody. She can't stand my mom, but they always had beef. Honestly, she never really liked me either, but I always loved her, and I want to be there for her during this time. I tried to visit her the other day, but she slammed the door in my face.

College is supposed to start in two weeks, and today is the last day to accept my acceptance if I'm gonna go to State. I been staring at this screen for the past ten minutes, wondering if I should do it or just let it go. I thought about everything that happened this year, and everything that's going on right now. Shit's crazy. Something's gotta change.

Finally, before I could change my mind, I scrolled down the screen and clicked Accept and then Submit.

I gotta get the hell up out of here.

Shaneece

It seemed like this year went by like a whirlwind. So much has happened. I am now in my last month of pregnancy, and the baby will be here any day now.

Something serious is going on with Twon. A couple of weeks ago, he went out somewhere, and when he came back, his entire demeanor was different. I tried to get him to talk, but he wouldn't tell me anything at first.

About a week later, he finally told me what was going on.

"I spoke to my mother."

I tensed at those words. "And?" I tried to brace myself for what he might say.

He sighed. "Well, she finally agreed to talk to me."

"Okay…" I said as I readjusted my position in bed. "So when are you guys meeting?"

"I don't know." His tone was flat. "I don't even know what she wants to tell me."

"Did you tell her about what happened with Charles?"

He nodded. "Yeah, and about the baby, and everything. Then she said she had something to tell me, but she stopped." He swallowed.

"Twon…" I tried to be careful with my wording. "You know what? Don't worry about it. Everything will be fine." I offered a weak smile for reassurance.

He stared at me like he wanted to believe me. "Are you sure?"

"Yeah, don't worry about it." I smiled again as my heart panged.

* * *

At about three o'clock in the morning, I felt like I had to use the bathroom. I barely made it to the toilet before everything let loose.

"Twon!" I called. "Twon!"

He appeared at the bathroom door.

I looked up at him in fear. "I think my water just broke!"

To be continued in book three in the series, *When Things Go Right*.

If you have not read the first book in the series, you can catch up by reading *When Things Go Left*.

A Note to My Readers

If you enjoyed reading *When Things Get Real*, please sign up for my email newsletter. One of the many benefits of joining the email list is that you get exclusive access to updates, excerpts from future novels, and information about book signing events that may be coming to a city near you! It's easy to join – just shoot me a quick email at tanishastewart.author@gmail.com. I love hearing from my readers!

Also, if you enjoyed this novel, please feel free to leave a review on Amazon. Not sure what to write? You can simply comment on your favorite character and your overall perception of the book (no spoilers, please ☺).

If you would like to connect with me on social media, here's where you can find me:

Facebook: Tanisha Stewart, Author
Instagram: tanishastewart_author
Twitter: TStewart_Author

I hope you enjoyed the novel. See you next time ;)!

Tanisha Stewart's Books

Even Me Series

Even Me

Even Me, The Sequel

Even Me, Full Circle

When Things Go Series

When Things Go Left

When Things Get Real

When Things Go Right

For My Good Series

For My Good: The Prequel

For My Good: My Baby Daddy Ain't Ish

For My Good: I Waited, He Cheated

For My Good: Torn Between The Two

For My Good: You Broke My Trust

For My Good: Better or Worse

For My Good: Love and Respect

Betrayed Series

Betrayed By My So-Called Friend

Betrayed By My So-Called Friend, Part 2

Betrayed 3: Camaiyah's Redemption

Betrayed Series: Special Edition

Phate Series

Phate: An Enemies to Lovers Romance

Phate 2: An Enemies to Lovers Romance

The Real Ones Series

Find You A Real One: A Friends to Lovers Romance

Find You A Real One 2: A Friends to Lovers Romance

Standalones

A Husband, A Boyfriend, & a Side Dude

In Love With My Uber Driver

You Left Me At The Altar

Where. Is. Haseem?! A Romantic-Suspense Comedy